BY

"*By Book or b...* ...stant librarian Lucy is ...ging cast of supporting c... ...malayan with attitude who can't seem to help sinking his claws into a murder."

—Sofie Kelly, *New York Times* bestselling author of the
Magical Cats Mysteries

"A charming new series by Eva Gates. A librarian in a historic lighthouse with a cozy apartment upstairs and a clever cat named Charles (Dickens) make for a book lover's dream. Lucy is a delightful and engaging sleuth surrounded by a cast of intriguing characters in an original and unique setting."

—Krista Davis, *New York Times* bestselling author of
the Domestic Diva Mysteries

"A library in a lighthouse? *And* a cat? Sign me up! A fun read for all cozy fans."

—Laurie Cass, national bestselling author of the
Bookmobile Cat Mysteries

"This is a first-rate cozy mystery featuring a spunky librarian, a captivating book collection, an intriguing lighthouse, and plenty of twists and turns to keep you reading until dawn."

—Daryl Wood Gerber, national bestselling author of
the Cookbook Nook Mysteries

continued . . .

"Gates writes with the clarity and dazzle of a lighthouse beacon. The first in her Lighthouse Library series is a puzzler peopled with a cast of Outer Banks eccentrics who delight from the first line to the end. A must for Austen fans, cat lovers, and library devotees!"

— Laura DiSilverio, author of the Book Club Mysteries

"Lucy Richardson is a funny, smart, and resourceful sleuth, a librarian fresh from Boston, finding a better life on the scenic Outer Banks of North Carolina. Is it so wrong to be jealous of her charming lighthouse library? Her quaint and possibly haunted apartment? That hint of new romance? Well, even if it is wrong, I'd still want to steal Charles, the splendid cat, and then eat all the gooey pecan tarts from Josie's Cozy Bakery. Then I'll demand the next book in this well-written and entertaining new series."

— Mary Jane Maffini, author of the Charlotte Adams Mysteries

"This charming, entertaining, and smart series launch by Gates ... features an unusual (and real) setting and a colorful cast of characters that sets it apart from other bookish cozies." — *Library Journal* (starred review)

"This great book is the first in a series. . . . The plot, characters, and locale make for an extremely creative story."

— *Suspense Magazine*

Previously in the Lighthouse Library Series
by Eva Gates

By Book or by Crook

Booked for Trouble

A LIGHTHOUSE LIBRARY MYSTERY

Eva Gates

AN OBSIDIAN BOOK

OBSIDIAN

Published by New American Library,
an imprint of Penguin Random House LLC
375 Hudson Street, New York, New York 10014

This book is an original publication of New American Library.

First Printing, September 2015

ISBN 978-0-451-47094-2

Printed in the United States of America
10 9 8 7 6 5 4 3 2 1

Penguin
Random
House

To Mom

ACKNOWLEDGMENTS

I always tell my creative writing students not to "write what you know" but to "write what you want to know." The Lighthouse Library series proves my point: I have had great delight in getting to know the Outer Banks.

I'd like to thank Mary Jane Maffini and Linda Wiken for their friendship, support, and encouragement and an introduction to the marvelous world of cozies. Thanks to my agent, Kim Lionetti, for taking me on and believing that I could do this, and to Laura Fazio, my wonderful editor at Obsidian.

AUTHOR'S NOTE

The Bodie Island Lighthouse is a real historic lighthouse, located at the Cape Hatteras National Seashore on the Outer Banks of North Carolina. It is still a working lighthouse, protecting ships from the Graveyard of the Atlantic, and is open to the public. The lighthouse setting and grounds are as wonderful as described. It is not, however, a library. Nor is it large enough to house a collection of books, offices, staff rooms, two staircases, and even an apartment.

But it is large enough to accommodate my imagination. And I hope the reader's also.

Chapter 1

I love my mother. Truly, I do. She's never shown me anything but love, although she's tempered it by criticism perhaps once too often. She believes in me, I think, although she's not exactly averse to pointing out that I'd be better off if I did things her way. She's a kind, generous person. At least, that is, to those she doesn't consider to be in competition with her for some vaguely defined goal, or else watch out—she'll carry a grudge to the grave. She may be stiff and formal and sometimes overly concerned with the observance of proper behavior, but she's also adventurous and well traveled. And above all, her love of her children knows no bounds.

I do love my mother.

I just wish she weren't bearing down on me at this moment, face beaming, arms outstretched.

"Surprise, darling!" she cried.

It was a surprise all right. My heart sank into my stomach and I forced out a smile of my own. I'd been living in the Outer Banks of North Carolina for a short time, making a new life for myself away from the social respectability of my parents' circle in Boston, and here she was.

"Hi, Mom," I said as I was enveloped in a hug. It was a real hug, too. Hearty and all-embracing, complete with vigorous slaps on the back. When it came to her children, Mom allowed herself to forget she was a Boston society matron. I loved her for that, too.

I pulled myself out of the embrace. "What are you doing here, Mom?"

"I've come for a short vacation and to see how you're settling in." She lifted her arms to indicate not only the Outer Banks but the Lighthouse Library, where I worked and lived. "Isn't this charming? I haven't been in this building since it was renovated."

"You were here before it became a library?" I asked with some astonishment. When the historic Bodie Island Lighthouse had no longer been needed for its original function as a manually operated light, it had slowly crumbled into disrepair. Then, in a stroke of what I considered absolute genius, it was renovated and turned into a public library. High above, the great first-order Fresnel lens flashed in the night to guide ships at sea, while down below books were read and cherished.

"Of course I was," Mom said. "Oh, I can remember some wild nights, let me tell you. Sneaking around in the dark, trying to break into the lighthouse. Up to all sorts of mischief." She must have read something in my face. "I was young once, Lucy. Although it sometimes seems like another lifetime."

She looked so dejected all of a sudden that I reached out and touched her arm. "It's nice to see you, Mom."

"You must be Mrs. Richardson." Ronald, one of my colleagues, extended his hand. He was a short man in his midforties with a shock of curly white hair. He wore blue-and-red-striped Bermuda shorts, a short-sleeved denim shirt, and a colorful tie featuring the antics of Mickey Mouse. "The resemblance is remarkable," he said. "Although if I hadn't heard Lucy call you Mom, I'd have thought you were sisters."

Mom beamed. I didn't mind being told I looked thirty years older than I was; really I didn't. Ronald was our children's librarian, and a nice man with a warm, generous heart. He'd only told Mom what she wanted to hear. And, I had to admit, Mom looked mighty darn good. Weekly spa visits, a personal trainer, regular tennis games, and the consumption of truckloads of serums and creams (and, perhaps, a tiny nip and tuck here and there) only accented her natural beauty. She was dressed in a navy blue Ralph Lauren blazer over a blindingly white T-shirt and white capris. Her carefully cut and dyed ash-blond hair curled around her chin, and small hoop earrings were in her ears. Her gold jewelry was, as always, restrained, but spoke of money well spent.

I, on the other hand, looked like the harassed librarian I was. Only the horn-rimmed glasses on a lanyard and a gray bun at the back of my head were missing. My unruly mop of dark curls had been pulled back into a ragged ponytail this morning, because I hadn't gotten up in time to wash it. I wore my summer work outfit of black pants cut slightly above the ankle, ballet flats, and a crisp blue short-sleeved shirt, tucked out. I hadn't gotten around to washing the shirt after the last time I'd worn it, and hoped there were no stains so tiny I hadn't noticed—because Mom would. I made the introductions. "Suzanne Richardson, meet Ronald Burkowski, the best children's librarian in the state."

"My pleasure," Mom said, before turning her attention back to me. "Why don't you give me the grand tour, dear?"

"I'm working right now."

She waved her hand at that trifle.

"You go ahead, Lucy," Ronald said. "My next group doesn't start for fifteen minutes. I'll watch the shop while you take your mom around the place. But," he added, "don't go upstairs yet. I want to show her the children's library myself."

Mom laughed, charmed. Ronald smiled back, equally charmed.

I refrained from rolling my eyes as she slipped her arm though mine. "Come on," I said. "I'll show you the Austen books, and then introduce you to my boss."

"Is he as delightful as your Ronald?"

"He's not my Ronald, and Bertie is a she." I liked Bertie very much, but if there was one thing she was not, it was delightful.

I proudly escorted Mom to view the Bodie Island Lighthouse Library's pride and joy: a complete set of Jane Austen first editions. The six books, plus Miss Austen's own notebook, were on loan to us for a few more weeks this summer. They rested in a tabletop cabinet handcrafted specifically to hold them, tucked into a small alcove lit by a soft white light. The exhibit had proved to be successful beyond the wildest dreams of Bertie and the library board. Not to mention the local craftspeople and business owners when crowds of eager literary tourists began flooding into the Nags Head area.

"I'd love to have a peek at Jane Austen's notebook," Mom said. "Written in her own handwriting—imagine."

"I'll get the key when we meet Bertie. I'm sure we can make an exception in your case and let you hold it." We'd learned the hard way to keep the cabinet locked at all times and to secure the only copy of the key on Bertie's person. She'd told me that if the library caught fire in the night, I had permission to break the glass and grab the books. Otherwise, only she could open it.

Bertie was in her office, chewing on the end of a pencil as she studied her computer screen. I gave the open door a light tap. Bertie looked up, obviously pleased at the interruption. I knew she was going over the budget this morning. Charles, another of our staff members, occupied the single visitor's chair. He stretched lazily and gave Mom the once-over.

Neither he nor Mom appeared to be at all impressed with what they saw.

The edges of Charles's mouth turned up into the slightest sneer and he rubbed at his face. Then, very rudely, he went back to his nap.

"Oh," Mom said, "a cat. How . . . nice."

Bertie got to her feet and came out from behind her desk. I made the introductions, and the women shook hands.

"I hope you're taking care of my only daughter," Mom said. Behind her back, I rolled my eyes. Bertie noticed, but she didn't react.

"Lucy's taking care of us. She's a joy to work with and I consider myself, and the library, very lucky to have her."

Mom smiled in the same way she had at parent-teacher interview day.

I'm thirty years old and have a master's in library science, but to Mom I'm still twelve and being praised for getting an A plus on my essay on the Brontë sisters. I felt myself smiling. In that, she was probably no different from most mothers.

"Are you staying with Ellen?" Bertie asked, referring to Mom's sister.

"I'm at the Ocean Side." Mom always stayed at the Ocean Side, one of the finest (and most expensive) hotels on this stretch of the coast. "I haven't been to the hotel yet, Lucy. I wanted to stop by and let you know I've arrived. Why don't you come with me and help me check in?"

"I'm working," I said. Work was a concept Mom pretended to be unfamiliar with.

"Go ahead, Lucy," Bertie said. "Take the rest of the afternoon off. You've been putting in so many extra hours—you deserve it."

"But . . ."

"I'll take the circulation desk."

Between Mom's wanting me to come with her and Bertie's wanting to escape budget drudgery, I could hardly say no, now, could I?

Not wanting to be left alone, Charles roused himself and leapt off the chair. He rubbed himself against Mom's leg. She tried to unobtrusively push him away. Charles didn't care to be pushed., He was a big cat. A gorgeous Himalayan with a mass of tan-and-white fur, pointy ears, and a mischievous tan-and-white face. We walked down the hallway, while Mom tried not to trip over the animal weaving between her feet.

"Did you drive all the way down today?" I asked. Mom loved to drive, and she'd often jump into her car and take off for a few days, giving the family no notice. "Me time" or "road trip," she called it. As I got older, I began to realize that "me time" usually corresponded with my dad's dark moods.

"I spent a couple of days in New York, left there this morning."

"New York," Bertie said, almost dreamily. "I haven't been there for ages. How was it?"

"Marvelous," Mom said. "I did some shopping, saw a play."

I grabbed my bag from the staff break room, leaving Mom and Bertie to talk about the delights to be found in New York City.

When I reappeared, Ronald had joined the conversation. He was from New York and had been a professional actor before giving that up to become a librarian. Broadway's loss, I thought. Ronald loved nothing more than putting on dramatic presentations with the kids. Ronald's children's programs were one of the most popular things at the Lighthouse Library.

"I'd enjoy showing you what we've done with what little space we have, Suzanne," he said. "If you have time, that is."

"Of course, I do," Mom said. "I'm on vacation after all."

"You go on up," Bertie said. "I'll take the desk and then show Suzanne the notebook."

Mom linked her arm though Ronald's. The children's library is on the second level. We climbed up the spiral iron stairs, while Charles ran ahead, leaping nimbly from side to side and balancing perfectly on the railing, his huge bushy tail held high.

The children's room was a riot of color and soft fabrics. The space was small, but Ronald had divided it into sections: primary-color beanbags for sitting on, stuffed animals and cartoon characters, and bright plastic tables for the little children; pastel shades and sports team posters for the preteens; darker colors, larger chairs, and big maps on the walls for the teenagers. A scale model of an eighteenth-century sailing ship sat in the deep alcove of the room's single window, overlooking the sea.

Mom clapped her hands. "This is marvelous. I have to bring my grandchildren here one day."

"They'd be more than welcome," Ronald said, clearly pleased by her enthusiasm.

"Has anyone seen— Oh, sorry. Didn't know you had company." The fourth member of our library team, Charlene, came into the room. Tiny blue buds were stuck in her ears and a cord ran down to disappear into her pocket. Charlene was our reference librarian, and when she was working, she enjoyed listening to music. What she considered music, anyway.

I made the introductions.

"You drove all the way down from Boston by yourself?" Charlene said. "That's quite a trip. What do you do when you're driving?"

"Will you look at the time?" I said. "Better be off, Mom. Thanks for the tour, Ronald."

Mom gave me a questioning look. As well she might, but she'd be grateful to me later if I could get her out of here. Charlene was hugely intelligent, a hard worker, and an absolute darling. I adored her, but for some totally unfathomable reason her passion in life was . . .

"I can lend you some CDs if you'd like, Suzanne. I find that you can really get into new music when you're alone on the open road."

"That would be nice of you," Mom said.

"Only on the condition, of course," Charlene said with a grin, "that you write back and tell me which ones you liked the best and what you'd like to hear from my collection next. I'll start you off with Nicki Minaj and maybe Kanye West."

"Who?" Mom said in all innocence.

Charlene's passion in life was hip-hop and rap music. Nothing wrong with that. Except for the fact that she was on a mission to convert the rest of us. No amount of protest could persuade her that we weren't on the verge of conversion.

"I'll run and make a list of what you might like right now," Charlene said. "I'll bring the CDs in tomorrow." She darted out of the room, clearly delighted to have found a willing subject. Mom was so polite that she would make an attempt to listen to the records. And then she'd feel obliged to write to Charlene with her thanks. Thus opening the floodgate of further recommendations.

"You're doomed," I said.

"Nicky who?" Mom said. "Is that the young Estonian concert violinist everyone's raving about?"

Ronald swallowed a laugh.

Footsteps pounded on the stairs and two girls burst into the library, followed by their mother.

"Phoebe. Dallas," Ronald said. "Great to see you." The younger girl dived into the pile of beanbags, while the older dropped to a crouch to examine the rows of books.

"Ronald," the woman said, "I have a bone to pick with you." She paid Mom and me not the slightest bit of attention. The look on my mother's face was priceless. Suzanne Wyatt Richardson was not accustomed to being ignored.

"What would that be, Mrs. Peterson?" Ronald asked sweetly.

"Chris Bernfoot had the nerve to tell me that you recommended a *seventh-grade* book to her Madison. Madison's six months younger than Phoebe. If she is reading seventh-grade material, then why isn't . . ."

I gestured to Mom and headed for the door.

"That was incredibly rude," Mom said as we descended the stairs. "Do you know that frightful woman?"

"Oh, yes. Mrs. Peterson is one of our most regular patrons. She is a devoted and doting mother to her five daughters. Devoted, I might add, to the exclusion of everyone and everything else in the world. She takes it as a personal affront when Ronald spends time with any other kids." Despite their mother's excessive attention, the five Peterson daughters were growing up to be great girls. I figured Ronald had a lot to do with that.

More running, laughing children passed us on the stairs.

"Did you like the children's library?" Bertie asked Mom.

"Totally delightful," Mom said.

"Now, let me show you our pride and joy. Although only temporary, I fear." Bertie unlocked the Austen cabinet with great flourish. I handed Mom the white gloves used to handle the valuable books, and indicated she could pick up the notebook. It was, of course, a precious and fragile thing, about four inches square and an inch thick, with a faded and worn leather cover. Mom opened the book. The hand was small, the writing faded with the passage of years. Mom smiled. "How marvelous." She carefully returned it to its place, and Bertie turned the key in the lock.

We stood quietly for a moment, no one saying anything. Then Mom shook the sentiment off, almost like a dog emerging from the surf, and said, "We'll take my car, Lucy. I'll bring you back."

We said good-bye to Bertie and headed for the door. As I reached for the knob, it flew open as if propelled by a force of nature. A woman about my age, all sharp bones and jutting angles, stood in the doorway. She spotted the bag tossed over my shoulder. "Lucy," she said. "Surely you aren't leaving work in the middle of the day."

"As a matter of fact, I am," I said, shoving Mom out the door. "Gotta run. Catch you later, Louise Jane." I dragged my mom down the path.

"Are we suddenly in some sort of a hurry?"

"Nope." I loved living in the Outer Banks and I loved working at the Lighthouse Library. My colleagues seemed to like working with me and I was making friends. But there is always a bug in the ointment, and Louise Jane was a skinny, lantern-jawed fly buzzing around my jar.

Mom's eye-popping silver Mercedes-Benz SLK stood out among the sturdy American vans and practical Japanese compacts pulling into the parking lot, bringing kids for the summer afternoon preteens program. Since she'd been in New York for a couple of days, she'd probably done a *lot* of shopping. More than would have fit into the suitcase-sized trunk of the two-seater convertible. She must have told the stores to send everything to the house.

"How's Dad?" I asked.

"Busy. Some silly deal with some silly Canadian oil company has run into problems."

My dad was a lawyer, partner in Richardson Lewiston, one of Boston's top corporate law firms. "You know your father. Always working." Mom gave me a strained smile. Outside, in the brilliant North Carolina summer sun, I saw the fine lines edged into the delicate skin around her eyes and mouth.

I climbed into the passenger seat of the car, and we roared off in an impressive display of engine power.

I knew perfectly well that Mom had not come for a visit, or to see that I was settling in nicely. She'd come to try to take me home.

Chapter 2

I pushed thoughts of Boston aside and stared out the window as the SLK pulled out of the lighthouse road onto the highway that wound through the Cape Hatteras National Seashore. It was a perfect Outer Banks summer day of blue sky, soft breeze, and warm sunshine. Not to mention plenty of tourists. Gulls circled overhead and sand drifted onto the road, but the ocean itself was hidden behind dunes and scruffy vegetation struggling to survive in the sea air and poor soil. The top of the car was down, and I took my hair out of its ponytail to let the wind, heavy with salt spray, blow through it. Mom chatted about the play she'd seen in New York, and I made the occasional grunt to indicate I was listening. After a few miles, the highway splits: left to the bridge to Roanoke Island and the charming town of Manteo, right to Nags Head and towns to the north.

We went right, down Virginia Dare Trail, past rows of brightly colored beach houses perched high on stilts to provide views over the dunes (and place them above hurricane waters), and hotels, restaurants, bars, and shops catering to summer visitors. Soon Mom slowed and turned

down a private drive. Sea oats and beach grass gave way
to a pebbled parking area outlined by huge pots overflowing with flowers in controlled colors of purple, white, and
yellow. The hotel had been built in the 1950s but made to
look much older, constructed in the memory of a grand
old Southern plantation: three stories, painted a pale yellow, with a wide white veranda wrapping around three
sides, a long balcony on the upper floors, framed in white
Greek-style pillars. To the side of the building, I caught a
glimpse of the weather-stained boardwalk leading to the
ocean.

The car pulled to a stop in front of the wide, curving
staircase, and the valet, dressed in a uniform of forest
green jacket and knee-length breeches, rushed to open
Mom's door. I clambered out without assistance. Mom
tossed the valet her keys, leaving him to bring in her bags,
and we mounted the stairs. While Mom checked in, I
glanced around. I hadn't been here in many years. When
my brothers and I were children, we used to come to the
Outer Banks every summer to stay with Mom's sister, Ellen, and Ellen's husband, Amos. I still think of those lazy,
happy summers as the best days of my life. Dad had never
accompanied us—work, of course—and Mom had come
less often as we got older. She never stayed at Ellen and
Amos's house, where she would have been welcome, but
always here. Always alone.

More me time, I guess.

Mom and Aunt Ellen came from a family of small
means. My granddad had been a fisherman. His father
had deserted the family when my granddad was only
days old, but my great-grandmother had worked hard
and raised her only child well. She'd died long before I
was born and I've always been sorry not to have known

her. My mom's mother, another hard worker, had been a cashier in a shop. I thought those were roots to be proud of, but Mom was never anything but ashamed of her hardscrabble origins.

I glanced around the hotel lobby. Marble floors, rich red carpets, wood-paneled walls, gleaming brass accents, lush palm trees in brass pots. Only one clerk was behind the reception desk and two people were ahead of Mom in the line. She was tapping the toe of her left espadrille impatiently. I leaned up against a wall. Plaster and paint were peeling where the ceiling met the wall. When I looked closer, I could see stains on the rugs, hairline cracks in the baseboards, a bad gouge in one wall, and a thick layer of dust coating the wide leaves of the potted palms.

The flowers on the round table in the center of the room were not fresh, but fading silk, covered in more dust. An air of neglect hung over the place, along with the overly strong scent of cleaning liquid. I wondered if the hotel was in financial trouble or merely trying to implement "efficiencies."

A van pulled up in front, and through the streaked glass doors, I saw a pack of almost identically dressed, camera-toting Japanese tourists spill out. The receptionist gave a quick glance out the window. Her shoulders visibly slumped and I sensed that no one would be rushing to help her check the new arrivals in.

"Suzanne Richardson," Mom announced. It was her turn at the desk. The receptionist switched her smile back on and said, "Mrs. Richardson, good afternoon."

Mom joined me, key card in hand, a minute later. "I swear the service here gets worse every time I come."

She'd been given a room on the second floor, and the elevator whisked us up. Now that I'd noticed signs of poor repair, I was seeing them everywhere. Scratched paint, a missing section of baseboard, ripped wallpaper, cracks in the elevator mirrors. Small and unobtrusive, but things like that didn't stay small—or unobtrusive—for long.

A cart loaded with towels, cleaning equipment, and an open garbage bag was parked about halfway down the corridor. A woman came out of a room as we approached, a bundle of sheets wrapped in her arms. She wore the plain gray dress of the housekeeping staff, and her thick black hair was pulled into a knot.

"Karen. Hi," I said.

"Lucy, what brings you here?" She pushed a wayward lock of hair off her forehead. She glanced at my mom.

"I'd like you to meet—" I began, but Mom was almost dashing down the corridor. "My mom's visiting."

"That's your mother?" Karen asked.

"Yes."

"Well, well. She's arrived at last, has she?"

We watched as Mom stuffed the key card into the slot. She shook the door handle, and when nothing happened, she ran the card through again. The door swung open and she disappeared at a rapid clip.

That was uncharacteristically rude. Mom could always be counted on to be polite, although not overly friendly, to waiters and hotel staff.

"What's she call herself these days?" Karen said, watching the closed door.

"Suzanne Richardson," I said. "Do you know her?"

"I did. Once."

It sounded to me as though, if they'd known each other in the past, they hadn't parted on good terms. I changed the subject. "Are you coming to book club tomorrow? Did you read the book?"

She turned back to me. "Yes, I did. I hope to make it. You know how much I love the book club. But they laid off two more of the maids and that means more work for the rest of us. Then I have to get home and make dinner, and . . ."

Since getting the Austen collection, we'd found—to our considerable surprise—a keen interest in the classics among Outer Banks residents and visitors. So far the classic novel reading club had been a great success, and the members had been able to discuss the chosen novels with much argument and enthusiasm.

"I understand," I said. I tried to like Karen—I really did—but her constant whining put my teeth on edge. Karen usually stayed after book club to help me clean up. But her real purpose, I thought, was to make sure I knew how hard done by she was.

"I'll let you get back to your work." I hurried after Mom.

She'd left the door open for me, and when I came in, she was standing in front of the French doors. The room opened onto a spacious balcony overlooking the beach and the ocean. People splashed in the waves, relaxed in deck chairs, or strolled along the waterline.

"That was rather rude, wasn't it?" I said. "Karen belongs to my book club and I was going to introduce you."

"I'm sorry, dear. Perhaps I'm more tired than I realized." She turned and faced me. "At least the view is as lovely as I remember. Let's go down for a drink. I'll unpack later."

"You have to drive me back to the library."

"One glass won't hurt."

"I guess. If you want, I can take your car and get someone to come back with me to drop it off later." My mom wasn't much of a drinker, so I had no problem with her having one now if she wanted. As long as she didn't try to drive.

She shrugged.

I looked at her closely. A heaviness I'd never seen before lay behind her eyes. "Are you okay, Mom?"

"Perfectly. Why wouldn't I be, dear? It's been a long day. Perhaps I'll have an early dinner tonight. You will join me, of course."

"Sorry, but I can't. I'm going out with Josie and some of her friends."

"You can cancel that."

"I'd rather not. You and I have lots of time to spend together. Why don't you come to my book club tomorrow night? You'll enjoy it. We're reading *Pride and Prejudice*."

"Perhaps. Actually, Lucille, darling, there's something I've been wanting to talk to you about. Let's go down to the lounge and have a little chat."

Oh dear.

The lobby bar was filling up with new arrivals, but we were shown to a quiet corner by the window. We settled into two wingback chairs covered in pink chintz. A dark stain marked the back of Mom's chair and I expected her to refuse to sit there, but she didn't even seem to notice. We admired the view while we waited for the waitress to arrive. A man dressed in overalls and a large straw hat was sweeping sand off the boardwalk, collecting plant refuse, and tossing it into a bucket at his feet.

"The hotel might be falling down around our ears," Mom said, "but if they can keep the grounds looking good, I'll continue to come here."

"Good afternoon, ladies. Can I get you something to drink?" A smiling waitress appeared at our table. She put down coasters and cocktail napkins.

Mom ordered a glass of Pinot Grigio and I asked for hot tea.

"If I remember correctly," Mom said when the waitress had bustled off, "they used to serve mixed nuts with the drinks in this hotel."

I glanced around. None of the other tables had small bowls. "Times change."

"Rarely for the better," Mom said. "Speaking of which, Ricky is simply beside himself."

I snorted. Finally, we had arrived at the true reason for this visit.

"My dear, he wants me to speak to you."

"How long are you staying?" I asked, choosing to ignore her last comment.

"A few days."

"That's fine," I said. "It's nice to see you. Why don't we invite Aunt Ellen and Uncle Amos to dinner one night? Did you know that Josie's boyfriend has opened his own restaurant? We can go there. He's having the official grand opening week after next, but the restaurant's already doing well. Josie's bakery's doing great, too. Every time I go, she's got a line out the door."

Josie was my cousin, Ellen and Amos's daughter, and one of my very favorite people.

"Lucille, we need to talk."

"No, Mom. We don't. And we aren't going to."

"You're making a terrible mistake."

I pushed my chair back and stood up. "If I am, I'll live with it. You enjoy your wine. I'll take your car and have someone help me drop it off before the library opens tomorrow morning. If you want, phone Aunt Ellen about that dinner."

Mom let out a long sigh. "Very well, dear. I'll say no more. Sit down and have your tea."

"Promise?"

"I promise."

The waitress brought our drinks and I took my seat. I had won the battle. But the war, I feared, was going to be a long one.

Mom chatted about the perilous state of my second brother's marriage; gave me the news from the country club; made a few nasty digs at Evangeline, wife of my dad's business partner; and debated going to Paris in the fall. I listened to her and thought that (other than trips to Paris) she led a boring and lonely life. A life that she was determined to see me re-create with Richard Eric Lewiston III, son of the aforementioned Evangeline and Richard Eric Lewiston Jr., my dad's law partner. That neither Ricky, as he was generally known, nor I was all that keen on getting married was irrelevant to Mom's plans.

Mom had two glasses of wine and I asked for a fresh pot of tea. It was coming up to six o'clock when I said I had to get home to have a quick bite before meeting Josie.

"No need to do that," Mom said. "You can have something here." She picked up the bar menu that had been left on the table, waved the waitress over, and ordered a plate of bruschetta and one of calamari.

"And another one of these, please," she said, lifting her glass.

Three glasses of wine was pretty much unheard-of in my mother's daily life. She must have noticed my expression because she said, "I am on vacation, dear." I wondered if there was another reason for this visit besides trying to drag me off home. Could there be trouble in my parents' marriage? For as long as I could remember, my mom and dad had lived together in a state of mild contempt. She had her tennis lessons and her country club friends; he had his business acquaintances and golf partners. They went to public functions together, holding hands and smiling affectionately at each other. At home, he escaped behind the closed doors of his den, where he disappeared into a cloud of cigar smoke, a glass of expensive whiskey resting on the table beside him, while she watched TV or went to bridge parties. Separate bedrooms, separate lives.

It had always been that way. I don't recall ever hearing a word of affection pass between my parents. But they must have had *some* romantic moments; I'm the youngest of four children.

At quarter to seven I pushed my chair back. "Gotta go, Mom."

"I'll walk you out." She wobbled only slightly as she stood up.

While we'd chatted, the lounge had filled with predinner drinkers. The van load of Japanese tourists were taking pictures of one another standing by the windows or posing with a potted plant.

A man, somewhat overweight, with a bulbous nose in a ruddy face and a greasy comb-over, was coming into the room as we left. He wore a dark suit with a name badge that said GEORGE, MANAGER. He stepped aside to let us pass.

"I think I'll go to my room and read for a while before sleep," Mom said. "Scarcely seven o'clock and I'm exhausted."

"Sue?" the man said.

She turned to him. "Yes?"

"Sue Wyatt?"

"Suzanne Richardson," she said.

"Wyatt's your maiden name, right, Mom?" I said, trying to be helpful. Mom's birth name was Susan. The family had called her Sue as a child. When she married, she'd subtly taken on what she considered to be the more sophisticated moniker of Suzanne.

The man grabbed Mom's hand, and began pumping it with an excess of enthusiasm. Mom looked as though her fingers had been thrust into a barrel of cold, wet fish. She snatched her hand back.

"It's me," he said. "George!"

"George? I know several Georges."

He laughed, trying to hide his embarrassment. "You haven't changed a bit, Sue. I recognized you right away. As beautiful as ever." Her back stiffened as he ran his eyes down her slim, well-dressed figure. Then he looked at me. "Hard to believe someone this old can be your daughter. Ha-ha."

For the second time that day, I'd been told how ancient I looked.

For once, Mom didn't look pleased with the compliment. I could tell she didn't have a clue who this man was.

I thrust out my own hand. "Lucy Richardson. Pleased to meet you, Mr. . . . ?"

"George Marwick." He shook my hand, but kept his eyes on Mom. Not a flicker of recognition crossed her face. His own face fell. "You must remember me, Sue. George. From high school."

"Oh," she said, "George."

The hostess was watching us. I suspected, by the way

her eyes lit up, that George, manager, wasn't all that popular with the staff and she was enjoying watching him being put in his place.

"Took you a minute there, didn't it? That's okay—it's been a long time since we were in school. Gosh, must be ten years now." He laughed heartily.

"Indeed. If you'll excuse us . . ."

George turned to me. "Your mother and I were engaged. We planned to be married—isn't that right, Sue? She was the one that got away. I've always been sorry about that." He snatched up her left hand. The giant diamond glittered in the warm lights of the bar entrance. "Gosh darn, I was hoping you were available again."

My mom might be polite to the hired help, but she certainly didn't allow them to touch her. She pulled her hand away. Her lips were set into a tight line, and her eyes blazed with fury. "I didn't know you *worked* here, George." Only I noticed the emphasis on the word "worked."

George kept smiling. "Yep, for about a year now. I've been in Raleigh since college. When this job came up, I jumped at it. Always wanted to come back to good old OBX someday. What about you, Sue? I've been married three times." He gave me an unattractive wink. "Like I said, I let the best one get away. How about you? Still with that Boston guy you dumped me for?"

"As I said to my daughter," Mom sniffed, "I am very tired."

"Sure, sure. We'll catch up tomorrow. I'll call your room. Maybe we can have lunch."

Mom walked away. I felt that I had to say something to the man. "Nice meeting you, George."

I don't think he even heard me.

The lobby was busy, new people checking in, some

heading into the lounge or the restaurant, others going out for dinner or a walk along the beach.

"Now I remember George Marwick," Mom said to me. "One of those odious little boys who used to follow me around at school. He doesn't seem to have changed a bit." She handed me her valet stub.

"I'll be here at eight thirty," I said. "Do you want me to park the car, or leave it with the valet?"

"Valet, please."

"Sure. See you tomorrow, Mom. Aunt Ellen and Josie are in my book club. We can talk about that dinner then."

She gave me a light kiss on the cheek and I hugged her tightly. She smelled, as she always did, of Chanel No. 5. It's still a scent I associate with love and comfort.

Karen came out of a side room, dressed in her house-keeping uniform, carrying her purse. She was pulling a pack of cigarettes out of the bag, but when she saw us, she stuffed them away and approached with a wide smile. "Sue. How nice to see you. You're looking great. Did you know that your daughter and I've become friends?"

I thought Mom had been less than polite to George, manager. That was nothing compared with the look on her face now. I have said that I love my mother. But at that moment I wanted to slap her. She was shorter than Karen, but managed to look down her long nose at the other woman. The edges of her mouth curled up in the sneer I had last seen when Rachel Ravensburg, who everyone knew had been thrown off the board of the abused women's shelter for embezzling funds, had approached Mom for a donation to the Red Cross. "Karen Whiteside." Mom didn't bother to lower her voice. "I can't say it's a surprise to see you working as a hotel maid."

"Mom!"

Karen recoiled. I swear conversation all around us stopped. George, manager, had come out of the lounge and stood watching. The hostess picked her jaw up off the floor. A stately woman, well into her eighties, tittered in embarrassment. Another woman, all gray—gray hair, gray eyes, a severe gray suit, and flat gray shoes—watched, not even pretending not to be listening. Even her frown seemed gray. I wanted to snarl at her to mind her own business, but I refrained.

"I need extra towels in my room," my mother said. "See to that, will you?"

Karen had approached Mom with a friendly smile and bright eyes. The smile remained frozen on her face, but her eyes darkened. I was reminded of the way the light outside my bedroom window changed when a storm moved in from the sea.

Mom began to walk away.

"I . . . ," I said.

"My name's Karen Kivas now, not that you care," Karen said in a penetrating voice. "Sue Wyatt, you were the most ambitious, greedy bitch in school. I'd heard you slept your way into money." The onlookers, hanging on to every word, gasped. Mom's back stiffened, but she did not turn around. "I still remember things about you, Sue. Things you might not want to get out, now that you're a pillar of respectability. What was it you were accused of? Oh, right, I remember. You were a common thief. And everyone knew it."

Chapter 3

Mom turned a corner and was gone. George rushed over. His face looked like an overinflated red balloon, about to pop. He grabbed Karen by the arm, and pulled her toward the nearest exit. Which happened to be the front door. I ran after them. Connor McNeil, the mayor of our town, stood in the entrance. He had to have heard the whole thing. Connor and I had become good friends; we might even be on the verge of becoming more than just friends. At the sight of him, my humiliation increased tenfold.

"Karen, wait," I cried. "Please."

George stopped at the bottom of the steps. He didn't let go of Karen's arm.

"I am so, so sorry," I said. "I can't believe what my mother said. I'll admit she can be somewhat imperious sometimes. It's just her way. She's . . . insecure."

"You think?" Karen said with a sneer. "Pardon me, Lucy, but your mother's a nasty piece of work. She always was. I'm surprised you turned out okay." She pulled her arm out of George's grasp.

"Let's not involve Lucy," Connor said. "She's not responsible for the actions of her mother."

"I'm sorry you had to witness that, Mr. Mayor," George said. "As for you, Mrs. Kivas . . ."

"Forget about it, George," Connor said. "I'd say Karen was provoked. No need to discipline her if she promises to stay out of Mrs. Richardson's way."

"As if I have any intention of seeing that . . . woman again," Karen said.

George hesitated. He'd probably been about to fire Karen on the spot. I knew Karen had recently separated from her husband. She needed this job.

Connor didn't give George a chance to speak. "Good, then we can consider the incident over."

"As if I don't have enough to put up with," Karen said, with a heavy sigh. "Good night. See you tomorrow, Mr. Marwick." She walked away, her back straight, her head high.

George shrugged, relieved to have the unpleasant decision of whether to fire someone taken out of his hands. He barked at the ramrod-straight valet not to slouch and marched back into the hotel.

I waved my ticket at the valet, who took it and went to get the car.

"Valet parking?" Connor said with a grin that made his gorgeous blue eyes dance. He was dressed in a gray business suit, a crisp white shirt, and a red tie. A trace of five-o'clock shadow darkened his jawline.

"Mom's car. She had several of glasses of wine and I don't want her driving. She doesn't drink much, and the wine seems to have gone to her head. That isn't like her. What happened in there, I mean."

"It's okay, Lucy. We're not responsible for our parents."

"Then why do I feel so bad?"

"Because we can't help *feeling* responsible for our parents. And all the other people we care about." His blue eyes always reminded me of the ocean on a perfect day. Connor and I had had a very short, very innocent romance one summer when we were young and I'd been vacationing in Nags Head. He hadn't been around the following year, but I'd never entirely forgotten him. I'd only recently learned that he'd never forgotten me, either, but he'd not tried to find me again, thinking that I wouldn't be interested in a boy from the Outer Banks, since my family had money. He'd done very well for himself as a result of intelligence, hard work, and determined parents. He'd become a dentist and then the mayor.

Connor let out a low whistle as the SLK pulled up with one looking-pleased-with-himself valet behind the wheel. "You're driving that?"

"It's a change from the Yaris, I will admit. I have to go—it's almost seven and I'm meeting Josie. I'll see you at book club tomorrow?"

"I'm sorry, Lucy, but I can't make it. I have a meeting I can't get out of. I loved the book, though. Perhaps you and I can discuss it another time. Over dinner?"

"That would be nice."

"What are we reading next?"

"I'm going to put it to a vote. Either *Jane Eyre*, for another look at the social restrictions on women of the age, or *Tess of the D'Urbervilles* for a nasty look at the life of women of the age. Feel free to send your own suggestions."

"I will," he said. "I gotta run. I'm late."

We said our good-byes and I drove back to the Bodie Island Lighthouse. I might have enjoyed driving the SLK a bit too much, and I made it in record time.

I quickly changed out of my work clothes into a short blue-and-green skirt, a blue blouse, strappy sandals, and loads of costume jewelry. I remembered to feed Charles, and then headed back into town to meet Josie and some of her friends at a bar featuring live music. Mom hadn't said I *couldn't* take her car out again, so I drove the SLK. Mindful of my responsibilities toward the beautiful car, I didn't dare have a drink, but I still had a lot of fun. Josie's friends were great, and they made room for me in their close-knit circle. We didn't stay late, since Josie started work in her bakery at the awful hour of four a.m. and some of her friends were early risers also. By the end of the night, I realized that I'd learned the secret of attracting male attention. Drive a flashy, expensive, European car. A pack of men of all ages had been gathered around the SLK as I left the bar.

The following morning, I wanted to burrow back under the covers when my alarm went off at eight a.m., but the thought of my cousin's intense schedule kept my hand away from the snooze button. I listened to Charles prowling around the minuscule kitchen, hoping some food might have escaped his bowl, and I rolled out of bed and started to get ready for work. Mom called as I was sitting down to my muesli and coffee. "I'm not feeling too well today, dear," she said. "Change in the weather, no doubt."

I thought I showed admirable restraint by not mentioning that several glasses of wine and no dinner will do that to a person.

"As a result, I'm going to have a quiet day and simply

relax. I'll spend the day by the pool, have a light lunch, maybe go for a walk to the pier later."

"That sounds nice."

"You can keep the car until it's time to pick me up for your book club."

"See you then, Mom. Have a nice day."

In the summer, traffic through the library doors is totally dependent on the weather. It was a beautiful sunny day, and thus we weren't very busy. Ronald is off most Tuesdays, so we don't have children's programs to fill the library with laughter and excitement. It was a good chance to get caught up on paperwork. Shortly before noon, our only patrons were two elderly sisters who never stopped squabbling and Harvey Spineta, a frequent visitor. Harvey had recently been widowed and I guessed that he mainly came to the library for the company. He'd taken his regular spot in a corner near the Austen alcove, and was reading magazines. The front door opened and a woman marched in. "Marched" being the operative word. Her back was ramrod straight and her steps were firm. She wore a gray T-shirt tucked into baggy gray knee-length shorts with a gray belt tied firmly around her thin waist. Her gray hair was tied into a tight knot at the back of her head. She ran her gray eyes over me, sniffed in a show of disapproval, and began studying the room.

"Good morning," I said. "Are you here to see the Austen collection?"

"No."

"Oh." I was momentarily taken aback, but plowed on. "We have a special exhibit for the summer. A full set of Jane Austen first editions. Also a personal notebook of Miss Austen herself. Written in her own hand." The widower put down his magazine and the sisters stopped berating each other over some long-ago, and long-forgotten, slight. I got to my feet. "They're in that alcove, over there. Let me show you."

"I can see it perfectly well. Thank you. Are you trying to find something to do?"

"No."

"You can get back to your work, then," she said.

I dropped into my chair.

As he always did, Charles was keeping Harvey company. Maybe the man came here to let the cat curl up on his lap as much as to read. As the woman passed them, walking firmly in her sensible gray shoes, Charles slowly stood up. The hair on his back lifted; he arched his body and hissed.

The woman stopped. "Are you allowed to bring your animal into the library, sir?"

Harvey blinked. "Isn't mine. Library cat."

The woman threw me a look that indicated the strength of her displeasure. But she said nothing and bent to examine the Austen collection. I went back to work.

She didn't stay long, and left in the wake of the still-squabbling sisters. There was something familiar about her, and I struggled to recall where I'd seen her before. Then it came to me: she'd been in the lobby of the Ocean Side Hotel last night, watching that scene between Mom and Karen. She'd been dressed in an all-gray suit then, too. A Gray Woman.

Not a very friendly one, either. I put her out of my mind and carried on with my day.

At six thirty I went to pick up Mom.

I took the SLK. I put the top down and enjoyed the feel of the salty wind on my face and in my hair. My hair is naturally curly, and it fuzzes into a ball resembling steel wool when exposed to sea air. But I'm from Boston and after many tearful mornings, I decided that I'd have to live with what I'd thought of as my curse. My mother, of course, has sleek, silky hair. As I might have said, my mother is extraordinarily beautiful. I am not. Josie, in fact, looks more like Mom than I do. And Josie has the added advantage of getting her height from her six-foot father rather than the much shorter Wyatt women.

I'd learned long ago not to wish for what I could never have.

At the lights at Whalebone Junction, a car pulled up beside me. Two young men whistled and waved and gave me thumbs-up gestures. I grinned at them, assuming they were referring to the car, not to me. When the light changed, I pulled away in an impressive display of horse-power.

Not your mother's librarian.

One of my mom's virtues is punctuality. Despite living in a world of the fashionably late, Mom never was able to get rid of some of the fisherman and shop-clerk habits she'd been raised with. She was always where she said she would be, when she said she would be there. Today she was waiting for me on the steps of the hotel. She climbed into the passenger seat and gave me a kiss on the cheek. She carried her Michael Kors purse as well as an enormous canvas beach bag. "What's in the bag?" I asked.

"A scarf in case it's cool later."

"Mighty big bag for a scarf."

"We are going to a library. I thought I might check out a book or two. I've almost finished the book I brought."

I turned the car around, and we headed out of town.

I glanced at the car's clock as I pulled into the library

parking lot. Five to seven. Most of the members of the book club had arrived and were milling about outside, waiting for me. I tried to look nonchalant as I put the roof up on the car. Theodore Kowalski and Butch Greenblatt came over to admire it. "New car?" Butch asked, almost drooling.

"Not for you, Butch," Theodore said, in the fake English accent he thought made him appear scholarly. "You would not fit."

I laughed at the image. Butch was a solid, muscular six foot five. A good-looking man in his early thirties with dark hair cut short, chiseled cheekbones, a strong jaw, and eyes of a deep brown speckled with flakes of gold.

"You'd always have to put the top down," I said.

He looked genuinely sorry. "I'd still like to take it for a spin, Lucy."

"If you're good in class tonight," I laughed, "I might ask Mom to let you drive around the loop." Meaning the loop that was the end of the lighthouse road. "This is my mother, Suzanne Richardson. She's here for a visit and is going to join us tonight."

Butch put out his hand and Theodore nodded.

Mom shook, and gave the men warm smiles. "I'm glad you like my car, gentlemen." She threw me a questioning look that I pretended not to see. Men don't usually join book clubs. And not a classic novel club such as ours. But Theodore had a degree in English lit and was a passionate (although impoverished) book collector, and Butch . . . well, I think Butch came because he liked me. I liked him, too.

Josie and Aunt Ellen waited for us with the group by the door. Mom and her sister exchanged enthusiastic greetings, and Mom gave Josie a big hug, which my cousin was unable to return because of the tempting-looking bakery box cradled in her arms. I unlocked the library door and we crowded in. I switched on lights and led the way past the circulation desk, through the main hall, and up the twisting, spiral iron stairs. The children's library was on the second floor, and the third level was where we housed research volumes as well as kept a small (very small) meeting room. It was my job to set out the chairs in the third-floor room and lay out glasses and napkins, and I'd done so before going to get Mom.

I glanced around the room as the members of the book club filed in, followed by Charles the cat. Drat, I'd lost Theodore. I'd been warned the day I started working here that Theodore had what Bertie called "wandering hands," meaning books would sometimes find themselves in his coat pockets, or make their way to the shelves in his home. We kept a small but impressive collection of rare books and old maps in a private room accessible by only the back staircase. The room was kept locked when not in use, but . . .

"Theodore," I bellowed. "Get up here."

His head appeared at a bend in the stairs, followed by his long, thin body. "I am coming, Lucy. This is a library. No need to shout." I didn't see any bulges in his pockets that hadn't been there a few minutes ago.

Mom and Aunt Ellen had taken seats, and (satisfied that Theodore hadn't nicked any of our collection) I helped Josie lay the contents of her box out on the table. Josie whispered to me, "How long's your mom here for?"

"She hasn't said."

"What's she want?"

"Me," I whispered. "She wants me. Back in Boston."

Josie stopped her work, a lemon square sprinkled

with a dusting of icing sugar in one hand. "Are you considering it?"

"Did Lizzy consider marrying Mr. Collins?" I said, referring to characters in *Pride and Prejudice*.

"Only briefly. Although her mother wanted her to."

"Exactly."

Butch pushed between us and reached for a raspberry tart. Josie hip-checked him. "Back off, buster—wait until I'm finished here." He snatched up the delicate pastry and quickly retreated.

"You know you'll never win," I said.

"Not when it comes to the Greenblatt brothers." Josie's almost-fiancé, Jake, was Butch's brother.

Butch grinned and bit into his tart. He looked around the room. "His Honor not honoring us with his presence tonight?"

"He had a meeting," I said.

"Gee," Butch replied. "That's too bad." He gave Josie an exaggerated wink and went to find a seat.

Josie moved away from the table, and the rush to the refreshments began. Grace Sullivan, who was Josie's closest friend and rapidly becoming one of mine, cried, "Let the festivities begin" in her usual flamboyant manner. She greeted Josie and me, whom she'd last seen only the previous night, with a European-style double kiss, one on each cheek. Mrs. Peterson, one of our most enthusiastic patrons, for once not accompanied by some combination of her five daughters, was next to arrive. "Charity is at some silly soccer camp," she declared to the room. "An entire week wasted chasing around after a foolish ball. As for Primrose, she's feeling unwell. Nothing to worry about, I'm sure. Just the sort of thing young girls get, you know."

Which I interpreted to mean that the teenage girls were grateful for any excuse not to have to spend their summer evening discussing classic works of literature with people their mother's age. Even I, who'd loved the classics the first time I was exposed to them, could understand that.

My mom and Aunt Ellen chatted happily while everyone helped themselves to refreshments and found seats. The sisters were not close and could go for a year or more without seeing each other, especially now that my siblings and I were older. Aunt Ellen and her husband, Amos, were true Bankers (as longtime locals were sometimes called) and their idea of a vacation was a weekend in Duck or Hatteras. They had built my uncle's law office together, and were both very active in the life of the community. My mom had different goals in life, which was why she left the area, planning to never return. She had obtained most of those goals.

Theodore took the seat on the other side of Ellen and my aunt introduced him to Mom. Ellen said something and Mom threw back her head and laughed. It had been a long time, I realized, since I'd heard my mom laugh with such abandon. She held the Michael Kors purse on her lap and slid her beach bag under her chair. Butch sat beside Mom and joined the conversation.

Everyone except for Karen had arrived and once they were clutching glasses of tea or lemonade and napkins full of pastries, I called the meeting of the Bodie Island Lighthouse Library Classic Novel Reading Club to order.

Most of our members had joined the group because they wanted to discover new books and to hear other people's opinions on what they'd read. Theodore came because he liked to talk about not only the book in question, but every other book of any possible similarity, the social and political issues of the time, the author's life and influences, and anything else he could think of to impress us with his range of knowledge. It was exhausting trying to get him to stick to the topic at hand and not let him dominate the conversation. Tonight he was dressed for book club in his usual wardrobe of three-piece tweed suit, paisley cravat, and gold watch attached by a chain to his vest pocket. He pulled out the plain-glass spectacles he wore for the effect and slipped them over his ears. He was only a year or two my senior, but unlike almost everyone else in the world, he tried to give the impression he was older than he was.

Louise Jane McKaughnan came because she wanted to sit beside Mrs. Fitzgerald, the chair of the library board. At the moment, Charles was curled up in Mrs. Fitzgerald's lap, allowing her to stroke his fur and coo about what a beautiful cat he was. Louise Jane's main goal in life was to work at the library, and she hoped her way in would be through Mrs. Fitzgerald. Louise Jane's second goal in life was to get rid of me.

Louise Jane was still fetching tea and squares for Mrs. Fitzgerald when I asked who'd read the book. Every hand, except for Louise Jane's, as it was occupied with bribes for Mrs. Fitzgerald, went up.

The bell at the front door rang. "Must be Karen," I said.

Josie jumped up. "I'll get it." She ran out of the room, and a moment later we could hear the iron stairs clatter as she came back up, accompanied by more footsteps than I'd expected. To my surprise, Josie was followed by not only Karen but also George, the manager of the Ocean Side Hotel.

"Sorry I'm late." Karen had changed out of her house-keeper's uniform and was dressed in a loose orange blouse and jeans. As usual, an aura of tobacco smoke hung over her. "I had trouble getting the car started. I don't know what I'm going to do if it gives out on me now. Everything's just so expensive these days. Oh, the raspberry tarts are all gone." She pouted. "They're my favorites."

Butch bowed his head.

"Hope you folks don't mind my dropping in," George said. "Karen here told me about her book club earlier this afternoon, and it sounded real interesting." He couldn't keep his eyes from wandering to my mom.

When Karen saw Mom, her mouth tightened into a thin line. She plopped herself into the last vacant chair, directly across the room from Mom. My mother suddenly remembered she had something urgent to attend to on her iPhone. She pulled it out of her bag and began pushing buttons and reading the screen, her brow furled with concentration. I didn't bother to point out that cell phones didn't get reception deep inside the thick stone walls.

All the chairs were taken, and George was looking around for someplace to sit. Butch jumped to his feet. "I can stand."

"I wouldn't want to . . . ," George said, practically sprinting across the room. "Gee, Sue. I didn't know you'd be here." George Marwick was one dreadful liar. He was dressed in a sports jacket that was too large for his body and jeans that bagged in the seat. Not a good look. His thin hair was freshly greased and neatly combed over his shiny bald pate.

Butch leaned against the wall and crossed his arms. I was about to suggest he go down to the children's library and get a chair, but when I thought about the tiny little stools, I changed my mind.

We had a successful meeting. I managed to keep Theodore under some degree of control. George hadn't read the book, but at least he didn't ask foolish questions. My mom had read the book, although a long time ago, and she seemed to enjoy the discussion.

"What would you like to read for next time?" I asked once we'd finished dissecting *Pride and Prejudice*. "I've had suggestions for *Jane Eyre* or *Tess of the D'Urbervilles*."

"Doesn't *Tess* have a murder in it?" CeeCee Watson said.

"Yes, it does."

CeeCee was the wife of Detective Sam Watson, of the Nags Head Police. She was an avid reader of mystery novels, although her husband claimed to hate them. "Let's read that, then," she said.

"I don't know," Mrs. Peterson began. "Is such a book suitable for Primrose and Charity?"

"This is an adult reading group," CeeCee reminded her. "The girls don't have to come."

Mrs. Peterson huffed, but made no further objections. Everyone else agreed on *Tess*, the meeting broke up, and most of the group headed off into the night. Josie and Grace left together, laughing at a private joke. Josie carried an empty bakery box. Butch pulled me aside and spoke in a low voice. "Jake's having the official grand opening of the restaurant next Thursday. Will you come with me, Lucy?"

"I'd like that."

"I am so proud of my older brother, I might just burst." He grinned and I grinned back. When he walked away, I could see Mom watching me. She did not look happy.

Karen lingered, as she usually did, to help tidy up. Mom stayed to wish me a good night, and George was determined to grab his chance to talk to Mom. She was icily polite, but the expression on her face clearly indicated that she didn't have the least bit of interest in hearing about the joys and challenges of running a five-star hotel. Or why George kept getting divorced. Every time he called her Sue, her face scrunched up as though she were sucking on a lemon. She busied herself gathering up glasses and crumpled napkins.

There were no leftover pastries for me to take upstairs to enjoy later. Drat.

Karen folded the chairs and stacked them in a corner and then we trooped downstairs. High above us, the lighthouse light flashed, as it would all through the night, in its rhythm of 2.5 seconds on, 2.5 seconds off, 2.5 seconds on, and then 22.5 seconds off. Most of the light was directed out to sea, but traces of it leaked into the building. I found the reliability of it extremely comforting. Charles showed off, walking beside us on the iron railing, his fluffy brown tail high. He leapt down when we reached the main floor.

"How about I give you a lift to the hotel, Sue?" George said.

"I have my own car," Mom said.

"You can come back and get it tomorrow. It'll be safe here overnight."

"I want to visit with my daughter," she said. "Good night, George."

Even he could take that hint, and he left, after suggesting they meet for breakfast in the morning. To which Mom didn't bother to reply.

"Guess I'd better be off, too." Karen shifted the weight of the cheap brown plastic purse on her shoulder, as though the weight of the world were in it.

Mom coughed. "Karen, I want to apologize."

Karen's eyes narrowed. "For what?" Instead of simply accepting the apology, Karen was going to force Mom to spit it out. I turned my back and fussed over the dishes.

"I was unpardonably rude to you yesterday. At the hotel. I am sorry. I hope you'll accept my apology."

With a cry that had me turning around, Karen launched herself into Mom's arms. "Oh, Sue. I can't tell you how happy that makes me. We were such great friends once." Over the other woman's back, Mom's eyes were large and startled. She made vague patting gestures.

Finally Karen unwrapped herself. She wiped her eyes. "Things are so difficult sometimes. Norm and I broke up— did you know, Lucy? I always said I'd kick the drunken bum out when the kids grew up, but then there were the grandchildren and never enough money. But he lost another job, and I couldn't take it anymore. He had to go." Karen linked her arm through Mom's. "Why don't you come over to the house tomorrow for dinner? We can have a nice long chat. I can't wait to hear all about your family. You are so lucky, Sue. . . ."

"I'm having dinner with my sister and her family tomorrow." Mom choked again and said, "How about lunch?"

I gave her a thumbs-up.

"Lunch," Karen said. "Must be nice to be able to go out for lunch. I only get half an hour at work, and I have to run errands or call my daughter and make arrangements for the grandchildren, do all the things Norm, my husband, used to do. Not that he ever did much. The drunken bum. But I don't complain. Friday and Saturday are the only days I get off. I don't even get Sundays. Work at the hotel doesn't let up, even for Sunday, you know."

I followed them through the dark and, except for Karen's droning voice, quiet main room to the front door and locked up after them. Without waiting to see their cars drive away, I switched the last of the lights off and made my way upstairs.

Chapter 4

My apartment, my beloved lighthouse aerie, was located on the fourth floor. I unlocked the door, and Charles ran in ahead of me straight to the kitchen area, where he exclaimed in shock when he found his food bowl empty. The apartment was tiny, only one small room plus a bathroom, but I absolutely adored it. The single window was a tall, narrow space that gave a million-dollar view over the marshes, past the beach, and out to sea. Set into four-foot-deep stone walls, the window had a bench seat covered in blue-and-yellow cushions, making it the perfect place to curl up with a cup of hot tea and a good book. Whitewashed brick walls curved with the shape of the lighthouse tower. A white daybed, piled high with pillows and matching cushions. Two wingback chairs around a low coffee table. The kitchen contained only a microwave and a toaster oven, so it wasn't good for much cooking. But I wasn't much of a cook, so that didn't really matter.

First things first. I filled Charles's bowl. Charles was the library cat; he was supposed to spend his time downstairs and eat and sleep in the staff break room. But as soon as I moved in, he had decided he liked my room better.

I loved having his company.

It was scarcely nine thirty and I was exhausted. Mentally more than physically. As I got ready for bed, I thought over the last couple of days. Mom could be prickly, haughty, self-absorbed, but she wasn't a mean person. She didn't exactly ooze friendliness to the hired help, but I had never before seen her behave in the outright rude way she had toward first George Marwick and then Karen Kivas.

Was there something personal about that? They both claimed to have been friends with her in her youth.

Fortunately, things with Karen had been resolved. Karen could play the martyr, but it would do Mom good, I thought, to reestablish some old friendships. I was quite proud of her for climbing down off her high horse and making the effort to be friends again.

As for George, manager, we've all had the experience of trying to get rid of an unwelcome suitor.

I sent a quick e-mail to Jake's Seafood Bar, requesting a table for five for tomorrow night, and then settled into my pillows while Charles curled up at my feet. I took one of the Fixer-Upper mysteries by Kate Carlisle (how could I resist a book with a lighthouse on the cover?) off the night table, and began to read.

Thick curtains cover the single window to keep out the light from the thousand-watt bulb flashing less than a hundred feet over my head, and the first thing I do on waking is pull them open to check the weather.

Today, the yellow ball of the sun was rising over the ocean in a sky of flawless blue. Another perfect Outer Banks summer day. Although here, on a razor-thin strip of land thrust into the Atlantic Ocean, the weather could, and often did, change dramatically in minutes.

Charles pointed out that his food bowl had somehow become emptied in the night. I fed him, and then got myself groomed and ready for the day. Then, as is my custom, I pulled up a chair to my small table and opened my laptop. I read the local and Boston papers online, enjoying my first cup of coffee and munching on yogurt and granola. At eight thirty, I put the dishes in the sink, told Charles it was time we went to work, and headed downstairs. When I'd worked at the Harvard Library, every morning involved a fight through the commuter traffic. For the improved commute alone, I cherished my life at the Bodie Island Lighthouse Library.

I was the first to arrive. I slipped outside before beginning work, as I usually did, to enjoy some sun on my face and get fresh sea air into my lungs.

Two cars were in the parking lot: my Yaris and a scratched, rusting, dusty Dodge Neon several yards farther away. At first I paid the Neon no attention. The lighthouse borders the marshes between Roanoke Sound and the National Seashore. Wooden walkways wind through the marsh, ending at a rough boat dock on the water. Plenty of people come at sunrise, to hike or catch birds beginning their day. It's a popular spot, and those who don't arrive by boat drive.

I greeted the morning with a few yoga moves—as Bertie, who had also become my yoga instructor, had taught me. And then I gripped first one foot behind me, and then the other, practicing my balance and getting the kinks out. It was so delightfully quiet here in the morning. Birds called as they passed overhead and the wind rustled the grasses in the marsh. I heard no voices, unlike on other mornings when people appeared, laughing and chatting about the birds they'd seen.

I glanced at the Neon.

I'd seen Karen's car only once. I wasn't sure, but it might have been one like this. And in much the same condition.

Was this Karen's car? It was possible.

I hadn't stayed downstairs to watch Mom and Karen drive away last night. She might have persuaded Mom to take her for a spin in the SLK. Maybe they ended up at the hotel, having a drink and chatting about old times.

I swung my arms in the air, breathing deeply. The air was fresh and clean, tinged with salt. Mom wasn't much for the beach. She preferred a hotel pool, with lounge chairs, umbrellas, paying guests, and hovering waiters. I'd talk her into coming to the beach with me on Sunday.

If she was still here. She hadn't said anything at all about going home.

I was about to head back inside when my attention was caught by a group of large black birds sweeping low out of the sky. They disappeared around the side of the lighthouse to be greeted by raucous cawing from their fellows who'd arrived earlier.

Nature was lovely and all that, but it did have its drawbacks. I hoped there wasn't a dead bird or small animal on the property. We got lots of kids visiting. I'd better have a look.

I rounded the corner, holding my breath, prepared to chase off a murder of crows and see something highly unpleasant.

I yelled and waved my arms, and the birds flew away, protesting loudly. A large purse had been tossed to one side, where it lay in the sunshine. Against the walls of the lighthouse, in deep shadow, I could see something made of denim. I blinked, my eyes focused, and I realized I was staring at legs, human legs, wrapped in jeans.

Chapter 5

First I called Bertie. After I'd told her what I'd found and she said she was on her way, I called 911.

I ran toward what I knew to be Karen Kivas's body. I dropped to my knees beside her, scarcely feeling the impact of the ground. She was lying on her back, staring up to the sky. I touched my fingers to her neck, checking for a pulse, and shuddered when I felt her icy-cold skin. Nothing moved. The ground under her head was wet. I could do nothing for her.

I was wearing a short-sleeved linen jacket over a T-shirt and a knee-length skirt. I slipped out of my jacket and draped it over Karen's face and head. Somehow it seemed like the right thing to do. Then I waited.

Only a few minutes passed before I heard the sound of help approaching.

The police arrived first, flashing blue and red lights and loud sirens. The car tore into the lane, and parked half on the lawn. Butch jumped out. He was in uniform, and did not smile on seeing me running toward him.

"It's Karen," I said. "She's dead."

"You stay here," he said.

Bertie arrived next, closely followed by an ambulance.

Butch ordered Bertie and me inside, told us not to leave until a detective had spoken to us, and went to meet the paramedics. I almost told them not to bother hurrying, but I bit my tongue.

Bertie slipped an arm around my shoulders and bustled me into the library.

I dropped into the chair behind the circulation desk.

"What happened?" Bertie asked.

I shook my head. "I've no idea. I went out for some air, heard the birds, and went to check. It's Karen Kivas." Charles leapt onto the desk and from there into my lap.

"You wait right there, honey," Bertie said. "I'm going to put on the kettle."

I stroked the cat's soft fur. From where I sat, I could see outside. More cruisers were arriving. Sam Watson pulled up in an unmarked car. He glanced toward the library, and I wondered if he could see me watching him. I pulled back.

When I looked again, he was gone.

Bertie brought me a cup of hot tea, thick with sugar. Then she phoned Ronald and Charlene and told them not to come to work until they heard from her. She didn't bother to explain. The news would be all over the Outer Banks in minutes, if it wasn't already. I hoped they'd be able to keep Karen's identity under wraps until her family was told.

Bertie pulled up a chair. "As we have a few quiet moments, why don't we do your performance review?"

"What?"

"Time for your first official quarterly evaluation. I was going to do it this week anyway. Might as well get it over with."

I looked at her. Her eyes were warm and a soft smile touched the edges of her mouth. She was trying to distract me from brooding on what was happening outside. I forced out a smile in return. Charles purred.

My performance evaluation went very well. Bertie was pleased with the job I was doing and would be informing the board of such. Basking in her praise, offering my own suggestions at how I might do a better job, sipping hot, sweet tea, and patting a contented cat, I almost forgot what was going on outside. But the pleasant feeling ended when the door swung open to admit Butch and Watson.

"The library will remain closed until you have my permission to reopen," Watson said.

"Now see here, Detective," Bertie said, rising to protest.

"The issue is not open for discussion, Ms. James," he replied.

Bertie muttered under her breath, but sank back into her chair.

"Officer Greenblatt says you made the nine-one-one call, Lucy," Watson said.

"Yes."

"Want to tell me what happened?"

It didn't take long. I'd heard nothing last night or this morning out of the ordinary. Karen had been here for my book club. "I can second that," Butch said. She'd left shortly after nine, but I didn't see what she did or where she went after she'd left the library.

I told them I'd been surprised to see her car here this morning. "She did say she was having car trouble. Maybe it didn't start, so she got a lift home. And then she came back this morning to try it again."

I didn't mention who was the last person—as far as I knew—who'd seen Karen.

My mom.

Watson flipped a page of his notebook. "I'll need the names of everyone in this book club."

"CeeCee Watson for one." The moment the words were out, I could have slapped myself. I don't mean to back talk when I'm under pressure, but somehow the wrong thing always seems to come out.

"We'll consider her carefully," Watson said drily.

"I can help you with the list," Butch said. "I left book club at the same time as Josie and Grace. We chatted for a couple of minutes, mostly about Jake's grand opening, and then went our separate ways. The parking lot was pretty much empty when I left. I think only Karen, some guy named George who I don't know, and Lucy's mother were still here."

"And Lucy, I presume?" Watson asked.

"Yes," I said.

"Your mother was here?"

"She's visiting."

"In what order did the last of them leave?" Watson asked.

I thought. I had to phrase this so it wouldn't look as though my mom was the last one to see Karen. But she had been. They were watching me. I opened my mouth.

The door flew open and a uniformed woman came in. "Coroner's here, Detective."

"I'll be right out. I need to talk to you, Lucy," Watson said, "but it will have to wait."

"Are you sure we can't keep the library open?" Bertie asked.

He gave her a look that spoke volumes.

"Just thought I'd ask," she said.

"Can I leave?" I said. "I'd like to go to the hotel and check up on my mom. Let her know what's happening."

"I don't see why not," Watson said. "I know where you live."

If that was intended to be a joke, it wasn't a very funny one.

The parking lot was jammed with emergency vehicles. Yellow police tape had been strung up around the side of the lighthouse as well as around the Neon. An officer had been placed at the boardwalk to turn the curious away, and a cruiser was stationed at the entrance off the highway, to tell everyone the library and the marsh were closed.

I just wanted to get out of there, so I didn't call Mom to tell her I was coming until I'd parked my car and was walking into the hotel.

"I'm at the hotel. I have to talk to you."

"I thought you were working this morning."

"Something's come up."

"I'm awake but still in bed. Why don't you join me for breakfast? I'll order room service and we can sit on my balcony. It's a glorious day."

"I don't feel much like eating, Mom."

"Just have coffee, then. Lucy, I spoke to Evangeline last night."

"I don't want to know." Evangeline was Ricky's mother. She was as keen on our marriage as my own mom was. Evangeline was hoping for an injection of funds into the rapidly declining fortune of the Lewiston family. Everyone in Boston knew the Lewistons were in financial difficulty, largely because of the gambling addiction and other not-quite-respectable indulgences of Ricky's dad. Not everyone knew that I myself had no money of my own other than what I earned through my job. My grandparents hadn't left me or my brothers anything, not even in trust. My brothers, not to mention their wives, were still mighty bitter about that. As for me, I'm happy with my quiet, comfortable life just the way it is.

"Evangeline told me Ricky brought that ridiculous Wallace girl to dinner the other night. The poor boy, he's so devastated by your abrupt departure, all common sense has deserted him."

"Mom!"

"Yes, dear?"

"I am not having this conversation. Anyway, I think Elaine Wallace is very nice. No one cares anymore about that incident when she was in college."

"I care. Evangeline cares."

"Evangeline can be hopelessly old-fashioned sometimes." I did not add that Evangeline cared only that Elaine's family wasn't rich enough. I ground my teeth. About two seconds ago I'd said I wasn't going to talk about it. And here I was, still talking about it. "The police are at the library, if you must know, because someone has died."

"Not one of your colleagues, I hope."

I shook my head. "No."

"I'm glad to hear it. Most unfortunate, and I'm sure it was a distressing occurrence, but I suppose you get a lot of elderly people at the library. If you don't want to eat on the balcony, we can go down to the dining room. Are they still open for breakfast? Did you notice, dear?"

I wanted to be mad at Mom for being so blasé when her childhood friend had died, but I reminded myself that she didn't know who I was talking about. "I'm coming to your room, Mom. Stay there."

"Where else would I go?"

I threw my phone back into my pocket and ran up the stairs.

Mom had propped the door to her room open and called, "Be right there, dear," from the bathroom in answer to my shout. I came in, shut the door behind me, and went to stand by the windows. The waves were high today, but walkers and joggers were out, and children erected sand castles while watchful parents set out beach umbrellas and blankets. Fishermen relaxed in their chairs, poles arching into the water.

I felt Mom beside me. "I'd enjoy a walk. This hotel is practically falling down around us, but the location is still perfect."

I turned to look at her. Sometimes it seemed as though it took hours for her to get ready to face the day, but when she wanted to, she could throw herself together in a flash. This morning she again wore Ralph Lauren. White capris, a black-and-white-striped sleeveless, scoop-neck T-shirt. A white linen jacket with black lapels, collar, and cuffs was hung neatly on the closet door. For today's jewelry, she'd chosen diamond stud earrings, a thick silver necklace, and a matching bracelet. Somehow, she'd managed to get her hair to fall in soft waves around her face despite the sea air. And her makeup had been lightly, but perfectly, applied.

By way of greeting she said, "You need a sweater or jacket to wear over that T-shirt. The sleeveless look is not at all professional, never mind that the First Lady seems to be able to get away with it. Much larger earrings would look better on you. I have something you can try."

I didn't mention that I had started the day with a jacket. "I'm not here to talk about accessories, Mom. You need to know—"

"I need breakfast. As I am dressed already, we might as well go to the dining room. If you won't talk about repairing your relationship with Ricky—"

"I don't have a relationship with Ricky to repair. Mom, don't you understand that Ricky and I don't *want* to get married?"

She gave me that smile. The one that said I might have *thought* I wanted a pony for Christmas, but I would be much happier with a pretty new dress for the children's New Year's party at the country club. Ricky had proposed to me, formally, down on one knee, extending a small blue box while Champagne rested in a silver cooler. That's what had precipitated my flight from Boston. I knew Ricky didn't really love me, any more than I loved him. He was simply doing what was expected of him. "I've been here more than a month, Mom. If he wants me, he can find me. Do you know that Ricky hasn't so much as sent me a text since I left?"

"You told us your cell doesn't always work in the lighthouse, so we're better off using the library landline."

"I told you that, Mom. Not Ricky."

She glanced to one side.

"Oh," I said, "you passed the message on. Well, he hasn't phoned me at that number, either."

"He's waiting for you to make the first move."

I doubted that. I forced my head away from thoughts of ponies and Ricky and back to the matter at hand.

"Mom, this is really important. Something has happened—"

A knock at the door. And then, even more unwelcome

than Mom's interruptions, the deep voice of Detective Sam Watson saying, "Mrs. Richardson, police. Open up."

Mom threw me a startled glance. I pasted a smile on my face and threw open the door. "Good morning, Detective," I trilled.

"Lucy, you got here mighty fast."

I could have said the same for him. Instead I smiled. "Detective Watson, may I introduce my mother, Suzanne Richardson. Mom, you met Detective Watson's wife, CeeCee, last night at book club." I might have been at one of my mom's bridge parties or charity luncheons, making sure everyone was made to feel welcome.

Unlike guests arriving to play bridge and nibble crustless (and tasteless) sandwiches, Butch stood slightly behind and to one side of Watson—as if I were about to pull out a gun and go down in a blaze of glory. "Come in, Detective. Officer. Mom, you remember Butch from last night."

"Nice to see you again, Mrs. Richardson," Butch mumbled, embarrassed at the intersection of his professional and social lives. Watson only grunted. Mom tried, but her hostess smile failed her. The two men walked into the room.

It was a big room, as hotel rooms go, with a king-sized bed, a two-seater sofa, a desk and chair, but Butch and Watson seemed to take up all the space. Watson strolled to the balcony doors and stood there, simply looking out. Butch shifted from one big foot to another, not looking at me.

For once, my mother was silent. She took a seat on the sofa. She crossed her legs at the ankles and rested her hands lightly in her lap. Her nails were pink. The same color was on her toes, the manicure and pedicure fresh and perfect.

Watson turned around. "Tell me," he said, "about Karen Kivas."

Mom couldn't hide her surprise. "Karen? Why on earth do you want to know about Karen?"

"I'll ask the questions, Mrs. Richardson. If you don't mind."

"She works here. At the hotel. I knew Karen many years ago when I lived in Nags Head. We spoke briefly the day I arrived here in the hotel, and met again last night at my daughter's book club." She glanced at Butch for confirmation. "We have nothing in common. We were friends for a short while back in school, but even then we soon went our separate ways. We had little to say to each other."

"What time did you leave the library after the book club broke up?"

"I didn't check my watch. Not long after nine, I suppose. Fifteen, twenty minutes after?"

"What time did Karen Kivas leave?"

"The same time as I did."

"Lucy," Watson asked, "did you see your mother and Mrs. Kivas leave?"

"Yes."

"Leave the building or the property?"

"Can you please tell me what this is about?" Mom said. "Lucy said someone died at the lighthouse. I assume by your questions it was Karen. I am very sorry to hear that. She was far too young. I don't know how I can help you. I didn't think she looked well. She was underweight and appeared haggard. A heart attack, I presume?"

"Answer the question, please, Lucy," Watson said, ignoring Mom.

Mom didn't like to be ignored. "Detective, I must insist—"

"I showed my mom and Karen out," I said. "Mom, tell these gentlemen what happened then."

"What happened? Nothing happened. I got into my car and returned to my hotel. I went straight to my room and watched TV for a while before switching out the light."

"Did Karen also get into her car?" Watson asked.

Mom thought. "I can't say I noticed. We said good-bye on the steps. My car was beside the path, hers a bit further away because she arrived late."

"Did you see anyone outside the library?"

"No."

"Were there any other cars in the parking lot?"

Mom shook her head. "No. Not that I saw. Everyone else had left before us. Lucy's Yaris was there, and Karen's old thing. No others."

"When I left," Butch said, "that guy named George was still there."

"He left before Karen and me," Mom said. "When we came outside, he'd gone. That is, I saw no other car."

"You met Karen the day before yesterday, you said. Here at the hotel. You spoke briefly."

"A short conversation." Mom picked at a nonexistent piece of lint on her capris.

"What was the nature of this conversation?" Watson asked.

My heart sank. He wouldn't be asking if he didn't already know they'd had words. Angry words.

Mom waved the question off. "We said hello. That was about it."

"Lucy, do you have anything to add?"

"What?"

"Were you there when your mother and Ms. Kivas first met?"

As if he didn't know full well I'd been there. I wondered who'd ratted us out this time. Could have been just about anyone. Most of Nags Head had overheard that hideous conversation.

"Yes."

"And?" Watson said.

I shrugged. "Mom was busy and didn't want to stop and chat. She told Karen so."

"I must insist on being told what's going on," Mom said. "I fail to see why you're asking me these questions. And being quite rude about it, I might add."

"Karen Kivas was murdered," Watson said, not bothering to beat about the bush.

Mom's eyes opened a fraction wider and she lifted one hand to her mouth. Only I knew her well enough to be able to tell that the news had shocked her to the core. "That's dreadful."

"You know anything about that, Mrs. Richardson?"

"Certainly not. Karen and I might have . . . not got on too well on our first meeting, but we made up later. Why, we were going to have lunch on her next day off."

"Did you?" Butch asked. "Make up, I mean. I was there, remember." He avoided looking at my face. "The air between you two was so chilly, I wanted to get myself a sweater."

"They made up after everyone left," I said. "Mom apologized and they hugged and everything."

"After everyone left?" Watson said. "So you, Lucy, were the only witness."

The interview went downhill from there.

Mom was an expert at dissembling. Years of oral combat at the country club and the top levels of Boston society had honed her verbal skills. As she'd parried Watson's questions with dexterity and great skill, I'd grown increasingly worried. He was no fool, and she was making a bad mistake by taking him for one. Every time I tried to interrupt, he slapped me down. I felt battered and bruised even though it had been only voiced. Mom had checked her watch, patted her hair, reminded him that she hadn't yet had coffee, pretended to struggle to remember the last two days, and then talked as though the argument with Karen had been a minor trifle in her busy day. Watson let her jabber on, while poor Butch looked as though he wanted to tell her to shut up himself.

Eventually Watson said, "Thank you, Mrs. Richardson," and headed for the door. Mom threw me a supercilious smirk at the very moment Watson turned around. "Do not leave the hotel without my permission."

"Don't be ridiculous," Mom said. "I'm on vacation. I have plans, things to do."

"I need to talk to other book club members as well as hotel staff and Karen's family. I may need to speak to you again. I expect to find you here."

"Okay," I said, interrupting Mom's objection. "She'll be here."

Watson and Butch left, the former with a warning glare at me, the latter still avoiding my eyes.

I turned to my mother. "As you're not going anywhere, can I have your car?"

"I don't know, dear. This whole thing will be cleared up in a few hours, and I scarcely want to be stuck here all day."

"Call me when the police are finished with you, and I'll bring the car back."

"I—"

"Great, thanks." I gave her a quick kiss on the cheek, grabbed the valet ticket off the desk, and hurried away.

I walked through the lobby as fast as I could without breaking into a sprint. A uniformed police officer was at the reception desk, and for a moment I thought Watson had put a guard on my mom.

"I demand you rectify the situation immediately!" An elderly lady, who looked as though she were preparing to take on the job of Maggie Smith's understudy on the set of *Downton Abbey*, pounded her bejeweled cane on the floor. She wore a purple sun hat big enough to serve as a soup tureen, and a voluminous, almost floor-length dress in a pattern of violet roses. Her crepe-paper neck was draped with yards of beads.

"Perhaps we can go someplace private." George, manager, attempted to ease the lady away without actually laying a hand on her.

"My great-granddaughter's birthday present has been stolen, and I want the person or persons responsible apprehended." Another whack of the cane. George flinched.

"If you'll just describe the item, ma'am." The cop struggled to get a word in edgewise.

None of my business. I headed outside and waved Mom's ticket at the valet.

In a few minutes I was heading, not south to the lighthouse, but north into the center of Nags Head.

I needed two things and I needed them fast: one of Josie's pastries and some of her calm advice.

I was pulling into the parking lot of the strip mall that contained Josie's Cozy Bakery when my iPhone told me I had a text.

Butch: You okay, Lucy?

I quickly texted back: My mother is not a killer.

He replied: Take care.

I was slipping the phone back into my purse when it buzzed once more.

Connor: Trouble at the library? Karen Kivas found on lighthouse grounds? You okay?

Me: I'm at Josie's.

Connor: You're okay then :)

I put the phone away.

The morning rush had died down at Josie's Cozy Bakery, and my cousin came out from the back when I asked one of the counter staff to get her. Josie wore her regular work clothes of holey jeans and loose white T-shirt under a calf-length apron with a bib. Her golden hair was pulled back into a high, tight ponytail and her nose and cheeks were dotted with flour. Even in that getup Josie looked sexier than I did after an afternoon of primping.

She took one look at my face. "What's the matter? Why aren't you at work? Do you want something to eat?"

"Coffee and a scone would be nice." It seemed like hours since my yogurt breakfast.

Josie made mysterious hand signals to one of her staff, and then she guided me to a table in a back corner. Fragrant steam rose from the espresso machine and the bakery was full of the marvelous scents of baking bread, warm pastry, and rich fillings.

Despite my worries, I took a moment to breathe it all in. A waitress arrived with two mugs of hot coffee and a large scone, plump with blueberries and drizzled with icing.

Only a few of the tables in the bakery were occupied at this time of day. Josie did most of her business in the morning, the seats taken by tourists relaxing after a run on the beach or a daybreak fishing trip and lineups of workers wanting coffee and breakfast to go. There'd be another rush at noon for crisp, healthy salads and sandwiches made with freshly baked baguettes or flaky croissants. The bakery closed at three, but Josie's evenings could be spent catering dessert buffets at private parties or after-business meetings.

Her boyfriend, Jake, had recently returned to the Outer Banks after ten years learning to cook in New York City and had opened a seafood restaurant, where he was the head chef. When Josie wasn't running her own bakery and catering business, she could be found at his place, chopping vegetables or sitting on a stool, watching him work.

Merely thinking about Josie's schedule was enough to exhaust me, but my cousin seemed to thrive on it.

Now her pretty face was pinched in concern. She peered at me over the rim of her coffee mug. "Talk to me."

"You know Karen, from the book club?"

"What about her?" Obviously the news hadn't spread to the bakery. Or, if it had, Josie's head had been buried in pastry dough or a hot oven.

"I don't know her well," I said, "but she always seemed nice enough. What's your take?"

"She's a lot older than us, more Mom's age. Local woman. Why are you asking, Lucy?"

"Just indulge me. What's your feeling about her?"

Josie leaned back in her chair. She cradled her mug. "Her husband, Norm, worked here for a while—did you know that?"

"No. When?"

"A couple of months ago. He didn't, shall we say, work out."

"Why not?"

"I'd been warned about him. That he'd been fired from a lot of jobs because he was so unreliable. But, well, I guess I wanted to help. Their youngest daughter worked here the previous summer, but she had a baby over the winter. Something went wrong and she's having a lot of health problems, and can't be on her feet for long hours. So I figured I'd do the family a favor and hire Norm. His job was to help get things up and running in the mornings, and make the deliveries." When Josie said "morning," Josie meant morning. She began work at four to get started on the first batches of bread and pastries that, as well as being sold in her shop, were delivered to hotels in Nags Head, Kill Devil Hills, and Kitty Hawk. "He'd only been with me one week—one week!—and he showed up drunk. I mean falling-down drunk, not just hungover, which would have been bad enough. He staggered into the kitchen, knocked over a bowl of bread dough, dropped a tray of croissants. I obviously couldn't send him out in the truck in that condition." Josie shook her head. "I had to call Jake, who had barely crawled into his own bed, to come and help me out."

"So you fired him?"

She shook her head. "Foolish me. I sent him home with a flea in his ear and another chance. Things were okay for a few weeks, and I figured he'd just needed some time to get into the routine of our hours. Then, same thing again. Out-of-his-mind drunk. That time I sacked him on the spot."

"How'd he react?"

"Not well. He threw me a couple of what he thought were withering insults. I threatened to call the cops, and he left. End of story. For me, anyway. I heard that Karen threw him out of the house and filed for divorce."

"He was angry with her?"

"Probably."

"Had they been married a long time?"

"I think so. I mean they're grandparents, and I don't think she'd ever been married to anyone else. Him losing this job was probably the last straw. Maybe she figured the kids were old enough and she was better off on her own." Josie shrugged. "But since you're asking, I never had much time for Karen."

"Why? I thought . . . I mean, I think she's nice." I didn't add that I'd had no patience for listening to her complaints. I was feeling guilty about that this morning.

"Maybe it's me, but she seems to play at being nice. Stuff like helping you clean up after book club. I mean, how hard is that? She told you about her marriage ending, right?"

I nodded. Karen had stayed after book club, chatting with me after everyone had left. "She needed . . . needs someone to talk to."

"Sweetie, Karen talks to everyone. I'm not saying she has an easy life, not married to Norm Kivas, but she has a steady job, reasonably good kids. She loves to play the martyr, though, milks it for all it's worth. Like last night. Can't just say she had car problems, but made sure we all knew she couldn't afford repairs. Oh yeah, she'll sigh and say she can't complain. And then she'll complain. And complain. She came here the day after I fired Norm. *Soooo sorry.* I had no idea of how difficult poor Karen had it all these years. But, mustn't complain."

"You don't like her?"

"Sweetie, I don't know her well enough to like her or

not. She was hinting that I should give Norm one more chance, and when I lied and said I'd found someone else, she was, shall we say, not polite. Of course next time she came in, she was all sweetness and light and *soooo sorry* about mean old Norm."

I nibbled at my scone, and thought about Monday's meeting between Mom and Karen at the hotel. My mom had been unpardonably rude to her. Karen had struck back, hard. *Was there anything wrong with that?* No, not unless she'd meant to take it further.

"You still haven't told me why you're asking all these questions, Lucy."

"Karen died yesterday."

"Wow! What happened? We saw her just last night."

"I don't know." I explained about Karen's body being found on the lighthouse grounds. "The police are there now."

Josie leaned back in her seat. "I feel bad about saying mean things about her."

"You were more honest that way." I licked the tip of my index finger and ran it through the remaining crumbs on my plate.

"There's more to this than your curiosity. Spill, Lucy."

"Is your dad in town? I mean, he hasn't gone to Louisiana to visit his family or anything?"

"Yes. And no. He's home."

My uncle Amos was a lawyer. He'd cut back on his workload in the past year, easing himself, he said, into retirement. He'd once been one of the top criminal lawyers in the state. "I might need to have him on speed dial. It turns out that my mom knew Karen back in the day and they had an unpleasant encounter recently."

"How unpleasant?"

"Mom was rude, and Karen threatened her."

"Threatened her. How?"

"Something about some secret Mom wouldn't want to get out."

"Yeah, I noticed they weren't exactly friendly at book club."

And that was the problem. Everyone had seen them being cold and distant. And no one, except me, had seen them make up.

"Forget about it," Josie said. "Karen was all talk. She'd never do anything to ruin her poor-little-me image."

"Mom wouldn't know that."

"You can't be thinking . . ."

"I'm not thinking anything. But Detective Watson is. And Mom didn't help her case by treating him like the hired help. I'm surprised she didn't tell him to use the servants' entrance. What a mess."

"You want another coffee?"

"No. I'd better get back to the library. See what's happening there." I dug my phone out of my purse and checked to see if I'd missed any calls. Nothing.

A family tumbled into the bakery. Mom, Dad, teenagers, preteens, grandparents, and an aunt and uncle or two. They were dressed in an assortment of brilliantly colored clothes and all had sunburned noses. "You have work to do. I've taken enough of your time."

My cousin gave me a radiant smile. She reached across the table and patted my hand. "Anytime, sweetie. You know that. I'll call Dad right now. Tell him he might be hearing from you. Just as a precaution. You have absolutely nothing to worry about."

Josie rose to her feet in one graceful motion. "Are we still on for dinner tonight?"

"Unless I hear otherwise. Watson told Mom not to leave the hotel, so we might have to change the venue. I'll let you know."

Josie raised a perfectly groomed eyebrow. She went back to her ovens and dough.

I went back to my work.

Chapter 6

The cop guarding the entrance to the lighthouse lane flagged me down as I pulled off the highway. I had the top of the SLK down, and the officer recognized me. She greeted me with a low whistle. "Nice wheels."

"Yup."

"How much do you make as a librarian, anyway?"

"Not enough to afford this car. It's my mother's. You know I live here, so can I go in?"

"Yeah." She waved me through.

Police vehicles still filled the parking lot, but Karen's Neon had been taken away. A woman clad head to foot in a white gown, booties, and cap climbed out of the back of a van as I drove up. I avoided glancing around the side of the lighthouse. I spared a thought for my jacket. Even if the police did return it, there was no way I would ever wear it again.

Bertie was at the circulation desk, working on the computer. She waved at me as I came in and pointed down the hallway. I could hear low voices and cabinet doors being opened. "What are they doing?" I asked.

"Searching."

"For what?"

"Karen was last seen here, in the library. They're in the break room now, and will be doing the third-floor meeting room next. They tried ordering me to go home, but I said I wanted to keep an eye on the place. The library is my responsibility. I've been told I have to sit here or in my office. No place else."

"Can I go upstairs?"

"You'll have to ask. Oh, and Diane Uppiton just called."

I groaned. The only reason Diane, one of our library board members, would call Bertie would be to cause trouble. "Let me guess. She heard about the death."

"On library property. To a library patron. She is horrified at this development. Unfortunately the board meeting's tomorrow, and I'm sure this ... incident will be brought up."

"It shouldn't reflect on the library," I said. "None of us can be blamed. Did you know Karen well?"

Bertie tapped her fingers on the desktop. "She was a regular patron. Brought her children, and then her grandchildren, to the library over the years. I had no opinion one way or another."

Hardly a ringing endorsement.

"I thought I heard your voice, Lucy." Watson's head popped around the corner. "I need to interview you. We'll use your office, Ms. James."

It was not a question, but Bertie answered as though it had been. "That's fine."

Bertie gave me an encouraging smile, and I fell into step behind the detective. Sad to say, Watson knew the way to Bertie's office. Butch and two other people were coming out of the break room as we passed. A woman nodded to Watson, and said, "Finished in there. Third floor next."

"Good," Watson said. "Greenblatt, you're with me."

I didn't want to sit in Bertie's place, so I took the visitor's chair. Watson seated himself behind the desk, and Butch leaned up against a wall, arms crossed over his chest.

"Tell me everything you did this morning," Watson said. "Until you phoned nine-one-one."

There wasn't a lot to tell, and I related the story quickly. I'd risen at my regular time, dressed and eaten my breakfast, and then come downstairs intending to start work. I stepped outside, as I usually did, to check the weather and take a moment to enjoy the peace and quiet. I'd noticed an unusual amount of bird activity. I investigated. I found (and here I had to stop for a moment and swallow) Karen.

"Did you hear anything in the night? People around, cars driving down the lane?"

"No. But it's quiet in my apartment. Solid stone walls, you know."

"When Officer Greenblatt left the library, Karen Kivas was still here. Along with you and your mother. Is that correct?"

"Yes."

"Anyone else remain behind?"

I thought. "George Marwick, from the Ocean Side Hotel, wanted to give Mom a lift, but she told him she had her own car. So he left."

"When was that?"

"We'd come downstairs, but not put away the dishes yet. He left about ten minutes before Karen. Maybe. I can't be positive about all the timing. . . ."

"Your mother and Mrs. Kivas had been cold to each other during the book club meeting."

"I told you. They had a silly spat but made up."

"So you say."

"Yes, I do say. They were great buddies when they left."

"Ah yes, when they left. Together."

"I mean . . ."

"You didn't see either of them drive away?"

"No."

"So you don't know if they left immediately, or perhaps stood and . . . chatted . . . for a while longer."

"No."

"Your mother says there were no cars in the parking lot other than your Yaris and what she presumed was Karen Kivas's car. She drove straight back to the hotel and went to her room. No one at the hotel can verify what time she came in."

"It's not a prison. People are not required to check in and out."

"True."

"Look, Detective. My mom and Karen had an unpleasant encounter earlier at the hotel. My mom apologized yesterday evening. Karen accepted her apology."

"So you say."

"I do say!"

"But no one else can verify that. Everyone we've spoken to"—Butch shifted uncomfortably—"says they were cold and distant. Hostile almost."

"It happened! My mom's a nice person."

"So's my mom," Watson said. "Tell me again about this encounter Monday afternoon. At the Ocean Side Hotel."

"We ran into Karen in the lobby as I was leaving."

"Your mother and Mrs. Kivas had words." It was not a question. "Tell me about that."

"Karen recognized Mom from years ago. They said hi. That's all." I shrugged, and checked my watch. Totally nonchalant. "Will you look at the time? Your forensics officers will be finishing upstairs now. Shall I go up and tell them you're free?"

"No need for you to act as my appointments secretary, Ms. Richardson."

"I'm only trying to be helpful." I threw a glance at Butch. He caught my eye and gave his head a slight shake. He was telling me, I assumed, to stop making things worse.

"As you won't admit it, let me tell you what others observed Monday," Watson said. "Your mother was rude and insulting to Ms. Kivas. Ms. Kivas was threatening in return. Does that sound about right?"

It came as no surprise to me that the cops were intimately acquainted with all the gruesome details of that hideous confrontation at the hotel Monday evening. Everyone in the vicinity had been enthralled, and no doubt happy to explain to the authorities, in great detail, what they'd heard.

"Well, yes, but only for people who don't know my mom. She doesn't do rude and insulting, you see. If she'd really meant to be rude—"

"Mrs. Kivas was heard to say that she knew something Mrs. Richardson wouldn't want to become general knowledge. I believe the word 'thief' was mentioned. Do you have any idea what she meant?"

"No. That's gossip, hearsay, isn't it? You can't use hearsay."

"We're not in a court of law, Lucy. I can ask whatever I want. Is she a heavy drinker, your mom?"

"Certainly not!" The picture on the wall behind Bertie's desk was of a woman doing a Downward Dog on the beach at sunrise. Bertie was a yoga practitioner and instructor. She practiced its calming rituals every day. I stared at the poster, trying to soak up some of that calm. It wasn't working.

I must have been doing it wrong.

"Three glasses of wine in quick succession with nothing to eat," Watson said.

"We had something to eat. Bruschetta and calamari. Delicious."

"*You* had bruschetta and calamari. Your mom's plate was unused."

I never liked having servants. I always suspected they were spying on me and laughing about me behind my back. Case in point: the hotel employees sure seemed to be keeping track of us. I imagined them in the kitchen, gossiping about the rich old broad who was vacationing alone and drinking so much her daughter had to take her car away.

"That's uncharacteristic of my mother. She rarely drinks."

"Is that so? I've found that folks often behave in unexpected ways when they have more to drink than they're used to. Quick to take offense, sometimes. Even to lash out."

"I didn't mean she *never* drinks. I just meant, before dinner, without dinner, instead of dinner. I . . ."

"Thank you, Lucy. You've been a great help."

"You mean we're finished?"

"Yes."

"You mean I can go?"

"Yes, Lucy," Butch said. This conversation had made him almost as uncomfortable as it had made me.

I got to my feet. "I'm having dinner with my mom and the family tonight. Can she leave the hotel?"

"I'll talk to her about that," Watson said cryptically. "By your family, do you mean Amos O'Malley?"

"He . . . uh . . . might come."

We were interrupted by a light knock. A cop popped her head in. "Detective. We've found something upstairs."

Watson got to his feet. "You're excused," he said to me again.

We left the office. I headed for the main library, and the three cops took the stairs, fast. I was so curious I almost followed, but self-preservation took over.

"How'd it go?" Bertie asked.

"Not well. They found something interesting upstairs. I wonder if Karen left something behind after book club. It can't be her purse. It was outside this morning with . . . uh . . . with her."

"Let's hope that, whatever it is, they can use it to sort this mess out. I have a library to run."

"I'm going to check my phone for messages. Be right back," I said.

I stepped outside and pulled out my iPhone. As soon as the No Service notice disappeared, the phone beeped, telling me I had a voice message.

"Lucy! Something dreadful has happened. Call your father. No, call Amos. I think . . . I think they are going to arrest me."

Mom.

Chapter 7

I was staring in shock at the phone in my hand when Watson ran out of the library, Butch hot on his heels. Watson was good at hiding his feelings, but Butch wasn't. The look he threw me was positively stricken.

Whatever they'd found upstairs had to do with my mom. I ran after Watson. "What's going on? You have to tell me what's happened. I know it's about my mother."

Butch got into the driver's seat of the cruiser. Watson stopped, his hand on the door. "There's been a development. Your mother's not under arrest at this time, but she is being brought into the station. You might want to alert Amos O'Malley. I'm going there now. You can follow us if you want."

He got into the car and they sped away.

I ran back into the library. "What on earth?" Bertie said as I charged past her. I dashed down the hall and into the break room, where my purse and car keys were. Good thing I had the SLK; if any cop dared to try to pull me over, I'd just lead him to the police station.

"Gotta go," I yelled to Bertie.

I leapt into the SLK and tore down the lighthouse

road in a spray of gravel. I sped down Highway 12 to the Croatan Highway. I didn't put the top down, and I didn't notice the scenery. I am well aware that it's highly dangerous to phone and drive at the same time, but I threw caution to the wind and called Uncle Amos. I told him what I knew—precious little—and he said he was on his way. I threw the phone onto the seat beside me. There'd been an accident on the Croatan by the outlet shops, and traffic slowed to a crawl. Up ahead I could see the red top of a fire truck and numerous flashing red lights. I pounded the dash in frustration. I inched the car forward and, when I figured I could make it, swung onto the verge of the road, squeezed past a van piled high with camping equipment and kids, and pulled into a driveway. I made a U-turn and edged back onto the highway, trying to squeeze the SLK through the double row of cars. If the SLK had been an inch longer, I wouldn't have made it, but eventually I was through. Taking my life in my hands, I shot into the briefest gap in the southbound traffic, speeding up as it escaped the bottleneck. Back toward the lighthouse, and then a sharp left into Virginia Dare Trail, and heading north again. Traffic was heavy as everyone tried to avoid the accident, but at least it was moving.

I can't say why I was in such a mad rush. It was unlikely that a mob of irate townsfolk had gathered outside the Nags Head police station with torches and pitchforks, intent on dragging Suzanne Wyatt Richardson off to an impromptu hanging. I shook away an image of Detective Watson standing on the steps, shotgun balanced loosely in his arms, pushing the brim of his hat back and telling them to "go off home now, folks."

Whatever they'd found upstairs had to have been

about Mom, but I couldn't imagine what it could possibly have been and what was so important about it that Watson immediately sent people around to arrest her (sorry—take her in for questioning). It all happened so fast; there must have been cops at the hotel. I'd seen an officer there earlier, talking to Dowager Countess Wannabe who was missing her granddaughter's birthday present. Had that officer then gone to talk to Mom? Had he been asking her about book club last night, and had Mom said something so stupid and condescending he thought she was confessing?

I pounded the dashboard once again.

It seemed like years, but was probably only ten minutes before I pulled into the Nags Head police station. If Butch and Watson got stuck on the Croatan, I might even be here ahead of them.

I ran into the building and demanded to see Detective Watson immediately.

All my hurrying had been for naught, as I was politely, yet firmly, told to take a seat. I then sat worrying and fuming for a good fifteen minutes until Uncle Amos strolled in. Tall and lanky and slow-moving with a deep Louisiana accent, he always reminded me of Gregory Peck in *To Kill a Mockingbird*. I had as much confidence in my uncle Amos as I did in Atticus Finch. And that was a comforting thought.

He said nothing to me but gave me a nod before speaking to the receptionist. He was told to come on in. I was not.

More worrying. More fuming.

Fortunately, I always have a book buried somewhere in the depths of my bag. When I calmed down enough to realize that all I could do was wait, I pulled it out. I hadn't yet started *The Haunting of Maddy Clare* by Simone St. James. A good ghost story seemed to be exactly what I needed right now. I'd been carrying the book around for a while. I wasn't superstitious, not in the least, but Louise Jane's stories of the lighthouse's history of hauntings had put me in the mood to *not* want to delve into a tale of the wandering undead before falling asleep. Even with the mighty Charles to protect me.

I hadn't phoned my dad. I probably should, but I figured I'd wait until I found out what was going on. It might be better if Uncle Amos called him, lawyer to lawyer. Although Dad was a corporate lawyer, and I didn't think he'd stepped foot in a courtroom since articling, he'd still know all the jargon and get mad at me because I didn't.

A steady stream of people came in and out of the police station. Feeling like a high school girl hoping for a date, I kept checking my iPhone, thinking that I might not hear it ring if Mom got the chance to make another call. Nothing. No encouraging text messages, either. Finally, the door to the inner sanctum opened. Out came Uncle Amos and my mom, followed by Detective Watson. I leapt to my feet.

Mom was pale and her face drawn into dark lines, but her Ralph Lauren jacket and pants were as immaculate as they had been this morning and scarcely a hair was out of place. She said not a word to me, but marched out of the police station, head high and back straight. Uncle Amos jerked his head in my direction, telling me to follow. I ran after them into the hot, bright sunlight. I couldn't have been in the police station as long as I thought I had.

"I came in the SLK," I said. "Do you want it?"

"Yes." Mom dug in her bag and brought out an enormous pair of Armani sunglasses. "That was quite the most embarrassing experience of my life. One I hope never to repeat. Thank you, Amos, for coming down. Can you take Lucy home?"

"This isn't over, Suzanne," Uncle Amos said.

She shrugged. "It is for now. I need to go back to the hotel and lie down. What time is our dinner reservation, Lucy?"

"Dinner?"

"You made the reservation, didn't you?"

"Yes, but . . ."

"Dinner's a good idea," Uncle Amos said. "We need to talk this over."

Mom held out her hand. "Keys."

I gave them to her. "Seven o'clock at Jake's. I'll pick you up at ten of."

"I'll drive myself."

"I'll pick you up."

"If you must." She headed toward her car. Then she stopped and turned around. "Did you call your father?"

"Not yet. I thought I'd wait until I could tell him what was happening."

"Good. Don't bother him with this."

"I still think—" Uncle Amos said, but Mom was walking away.

Amos and I exchanged glances, and then we walked to his car.

"I've just remembered," I said. "My car's at the hotel. Can you drop me there instead of at the lighthouse?"

"Of course," he said.

"What happened?" I asked once we were seated in Uncle Amos's comfortable Camry.

He pulled into traffic. "We'll talk about it at dinner, but it doesn't look good. I don't know if your mother's putting up a brave front—the Wyatt girls are good at that—or if she genuinely doesn't understand. I wish I could call your dad, but she ordered me not to."

"They didn't charge her with anything, did they? She wouldn't be out this fast, not for a murder, if they had."

"She's not to leave Dare County."

"Why? What could they possibly have on Mom for the death of Karen? The very idea's preposterous."

"We'll discuss it at dinner," Uncle Amos said. "When Suzanne can give me a full explanation. At this time, she's not been accused of murder. Only of theft."

For a moment I thought he was joking. But there was no smile on his face or twinkle in his eyes. "You can't be serious."

"Your mother owns a beach bag? A big white canvas one with a blue sailing ship on it?"

"Yes."

"Have you seen it recently?"

"Last night. She brought it to the library in case she wanted to select some books for the rest of her vacation."

"Did she take it with her when she left?"

"I don't know." I thought. "Now that you're asking, I don't remember seeing it again."

"It was found in the third-floor room of the library. On the floor behind a pile of chairs."

"Karen folded the chairs and stacked them. Maybe she pushed them against the wall and didn't notice the bag was still there. Why does this matter, Uncle Amos?"

"Inside the bag, they found a necklace. A diamond-and-gold necklace."

"So, my mother owns lots of nice things."

"Unfortunately, the necklace didn't belong to her. It had been reported stolen from the Ocean Side Hotel just a few hours earlier. Your mother insisted she'd never seen it before."

I drove back to the library in a daze. Bertie was in the break room, pouring herself a drink of water. She took one look at my face and handed the glass to me. I downed it in one go. "What's happening, honey? Here, sit down."

I dropped into a chair. Charles leapt into my lap. He rubbed his big white-and-tan head against my chest. I scratched his throat and felt some of the tension dissolving from my shoulders. "What a mess."

"You don't have to tell me if you don't want to, Lucy. Do you need to take some time off?"

"No. I mean, I don't know. I might have to, although I'd prefer to keep working."

Bertie was my aunt Ellen's closest friend. I'd quit my job at Harvard and fled Boston after turning down Ricky's marriage proposal. I'd come to the Outer Banks, wanting to be cosseted and pampered by my family while I decided what I was going to do with my life. Instead, Ellen had invited her best friend to tea, and by the time tea was over, I had a job at the Lighthouse Library. "I simply don't know what's going on," I said to Bertie now. "Karen's dead. And my mom's been questioned about, of all things, theft."

Bertie's eyebrows twitched, but she made no comment.

"That's all I know. We're having dinner at Jake's tonight, so I'm hoping to hear more. Mom doesn't seem to be worried, but Uncle Amos is."

"It's almost three. Why don't you take the rest of the afternoon off?"

"Thanks, Bertie, but work is always better than worry." I gave the cat a scratch behind the ears. "Isn't that right, old boy?"

Charles purred in agreement. I reluctantly lifted him off me and set him on the floor.

"In that case," Bertie said, "stay in the main room. I want to be sure that one of us has an eye on the Austen collection at all times."

"You can't think the cops are going to take the opportunity to snatch a book." I said, shocked. "Anyway, isn't the cabinet locked?"

"They took all my keys. Who can say in what heart lurks a ruthless bibliophile?"

She wasn't joking.

"We have a bit of financial leeway, Lucy. If you need some time to look after your mother, I can afford to ask Louise Jane to fill in temporarily."

I left without commenting on that. No way was I was prepared to let Louise Jane get another crack at replacing me.

If I hadn't been worried about my mom and upset over the death of one of our patrons, I would have enjoyed the rest of the workday. Nothing like an empty library to allow one to work in peace. The police had told Bertic and me that as long as we stayed away from the third floor, we could go about our business.

Watson and Butch did not return, but other officers and various personnel kept coming and going throughout the afternoon. Around five o'clock, a dark van pulled up and a stretcher was unloaded. Bertie and I stood at the window and watched as Karen Kivas's body was taken away. A woman I didn't know, identifiable by the badge pinned to the belt beside her holster, came in and told us they were finished. She handed Bertie her keys.

"Can we open the library?" Bertie asked.

"Detective Watson sees no reason why you can't get back to business tomorrow. We've marked off the side of the building and don't want anyone venturing there." She gave me a steely-eyed stare.

No worries there. I had no interest in going back to that spot.

Bertie called Ronald and Charlene to tell them to come in tomorrow. She took the opportunity to get to her yoga studio early, and left me browsing publishers' catalogs, checking out what was new for the winter.

By six fifteen Charles was leading the way, tail held high, up to our lighthouse aerie. What a day, and it wasn't over yet. My book nook beneath the window looked mighty inviting, but instead I attacked my closet. I'd planned on wearing my new yellow dress, bright and light and flowing. Something fun yet suitable for dinner with the family. But now it didn't seem as though summer fun was going to be the tone of the evening.

I pulled clothes off hangers, held them up against me, and then tossed them onto the bed. Josie would be wearing something perfect for the occasion, yet drop-dead sexy at the same time. I'd learned long ago not to even try to compete with Josie, and had been much happier for it. Just as well I was the librarian and she the baker. She could tell whether the dough needed more salt by a look, but whenever I cooked, I had to taste everything. I could only imagine what I'd weigh if I worked in a bakery.

With that cheerful thought, I selected a plain black linen dress and a navy blue scarf.

Mom, as could be expected, was flawlessly turned out in an oatmeal pantsuit with a bright pop of color provided by a red shirt and ruby earrings. She climbed into the Yaris and gave me a peck on the cheek. Then she pulled back and studied my dress. "Is that the best you could do for dinner out? We're not going to a librarians' convention, dear."

"Yes, Mom."

At the restaurant the hostess showed us to a table on the deck where Josie, Aunt Ellen, and Uncle Amos were already seated. They got to their feet as Mom and I approached. Ellen gave her sister a hug and Mom briefly allowed herself to be enfolded before pulling away.

The restaurant faced west, overlooking Roanoke Sound, boats bobbing on the dark water, the bright lights of Manteo, and the rhythmic flashing of the fourth-order Fresnel lens on the reproduction Roanoke Marshes Lighthouse. A light breeze ruffled the warm night air. The restaurant was full, inside and out, but the seating was spaced well enough apart that we could talk in privacy.

The unpleasant matter of murder and theft squatted on the table like an unwelcome toad while we exchanged greetings, ordered drinks, and consulted the menu.

"I popped into the kitchen when we arrived," Josie said, "to check what Jake's cooking. The flounder's super fresh and he recommends it. He says he'll send out an extra-large plate of hush puppies, soon as we're ready, because he knows how much you love them, Lucy. He has a few bottles left of that Merlot you like, Dad. He's been saving one for you."

"I'm afraid he'll have to keep saving it," Uncle Amos said. "This isn't a night for drinking."

"Well, it is for me. As I'm not driving, I'll have a martini to begin." Mom handed the waiter her menu without even glancing at it. "Whatever you suggest for dinner will be fine."

"Now that we're here," Uncle Amos said once the waiter had gone in pursuit of drinks, "and out of the police station, do you want to tell us about that necklace, Suzanne?"

"I have absolutely no idea what that thing was doing in my bag. Obviously someone stole it and then tried to ditch it by putting it in the first available container."

"I think I overheard something about that," I said. "When I left the hotel this morning, an old lady was in the lobby, saying her granddaughter's birthday present had been stolen. A cop was with her, and George, the manager, was trying to get them out of the lobby. He can't have been happy at her broadcasting it all over the hotel."

"Where was your bag yesterday?" Uncle Amos said.

Mom shrugged. "I took it with me down to the pool."

"Did you look in the bag?"

"I told you and the police all this," she said.

"Indulge me, Suzanne. I'd like to go over it again. See if you can remember anything else."

"Very well. I might have tossed a towel inside without checking it first. When I got back from the pool, I took out my towel, beach wrap, and book. It's possible I could have missed seeing the necklace. I put a scarf in the bag in case it was cool later. I dressed for dinner, and dined early so as to go to Lucy's book club."

"Did you eat in the hotel restaurant?"

"Yes."

"Did you bring the beach bag with you?"

"No."

Uncle Amos stopped talking when the waiter returned with the drinks. Mom practically snatched her martini out of his hand. She took a long gulp. "Really, Amos. I do not know how it got there."

"Can you take a guess?"

"Hold on," I said. "You're going too fast. Has Mom been charged with stealing this necklace? You said it was expensive. Like really, really expensive or sorta expensive?"

"Really, really," Amos said. "Diamonds, of a good size."

"Oh. Is it big?"

"Watson showed us a picture. It's quite small, and probably very light. A gold chain, of a size that would fit snugly around a woman's neck, with five diamonds, each of which is a carat or more. Suzanne has not been charged with the theft. The bag was left, unattended, in her hotel room for an hour at least while she was at dinner, and the necklace might have even been there earlier, as she didn't empty it during the day. I reminded Watson that a hotel room is not a secure place. Staff come and go all day long. Management, maintenance, and housekeeping have master keys. Pretty much anyone who works there can get access to a room if they want."

"That's a comforting thought," Aunt Ellen said.

"Guests can slip in and out of someone else's room while a housemaid's back's turned. Watson had to agree, reluctantly, that any number of people could have put the item in Suzanne's bag."

"Why would someone do that? And what do you think this has to do with Karen's death?" I asked.

"The necklace might have nothing to do with the killing. Not directly, anyway. I also pointed out to Watson that it's entirely possible the thief feared he or she was about to be discovered yesterday, and for some reason he or she decided they had to get rid of it, and fast."

I didn't say that in that case we were talking about a pretty incompetent thief. Why not stick the darn thing in the depths of a plant pot or something and come back for it later? Not hide it where it was certain to be found, and very soon.

Almost anything might have happened, but the only thing that made any sense at all was that someone was trying to frame my mom. I couldn't see that this was a coincidence, particularly after Karen had said, in front of a roomful of witnesses, that Mom had been called a thief in school. The idea was ridiculous. I knew my mom. If she wanted something, she bought it. I know there are those to whom thievery is a compulsion, the act an end in itself, but if my mother were a kleptomaniac, she—and my father—wouldn't have been able to keep it a secret all these years.

If someone was trying to frame Mom, the only person I could think of with a motive, as well as the meanness to do it, had to be Karen. Who was no longer around to be questioned about it.

"It's perfectly obvious to me," Aunt Ellen said. "That's exactly what happened. Suzanne's bag was nothing but a convenient depository. I trust they will be fingerprinting this necklace?"

"It's been sent to the lab."

"And we all know how long it will take to get those results back," Aunt Ellen said.

"It might be faster than usual," Uncle Amos said, "if Watson makes the case that the necklace is tied up in the murder."

"But Lucy overheard the owner reporting it missing this morning," Josie said. "Not yesterday."

"The woman says she saw it last when she checked

into the hotel and unpacked on Sunday. She's visiting for the birthday of her great-granddaughter. The necklace was to be her gift. When she went to get it this morning to take to the birthday lunch, she found it missing and called the police."

"I don't see what it can possibly have to do with Karen," I said. "The necklace was stolen at the hotel. Karen was killed at the lighthouse." I stopped talking. Karen. Had Karen stolen the necklace and hidden it in Mom's bag to get it out of the hotel, planning to retrieve it later at book club?

If so, had someone killed Karen for the necklace? Without realizing that she didn't have it on her?

The expression on Uncle Amos's face indicated that he was thinking the same thing. "We can't forget that those two incidents happened around the same time. You can be sure Watson isn't forgetting it."

"I thought him perfectly capable of forgetting his head if it wasn't attached," Mom said, as she signaled the waiter to bring her another martini. We hadn't even had time to order food yet. I buried my head in the menu, trying to unobtrusively eye my mother at the same time. She looked as she always did, perfectly dressed, perfectly groomed, perfectly composed. But there were fissures beneath that composure. I could tell, by the way Ellen threw worried glances her way, that my aunt noticed them also.

"Do you have something wrong with your eyes, Lucille?" Mom asked.

"No."

"I ask because you seem to be staring. I do not need to explain my behavior to you, but I will anyway. I have had a most trying day."

"I know that, Mom."

"I wonder if you do."

"Don't mistake Sam Watson for a fool, Suzanne," Uncle Amos said. "Or for a small-town, hick cop. He spent years with the NYPD. Homicide."

Mom sniffed, not impressed.

But I was. "Oh," I said.

"Homicide," Josie said. "We seem to almost be forgetting about Karen's death."

"Karen and Mom were in high school together," I said. "Did you know her, too, Aunt Ellen?" Ellen was the older of the sisters.

Aunt Ellen's lips pinched together. "She was in your mom's year, so I didn't have anything do with her at school, but Sue brought her around to the house sometimes."

"Rarely," Mom said.

"Quite often in junior year, as I recall. Then, when you were both seniors, you had other things on your mind than your school friends." Meaning my dad and getting out of Nags Head. "After we left school, I'd see her around town and we'd say hello, but that was about it. She had children and the children got bigger, and then she was with little children again. Her grandchildren. Must be nice to have grandchildren."

"Yes, Mom." Josie rolled her eyes at me.

My mom could usually be persuaded to pull out pictures of my brothers' children at even the slightest mention of offspring. That she didn't take this opportunity, presented to her on a silver platter, showed me how preoccupied she must have been.

"I'll admit that I didn't like Karen, not in school or after," Aunt Ellen said. "She was always—I don't know—

'manipulative' might be the word. But I did feel sorry for her. She seemed to be steadily going down in the world as the years passed."

"She made sure everyone knew how hard done by she was." Josie sipped at her glass of white wine. It looked delicious, but I was sticking to iced tea tonight.

"You're right about that, honey," Aunt Ellen said. "But still, things were hard for her."

"Speaking of Karen Kivas's hard knocks, folks," Josie said. "Don't turn around, but look who just walked in."

Is there any phrase in the English language more designed to make one look than "don't turn around"? As one, my mother, Aunt Ellen, and I swiveled. The hostess was showing a couple to seats at the bar. The man half tripped over his own feet and grabbed the back of a chair to save himself. The woman seated there gave him a look that would curdle milk.

Aunt Ellen sucked in a breath. "I can't believe it."

So much for looking: I didn't recognize either of them. The man was about my parents' age, with a more-than-adequate beer belly, a few strands of gray hair, and a goatee streaked gray and brown. He was dressed in jeans that needed a good wash and a flannel shirt worn open over a gray T-shirt advertising a trucking company. The woman was young enough to be his daughter. She was painfully thin in distressed skinny jeans, a tight blue tank top, and sky-high stilettos. Bleached-blond hair cascaded around her shoulders. He climbed onto a barstool and she wiggled her bony behind to get comfortable on hers.

The bartender slapped cocktail napkins on the counter in front of them and asked what they wanted.

We were momentarily distracted as our waiter placed an overflowing plate in the center of the table. "Compliments of the chef," he said with a grin at Josie. Hush puppies, plump and perfectly crisp. Yum. "Are you folks ready to order?"

Uncle Amos had the clam chowder, which would be made in the traditional Outer Banks style as a clear broth, followed by the rib eye, rare. Aunt Ellen ordered two crab cakes, and Mom said, "Same for me." Josie asked for a burger with a side of sweet potato fries. She glanced at me apologetically. "I get all the seafood I want. Tonight I'm in the mood for something different." I was most definitely not in the mood for anything different. Nothing I love more than real Outer Banks cooking. "Crab and flounder, please. And the littleneck clams to start."

We handed our menus to the waiter before returning to the matter at hand. "I can't believe he's here. Tonight of all nights," Aunt Ellen said.

"I can't believe he's here any night," Josie said.

The restaurant was full of the sound of conversation and laughter. Lamps hanging above the bar and along the railing cast long shadows. While the thin woman studied the menu, her companion glanced around. He gave our table a long, hard look and his eyes settled on Josie. Now, men always look at Josie. But not usually in that way. As though they're going to spit on the floor. She did not look away, and the man broke eye contact first.

"Who's that?" I asked.

"Norm Kivas. Karen's husband."

Chapter 8

Despite myself, I turned again. The bartender brought a beer for the man, a glass of wine for his companion. Norm lifted the drink and took a long swallow.

"You said they were divorced," I said to Josie. "Maybe he doesn't see the need to pretend to be grieving."

Aunt Ellen harrumphed. "They were married for thirty years. She's the mother of his children, grandmother of his grandchildren. Is it too much to expect him to show some signs of respect?"

"Yes," Josie said.

Josie had told me she'd had to fire the man for showing up to work drunk. Twice. That had been the final straw in the marriage, and Karen had thrown him out of the house.

"Why wouldn't you expect to see him here any night?" I asked. "Does he have a problem with Jake?"

"Norm Kivas has a problem with everyone," Josie said. "But specifically with Jake? Nothing I know about. No, this place is out of his price range, and way out of his comfort zone. Look at him. He's already been drinking.

I don't know who that girl is, but I bet she insisted they come here."

Jake's wasn't a fancy restaurant, but it was in the higher end price-wise for the Outer Banks. Still, I thought, a beer couldn't cost much more here than it did anyplace else.

The waiter arrived to take their food orders. Through a brief lull in the hum of conversation, and because he almost shouted it out, I heard Norm ask for a large Caesar salad followed by the surf and turf meal of prime rib with lobster, which I'd noticed was a heart-attack-inducing fifty bucks.

"Perhaps," Uncle Amos said, choosing his words slowly and carefully, "he's come into some money."

"Or is expecting to," Aunt Ellen said. "I can't imagine Karen left much in the way of an inheritance."

"Insurance?" Uncle Amos said. "Couples sometimes take out cheap policies when they're young, pay automatically so they scarcely even remember, and then get a surprise windfall if one of them cashes in."

"Maybe not such a surprise," Josie said.

"Where is that waiter?" Mom said. "My glass is empty."

Norm Kivas laughed uproariously at something his friend said. He was pretending to ignore us, but couldn't help taking sideways peeks at our table at regular intervals.

"Did the police tell you anything about Karen's death?" I lowered my voice and leaned toward Uncle Amos.

Aunt Ellen got the hint and turned to her sister. "How are the boys doing, Suzanne? That youngest grandson of yours must be getting awful big. I wish they'd come here for a vacation one year."

"They won't say anything official, of course," Amos said, "until they get the results of a full autopsy, but it looks as though it was some time before she was found. Time of death was probably late evening."

"Right after book club."

"Yes."

I avoided looking at my mom, who was pulling up photos on her iPhone. If Karen hadn't left the lighthouse grounds, Mom quite likely was the last person to see her alive. The last person, I reminded myself, other than the killer.

First courses arrived. Mom asked the waiter to bring another martini.

"Cause of death?" I asked Uncle Amos.

"A blow to the head. Initial speculation is a rock." I thought of the lighthouse grounds. Mostly tough marsh grasses, but some good-sized rocks and stones were scattered about. "Nothing has turned up."

"Suspects?"

Uncle Amos dug into his chowder. "That I don't know. They wouldn't tell me."

I popped a clam into my mouth. Delicious.

"Butch," Josie said.

"What?" I said.

My cousin grinned at me. "I was telling Aunt Suzanne that Jake's brother and you have become great friends. Isn't that right, Lucy?"

"He's very nice."

"The official grand opening of the restaurant's next Thursday. Butch told Jake that he's bringing Lucy I'm sure you'll like him very much, Aunt Suzanne."

"It's nice that Lucy's made friends," Mom said, as though I were five years old and heading off to first grade. "I met him at book club last night." She noticeably omitted mentioning having met him again this morning when the police called on her at the hotel or at the police station. "He seemed pleasant enough, but if he's interested in Lucy, he's going to be sadly disappointed. Ricky's waiting at home for Lucy's summer vacation to be over. Just like when they were young. Lucille always came home at the end of August."

Wow! That really was shucking off reality. I watched Mom nibble on a hush puppy. Instead of being mad, I leaned across the table and touched her other hand. She looked up, startled, and I felt a sudden stab of pure love for her. Mom had more than enough to worry about right now. If she wanted to persist in believing I still intended to marry Ricky, I'd let her. For now.

Josie threw me a questioning look, and I gave her a slight shake of the head.

Despite the cloud that hung over our table, we enjoyed our meal. Jake came out to meet my mom and she showered him with praise about the ambience of the restaurant and the quality of her food. Clearly charmed, he gave her a little bow. He was slightly shorter and a bit thinner than Butch, but the family resemblance was strong. They were two mighty handsome brothers.

For some reason, an image of Connor McNeil jumped into my head. I'd missed him at book club last night.

Josie got to her feet and drew Jake aside. She nodded toward the bar, where Norm Kivas had polished off his steak and lobster, accompanied by a bottle of red wine. His friend was looking none too stable on her stool.

Norm had spent most of the evening pretending not to notice us, while peeking out the corner of his eye at our table and laughing uproariously at whatever his companion had to say. All the while drinking steadily.

Now he turned to watch Josie and Jake. Jake made a signal to the bartender, and the bartender said something to Norm that I didn't catch. Norm got off his stool and swaggered over to Jake and Josie. Uncle Amos placed his napkin on the table and slowly got to his feet.

"You got a problem with me eatin' in this here establishment of yours?" Norm jabbed Jake's chest with one finger.

The dinner rush was over and the patio was thinning out. Around us, conversation died and people turned to stare.

"You're welcome here," Jake said quite pleasantly. "We're happy to call you a cab. On the house, as I think Ryan there told you." He didn't look particularly tough in his checked gray pants and white jacket, but I noticed he'd taken a step away from Josie and planted his feet apart. "Did you enjoy your dinner?"

"Meat was overcooked."

His companion hopped off her stool. She wobbled when she hit the floor and staggered over to the men. She plucked at Norm's sleeve. He shook her off. He turned to Josie. "How about you? You have a problem with me eatin' here?"

"Not at all," she said. "But it looks to me as though you've had enough to drink for one night." Jake attempted to shush her with a gesture. Not one to be shushed, Josie added, "That seems to be a regular occurrence."

"And you're the judge, are you? Take away a man's job, see him banned from restaurants in his own town—"

"You're not being banned," Jake said.

"Come on, honey," the young woman said, plucking once again at his sleeve. "Let's go."

"That was a mean trick, sending your cop brother over to harass me. Went down real well at my new job. Think you own this town, all of you." He swung around and faced our table, pointed at Uncle Amos. "You got the lawyer man right here, too. Judge, jury, executioner."

A waiter came out from the main building and stood filling the doorway. He held a phone in his hand and looked to Jake for instructions.

"If someone called the cops on you, it wasn't us. I'd suggest you leave, if you don't want us to do so now," Josie said.

Norm opened his mouth and said something to Josie. I didn't hear what it was, but Jake obviously did. He grabbed Norm by the arm and jerked the man off-balance. "Now you *are* banned. Get out."

Norm swung. It was hardly a fair fight. Norm was thirty years older than Jake, overweight, out of shape, and drunk. Jake ducked and the blow sailed past his jaw. Norm's companion squealed and leapt toward Jake, her long red fingernails outstretched. Josie shoved her, and the woman hit the floor, yelling a blue streak. People jumped up. Women screamed. Phones were pulled out of pockets. Some people punched in 911. A few took pictures. Uncle Amos made as if to intervene, and Aunt Ellen yelled at him, "No!"

It was over as quickly as it had begun. The hovering waiter grabbed Norm by one arm, Jake took the other, and they dragged a bellowing Norm away. Josie reached out her hand to the woman lying on the floor in an undignified heap. I came to my senses and hurried to help. The woman took the offered hand and pulled herself upright. "Thanks," she mumbled. I scooped up a lost shoe and handed it to her.

"Are you going to be okay?" Josie said. "You can stay for a while, if you want. We'll call you another cab."

"Nah. I'm fine. Norm's all bluster. He wouldn't have done nothin'. He's kinda upset tonight, you see. His ex-wife died this morning."

"We all grieve in our different ways," Josie said drily.

The woman failed to notice the sarcasm. "I'm glad you understand. You're Josie, right, from the bakery?"

"Yes?"

"Y'all got any positions open? I've got tons of retail experience. My name's Sandy, by the way. Sandy Sechrest." She thrust out her hand.

Josie took it. The women shook and then Sandy offered me her hand.

"Lucy."

"Pleased ta meet ya, Lucy. I better run. I'll pop around tomorrow, Josie. Ask about that job. Bye."

"Bye," my cousin and I said in chorus.

Sandy skipped away. Josie and I looked at each other and burst out laughing.

"I'm glad someone found that incident amusing," Mom said when we made our way back to the table, clutching our sides with laughter.

"Norm Kivas wasn't a bad man," Aunt Ellen said. "But the drink got to him, and then the downward spiral began. He spent some time in prison for robbery, as I recall. Amos?"

Uncle Amos sat back down. "The usual story. He's never been brought up on domestic violence charges, though. Still . . ." His voice trailed off.

"Anyone for coffee?" Aunt Ellen said.

*   *   *

Josie headed into the restaurant kitchens to spend some time with Jake, and Mom and I said our good-nights to Aunt Ellen and Uncle Amos in the parking lot. Rather than drop Mom off in front of the hotel, I figured I'd better see her to her room. She had a slight smile on her face and a wobble to her step.

The lobby bar was full and conversation and laughter spilled out of the restaurant. George was standing by the reception desk. He spotted us when we came in, broke into a huge smile, and hurried over. "Sue. Did you have a pleasant evening?"

"Yes, we did. We dined at Jake's Seafood Bar. Do you know it?"

"A new place, isn't it?"

"Very new. You should direct your guests there. Excellent seafood, isn't that right, dear?"

"Uh, right, Mom."

"I can't apologize enough," George said, "for that unfortunate misunderstanding earlier." I wondered what misunderstanding that might be. The murder of a staff member or the theft of a diamond necklace from a hotel guest?

Mom waved her hand. "I explained to the police that I had nothing to do with it. It's all settled now."

Ah, the necklace. It wasn't exactly settled, but I let it go. Mom wasn't going to explain to a man she hadn't seen for more than thirty years that she was still under investigation, was she? I wondered if I was making too many excuses for my mom on this visit.

"Can I offer you a nightcap?" George asked. "You and your lovely daughter."

I braced myself for Mom's version of an explosion,

which was more like a localized quake, knocking the feet out from under those standing close, while no one else noticed what was going on. He was a brave man, that George. Mom had put him firmly in his place on their first meeting, and I expected her to do so again. But I had to pick my jaw up off the floor as she said, "Are you allowed to? Surely you're on duty?"

He grinned. "I'm the boss. I give myself permission."

Mom's laugh was a delightful tinkle. "Lucy's off home now. A glass of Drambuie would make a lovely night-cap." She gave me a peck on the cheek. "Remember, dear, I still haven't seen your apartment. I'm having lunch with Ellen tomorrow, so I'll come by and pick you up when you finish work. When is that?"

"I get off at five on Thursdays."

"You can show it to me, and then we can go out for a drink and a nice chat." She turned back to George with a smile. He held out his arm, and she accepted it. They walked together into the lobby bar.

Weird.

I turned around and almost ran smack into a woman standing directly behind me. If I was the suspicious sort, I'd say she'd been listening in on our conversation. She was dressed in gray Bermuda shorts and an unadorned white T-shirt. Her long nose and small black eyes put me in mind of a hawk. Her gray hair was cropped close to her head and she wore no makeup. She appeared to be alone, and carried a hotel key card.

"Excuse me," I said. Then I recognized her. The woman who'd been in the library yesterday, and been very unfriendly to boot. The one I had thought of as the Gray Woman. I was about to say hello, but she marched away without a word.

Weird.

This whole day had been weird. Finding a body on the lighthouse grounds. My mother dragged down to the police station to be accused of theft, her abrupt change of heart toward George, manager. A fight at a restaurant.

My phone rang. I groaned. I didn't think I could take any more weirdness today.

I checked the display before answering, to make sure it was a perfectly normal person calling. It was. "Hi, Connor. What's up?"

"I was wondering if you have time for a drink. Dinner would be on offer, but I'm assuming you've eaten. I know it's late to be calling."

"I went to Jake's with Mom and the family, so a drink would be nice. I'm at the Ocean Side, dropping Mom off."

"I can be there in a couple of minutes."

"I'm sick and tired of this place," I spoke before thinking. "Why don't you meet me at the library? I have an unopened bottle of wine in my fridge that I've been saving for company."

"Good idea. See you in a few minutes."

I hung up. Then I panicked. What on earth had I done? I'd invited a man—Connor McNeil, a highly attractive man—to my apartment. At ten o'clock at night. Would he read more into the invitation than I'd intended?

Once again, I made it home in record time. Connor's car was not in the parking lot, and I was pleased to see no police vehicles, either. I ran up the path, fumbled to get my key in the lock, sprinted up the stairs—round and round, I went—fumbled once more with the lock to the apartment, and burst in. I grabbed the bottle of wine, snatched up two glasses, and sprinted out again. My apartment has only one main room. My mother would never approve of me entertaining a gentleman in the equivalent of my bedroom. Charles was standing on the landing, glaring at me, quite put out at not being effusively greeted the moment I'd arrived.

I switched on a single light in the main room of the library, pulled two chairs up to a small table, cleared books off the table, and laid out the bottle and glasses. I was relaxing comfortably, not sure if my heart was pounding so hard because of the burst of exercise or in anticipation, when lights washed the front of the lighthouse. Charles reached the door first, because I was strolling toward it so casually.

Connor's hair was mussed as if he'd been running his fingers through it. His tie was askew and his top shirt button undone. He gave me a strained smile and I invited him in.

"You don't look too well," I said. "Is something wrong?"

"Rough day." He spotted the wine and the chair grouping and his blue eyes widened.

"I thought," I said, "it would be nice to sit down here. I love a library at night. It's so peaceful and quiet. I sometimes think I can hear the books whispering among themselves."

A smile touched his face.

"Does that sound silly?" I said.

"It sounds perfect. Perfectly Lucy."

"Wine?"

"I'd love one."

I always buy a bottle with a twist cap when I can. Just as well, as I don't own a corkscrew. I poured two glasses while Connor dropped into one of the wingback chairs with a weary sigh. I handed him his drink and he leaned back and closed his eyes. His handsome face was darkening with end-of-the-day stubble.

"How's your mother's visit going?"

"Dramatic, to say the least. I suppose I should tell you that we were at the police station earlier with Uncle Amos, because the police questioned Mom about the theft of a necklace from a guest room at the Ocean Side."

"That doesn't sound good."

"No. It sure doesn't. The necklace was found in my mom's bag."

"Why'd they search her bag?"

"They found it. Here, upstairs. She forgot it after book club."

"Do you think your mom took it?"

"No. If she had kleptomaniac tendencies, they would have shown up by now. She can afford to buy anything she wants, and she usually does. But I'm worried about what the cops think. Frankly it's unlike her to leave her property behind, to not even know what's in her beach bag. She's normally highly organized and superefficient. She's been acting so strangely on this visit."

"Strangely, how?"

"Drinking far more than she's used to, for one thing. I don't like it. I'd be worried about her even if a cloud of murder and theft wasn't hanging over her. Over us."

He sipped his wine. The setting was so peaceful with the dim lights, the quiet books, and the curving whitewashed brick-and-stone walls surrounding us. I wished I'd thought to bring out candles. Charles leapt onto Connor's lap and settled down with a loud purr.

"As long as we're talking about going to the police

station," Connor said, studying the wine in his glass, "I had a visit from Watson, too."

"What?"

"I wasn't at book club last night. He wanted to know why. A previously scheduled meeting, I told him. I'd already heard about the death of Karen Kivas. I also heard you were the one who found her. That must have been hard."

"It was. The whole day has been nothing but dreadful. One thing after another." I lifted my glass. "It's nice to sit back and relax."

"Watson had some questions for me about Karen's brother."

"Who's he?"

"Guy by the name of Doug Whiteside. Doug's planning to run for mayor next time around."

"Against you?"

"I don't intend to be mayor forever, but this is my first term, and I have things I want to accomplish that I haven't had time for yet. Whiteside, well, let's say it's my opinion that he'd be a disaster of a mayor."

"Why?"

"Strictly between you and me, Lucy?"

"Yes."

"I suspect he's on the take. From developers. I have no proof, so I can't start spreading it around, but there arc strong indications that that's the case. There are some important environmental issues coming up, things that developers might not be happy about."

"I understand." The Outer Banks is a thin, very thin, strip of sand jutting into the Atlantic Ocean. The shore is constantly being pounded by waves and washed by currents, and the hotels and beach houses perch precariously on the sandy shoreline. If the land is going to be habitable in the future, strong protections are needed. The sort of protections that might interfere with some people's building plans.

"You think her brother had something to do with Karen's death?"

Connor shook his head. He absentmindedly stroked Charles's soft fur. "No, I don't. They were not close. Estranged, in fact. But blood is thicker than water, and Detective Watson was idly wondering if I might have taken the opportunity to kill Karen to knock Doug out of the race."

I almost laughed; the idea was so ridiculous.

Then again, it wasn't any more ridiculous than my mom stealing a diamond necklace and forgetting it was in her beach bag.

Connor gave me a smile. "I think even Watson realized how far-fetched that was as soon as he said it. I have a lot of confidence in Sam Watson. He's a good cop. How was your dinner?"

"Dinner was good. The food's fantastic and Jake's is at a perfect location. Do you know Karen's husband, Norm?"

"I know of him. Why do you ask?"

"He was there, at Jake's. He was drinking heavily, and caused a nasty scene with Josie and Jake. Apparently earlier this year Josie fired him for coming to work at the bakery drunk, and he thinks that was part of some grand conspiracy to keep him down. A conspiracy that includes the police. I'd think a visit from the cops to tell you your wife's dead would be standard police procedure, but Norm didn't take it that way."

"Was he drunk?"

"Oh, yeah. He was with a young woman. At first I thought she might have been his daughter, but I think she was his date. She didn't seem to have a brain in her head. The sort, I'd imagine, who wouldn't have given him the time of day if he'd suggested going for beer and wings. He was spending big, too, the most expensive dishes and a bottle of good wine."

"That's interesting. Karen worked as a hotel maid, she was helping to raise her grandkids, and Norm can't hold down a job. Then, the day after she died, he can afford to take a woman to Jake's? Is it possible she, the date, was paying?"

"I suppose it might have been." I hadn't noticed who'd taken care of the check.

While we chatted, Connor had stopped patting Charles. The cat swatted his hand as a reminder, and we laughed before going on to talk about more pleasant things. Eventually Connor refused a top-up, put his glass on the table, and got to his feet. "I'd better be off. Thanks, Lucy. You're a good listener."

"I did as much talking as listening."

"It's nice just to be with you."

I flushed, and hoped the rising color wouldn't show in the soft lights of the library. Connor and I walked to the door as Charles wound between our feet before leaping to the top of the returns shelf. Connor hesitated. Charles butted His Honor with his head, and then Connor said, "There's something I've been wanting to ask you, Lucy. Next Thursday's the official Mayor's Ball. It's the highlight of the summer season, or so I've been told. I'd like you to accompany me."

"To go to a ball?"

"Very formal, I'm afraid. Totally stuffy. Suits and evening dresses and pressing the flesh. It's work for me, but I'd like it very much if you'd be my date."

"I'd love to."

Connor grinned. "Great! And thanks for a nice evening." He leaned over and gave me a kiss on the cheek so soft it was like air brushing against my skin.

He went out into the night. I closed the door, and leaned up against it, my cheek burning with the feel of his kiss. I liked Connor. A lot. I liked Butch. A lot. I'd have to decide, and probably soon, if I was going to take things further with one of them.

But which one?

Then Charles reminded me he hadn't yet had his dinner.

Chapter 9

Over a breakfast of coffee and a parfait of Greek yogurt, granola, and fresh berries, I checked the local news. The police had not yet made an arrest in the "brutal murder" of Karen Kivas, but were "expecting to shortly."

Which I translated to mean they didn't have a clue.

Or maybe they had too many clues. I thought of Mom, Norm Kivas, and even Karen's brother, Doug. Connor had said Doug and Karen were estranged. I wondered how far that went.

I picked up the phone.

"Greenblatt."

"Hi, Butch. It's Lucy."

"Lucy!" I heard a smile creep into his voice. "How are you this fine morning?"

"I'm afraid I'm calling about business, Butch."

"Whose business?"

"Yours."

"Shoot."

After the day I'd had yesterday, I should have fallen asleep immediately. Instead I'd lain awake most of the night, listening to the wind rattling the lighthouse and Charles snoring. I thought of poor Karen. Tragic as her murder was, I'd barely known her, and her death didn't have anything to do with me. But my mom had become involved. I couldn't simply ignore the fact that she might find herself falsely accused. I decided that I'd do what I had to do, and with that, I finally fell asleep.

"I was at Jake's last night," I said. "Norm Kivas came in, Karen's husband."

"Go ahead."

"He was drinking. Heavily. I gather that's not unusual. He was spending a lot of money and was with a woman, a young woman, who seemed to be his date." My voice trailed off. "I thought you should know."

"Thanks, Lucy. I'll tell Detective Watson." Butch didn't sound terribly excited at my news. Jake had probably told him.

"He tried to start a fight with Jake and Josie. Accused Jake of sending the police around to harass him. Did you?"

"Harass him? No, Lucy, we didn't harass him. I was with Watson when he broke the news of Karen's death to Norm. Can't say he was particularly upset, didn't seem too bothered by it, but we knew he and Karen had split up. We asked the usual questions about where he was at the time. I suppose he could consider that harassment. If he had something to hide."

"Does he have an alibi?"

"No. He says he was at home, alone. He didn't say passed-out drunk, but that was the impression we had."

"Do you believe him?"

"I don't believe or not believe. Most murders are committed by family members, and the odds are even greater when there's been a recent divorce or separation. We're looking into everyone who might have had reason to kill Karen Kivas."

"Including my mom?"

"I'm not going to answer that, and you know it."

"She would never have stolen a necklace. She'd have no reason to. My parents are . . . financially comfortable."

"You'd be surprised at how many people steal things they don't need. Or even want."

I thought of the Jane Austen first-edition collection on display in the library. And who had stolen some of the volumes a few weeks ago. "I get your point. But not as it regards my mom."

"I gotta go—Watson's giving me the evil eye."

"One more thing. Don't you find it strange that Karen was alone outside the lighthouse last night?"

"The thought did cross our minds, Lucy."

I pretended not to hear his tone. "She was parked there. Why didn't she get into her car and drive away? If she had car problems, she could have phoned for help, or knocked on the door and asked me to give her a lift into town. Was there a problem with her car?"

"It started straight off the bat when they gave it a try."

"So, if she wasn't having car problems, maybe she saw something, or someone, creeping around, and went to check. Have you considered that?"

"Lucy, Detective Watson knows how to conduct an investigation."

"I'm just tossing out ideas."

"I have to go. We'll be busy with this murder investigation, but I will, no matter what's happening, be there for my brother's big night. I hope you're still on for that, Lucy."

"Looking forward to it."

We hung up and I went to work.

Charlene and Ronald, my coworkers, were arriving as I came down the stairs. They fired their questions at me at the same time.

"Lucy, what on earth is going on?"

"Karen Kivas died, right here in the lighthouse?"

"Not in the lighthouse," I said, "but outside."

"The police think it's a suspicious death," Ronald said. "Is that true?"

"I'm afraid so." I told them all I knew, which wasn't much. I left out the stuff about the diamond-and-gold necklace and my mother being under suspicion of having stolen it.

"I'd hate to think," Ronald said, "that someone was hanging around outside, in the dark, waiting for a woman to come out of our library."

I lived here alone; I tried not to think about that, either. Of course I then I thought about it. It was possible that this had been a random killing. But the question remained as to why Karen had lingered after I'd closed the door and Mom had driven away. Had Karen taken time for a smoke? That was possible. She did have grandchildren, so perhaps she never smoked in her car because she drove them around. Or had she made a phone call and been sitting in her car, alone in the dark, when someone tapped on her window asking for help?

I was about to head for the phone to let Butch know my new theory, but I remembered that he'd told me to butt out. Very politely of course.

"Nasty business," Ronald said with a shake of his head. His tie featured Donald Duck today. I took my seat at the circulation desk, and Charlene flipped the sign on the door to OPEN.

"I'll be upstairs if you need a break." Charlene dug in her pocket for her iPhone and earbuds.

Thank heavens for earbuds, was all I could say.

Charlene had headed upstairs, the muted sound of Jay Z trailing behind her, when Bertie came into the room. She did not look happy. "I had a call from Eunice Fitzgerald. The restaurant has apparently had a fire in the kitchen and had to cancel the board meeting lunch today."

"A fire! Was anyone hurt?" Ronald asked.

"No. It was quickly brought under control, I hear, but the kitchen will be closed for a couple of days."

"Isn't that a good thing, then? No board meeting," I said.

"Never one to be put off, Mrs. Fitzgerald has decided to have the meeting here. She will be bringing sandwiches." Bertie rolled her eyes. "As my office is hardly big enough, we'll meet in the staff break room. I can only hope they won't have a quorum. Lunch in the back room of a library with sandwiches and bottled tea is no substitute for a fancy meal, heavy on the wine and beer, enjoyed on the veranda of a nice restaurant. I won't mention any names, of course, but some of our board members seem more interested in enjoying the perks of the job, on *my* budget, than actually doing the work of running a library. They'll be here at noon."

"I'll send them back," I said.

Shortly before eleven a steady stream of parents with two- to four-year-olds in tow began coming through the doors, heading upstairs for Thursday Toddlers Theater.

The kids were jumping with joy, in some cases quite literally. Ronald and his wife, Nora, had both had moderately successful show business careers in New York in their youth. But acting, as he'd explained to me, is a tough, unreliable business, and they'd given up the greasepaint and floodlights to move to the Outer Banks. Now Nora taught dance, and Ronald had become a librarian. But you can't take the theater out of the boy, and one of his most popular initiatives at the library was Toddlers Theater. He wove stories from the rich history of the Outer Banks, and the children dressed up in a wild assortment of costumes to play Elizabethan settlers, Indians, pirates, and crusty sea captains.

Charles always seemed to know when the children would be arriving, and he sat on the second level of the returns shelf, accepting the pats and praise he took as his due.

Shortly before noon, the phone on the desk rang. For a moment my heart lifted when I recognized Butch's number on the display. It fell back with a thud when I remembered that he was working and what that work entailed. It was unlikely he was calling to ask either for a date or for my help.

"Ms. Richardson," he said, his tone deep and formal. Not good.

"Speaking," I chirped.

"Detective Watson wants to interview you once again about the events on Tuesday night. I called your cell phone and was told you were out of range. Are you at the library?"

"Yes." The thick stone walls of the lighthouse interfered with cell phones. To get a signal, we had to stand by a window or find the exact spot by the sink in the break room where modern plumbing penetrated the nineteenth-century wall. Upstairs in my apartment, I could use my iPhone if I opened the window, stood on the bench seat, and leaned out.

"We'll be around shortly," Butch said.

"But we're working. We're very busy today." I mentally crossed my fingers. Ronald was busy—children's laughter poured down the staircase—but the parents had gone for coffee and a good gossip, leaving the main floor of the library empty.

"We'll be there in ten minutes." He hung up.

If I hadn't been in a library, I might have sworn. I used the phone to call Charlene and tell her she was needed on the desk. She grumbled, but agreed to come.

According to the big clock on the wall, it was ten to noon. Oh, goody. The cops would be here at the same time the library board began arriving for their meeting. I abandoned the circulation desk and dashed up to the second floor. Ronald needed to know I'd be tied up for an indeterminate amount of time. I stuck my head in the door of the children's library. Today must be pirate day. Ronald wore a big hat with a plume and had a black patch tied around his head to cover one eye. A stuffed parrot perched on his shoulder. I swear, he had the costume for every occasion. The children were seated on the floor in a circle, dressed in an assortment of long dresses, vests, and hats, waving plastic swords or pushing wooden sailing vessels around their feet.

Ronald glanced up when I arrived, but kept reading without missing a beat. I mouthed "cops" and made a signal as if I were pulling out and aiming a gun. The kids laughed and fired back. I held up ten fingers and Ronald nodded. I ran down the stairs.

When I got back, the Gray Woman was browsing the stacks, and Diane Uppiton was standing by the circulation desk, tapping her feet. "Why is no one here?" she demanded. "Anyone could march in and rob you blind. Does Bertie know you've abandoned your post?"

As if I were the only remaining sentry on guard duty at Fort Knox. "Good thing I locked up the silver. You're right, Diane—anyone could come in."

Diane had made it perfectly clear that she didn't like me. For some reason she'd decided I had designs on her husband, the former chair of the library board. That Mr. Uppiton was now, unfortunately, deceased made no difference to her.

"All alone, today, Diane? Mr. Gardner not around?" I said.

"I'm here for the board meeting. Curtis has been unavoidably detained. An emergency at work." Curtis Gardner was not only Diane's paramour (and had been when the aforementioned Mr. Uppiton was still alive) but also a member of the library board. I had no doubt that the work emergency was more related to the sudden change in venue of the meeting, meaning that beer would not be served.

The rest of the board began to arrive. Mrs. Fitzgerald held the door for her granddaughter, bearing a sandwich box from Josie's Cozy Bakery and a bag of drinks. Only Curtis and Graham Luffe, the one board member who was also a town commissioner, hadn't come. They had a quorum. Bertie would have to present her budget after all.

"I'll take you to the meeting room," I said.

Curses! I wasn't fast enough. The door opened once again, and in came Butch and Detective Watson. Butch was in uniform, and Watson had his badge pinned to his belt. No one would mistake this for a social call. "Be with you in a minute, gentlemen," I said. Not a single member of the board made a move to follow me.

"Is there a problem, Detective?" Mrs. Fitzgerald said. Her granddaughter, a gangly girl of about fourteen, cocked her hip and smiled at Butch through a serious set of braces.

"Not a problem, ma'am," Watson said. "We have a few questions for Ms. Richardson."

"I told you!" Diane shrieked. "Another theft. The way this library is managed is a disgrace."

The Gray Woman looked up from the S shelf, full of attention.

"There's been a theft?" Butch said.

The granddaughter shivered and edged closer to Butch. "No," I said.

"If there hasn't been, there might well be," Diane said. "The way the staff are allowed to behave around here. Bertie doesn't enforce discipline. I'm so glad you're being proactive, Detective Watson, to provide them with helpful tips on crime prevention." She gave him what she considered to be a warm smile. Diane dressed for board meetings in the style I thought of as politician's-wife-trying-too-hard. Today she had on a Pepto-Bismol pink suit with a three-quarter-length-sleeved jacket, skirt cut right at the knees, buttoned shirt, and pumps with two-inch heels. Gold hoops were in her ears and a diamond tennis bracelet was around her wrist. In contrast, only Watson was in a tie, although the knot was loose, and even Mrs. Fitzgerald, a proper Southern matron of the old school, wore a comfortable summer dress.

Watson didn't look pleased at being mistaken for a

part-time community officer. Butch tried, not very successfully, to hide a grin.

Bertie walked into the room. "What's going on?"

"The police are here to give your staff a lecture on crime prevention," Elaine Rivers, one of the board members, said. "I agree with Diane. You need to protect the valuables in this library. It's a historic building, you know."

"What on earth are you talking about?" Bertie asked.

"As we're all here," Elaine said, "I propose we postpone the formal board meeting so we can all attend the lecture. I'm sure we have things to learn also."

The board nodded their agreement.

"Oh, for heaven's sake. I'm not here to give any lecture," Watson said. "Ms. Richardson, we need a private room. Or we can go down to the station."

"You're questioning her?" Diane said. "You mean Lucy's our thief? I knew it was a bad idea to have all that computer equipment not tied down. Never mind the Austen collection."

The Gray Woman, not even pretending not to be paying attention to our private conversation, nodded in agreement.

"There's been no theft," Watson said, "of computers, rare books, or anything else. As far as I'm aware. I have some questions about the death that occurred here. We'll use the staff break room."

"You mean that murder!" Diane shrieked. "It happened here?" She glanced around, as though expecting to see blood spatter on the walls. "The news said the body was found outside in the marsh."

Board members began to murmur. "I didn't know it had anything to do with us," Elaine said.

"It doesn't," Bertie said sharply. "But as the body was found on lighthouse property, the police are, of course, questioning anyone who was in the building."

I waited for more objections. There were none. Thank heavens Karen's attendance at our book club hadn't made it into the news reports.

"The board's meeting in the staff room. You can have my office, Detective," Bertie said. "Come along, everyone."

Diane looked momentarily confused. Then she swung back onto the attack. "Goodness gracious, Lucy, not you again!"

"I didn't have anything to do with it."

"Please, people," Watson said in a voice he must once have used when trying to control a riot. "Go and have your meeting. No one here has done anything, as far as we know at this time. Lucy might have seen or heard something; that's all."

"I see you brought lunch," Bertie said. "How nice. Eunice, why don't you show your granddaughter where we keep the plates and napkins? Everyone, let's let these officers go about their business. You know where my office is."

They certainly did.

The Gray Woman seemed to be far more interested in the chatter around the circulation desk than in looking for a book to check out. She was holding *Outer Banks* by Anne Rivers Siddons upside down.

At first my interview with the police was nothing more than a rehash of yesterday's. When had I last seen Karen? Whom had she left the library with? (Unfortunately, my mom.) Then Watson moved on to the beach bag. I had to say I'd noticed Mom carrying it into the library and putting it on the floor under her chair. I had not seen it again.

I was about to ask Watson if he'd heard that Norm Kivas was at Jake's last night, when there was a knock on the door, and Charlene's head popped in. "Call for you, Detective. They said they tried your cell but can't get you. You can use that phone. Press nine."

Watson reached for the desk phone. "We're finished here, Lucy. Thank you."

"I'll walk Lucy back to the front," Butch said. He held the door open for me, followed me out, and pulled it shut behind him.

I turned to face him. "Watson doesn't seriously think my mother had anything to do with . . . with what happened to Karen, does he?"

"I don't know what he's thinking," Butch said, carefully avoiding my eyes.

"You must. Surely he talks to you."

"Total truth, Lucy. He doesn't. He plays his cards very close to his chest."

The door to the staff room flew open. "Do you mind?" Diane Uppiton said. "We're having a meeting in here. Oh, it's you. I might have known. Really, Lucy, can't you keep your personal problems to yourself while at work? I would expect more professionalism from you."

I flushed. We'd hardly been shouting. Diane must have had her ear pressed up against the door, hoping to hear the sounds of screaming as I was dragged away in handcuffs.

Charles took the opportunity to slip into the room, crouching low, tail down, as if trying to be unobtrusive.

"Mrs. Uppiton, I am waiting for your vote," said the commanding voice of Mrs. Fitzgerald.

Diane huffed and slammed the door.

"Lucy—" Butch said.

I never did get to hear what he wanted to say. A screech came from inside the break room. "Who let that horrid beast in? Look what he's done to my stockings." The door flew open once more and Charles strolled out, his pointed ears up and fluffy tail held high. If he'd been human, I would have said he smirked.

Chapter 10

The Gray Woman was still in the main room, poking through the shelves. She looked, I thought, more as though she were checking for dust than seeking something to read. Waiting for her family to meet up with her, maybe. This was a tourist town, and it was tourist season, so we got a lot of seasonal people through our doors. Some of Ronald's children's programs were specifically designed for visitors, to introduce the kids to not only the history of the Outer Banks but also the flora, fauna, and spectacular natural features of this marvelous part of the world.

"Thanks, Charlene," I said. "I'll take over now."

"Everything okay?"

"As okay as can be."

I jerked my head in question toward the shelf behind which the Gray Woman had disappeared, ALCOTT–CAPOTE. Charlene leaned forward to whisper in my ear. "Been here for ages. Says nothing."

"Can I help you?" I peeked around the shelf as Charlene went upstairs. The Gray Woman jumped and slid the book she was holding back into its place. "No, thank you. You have an impressive collection, for such a small space." She spoke in a Midwestern accent as she stared at me down that long nose, through those black eyes.

"A small space means we have to know what's important," I said.

"True."

"I'm Lucy Richardson."

"Are you?"

"I mean . . . well, let me know if you need anything."

She turned her attention back to the shelf.

Perhaps she was still feeling chilly from a long Midwestern winter. A bit of North Carolina sun might warm her up a fraction.

Then again, maybe not.

She soon left. She didn't say good-bye or thank-you and she didn't check out any books. I assumed she'd been killing time, probably while her family did something she didn't approve of—like have fun—and I put her out of mind.

The board meeting finished at long last and the members streamed back into the main room. One of the men said to the others, "Anyone up for going for a drink?"

"How'd the meeting go?" I asked Bertie once they'd all left.

"As well as can be expected. If Diane knew anything at all about accounting or how to read a budget, she would have made plenty of objections, but even she knows when to keep her mouth shut. Sometimes. She does seem to have gotten a bee in her bonnet about security around here. Some idea of having the police give us tips on theft prevention."

"She mistook Sam Watson for a community services officer. He wasn't impressed."

Bertie laughed. Watson and Butch had left right after getting that phone call. Watson hadn't given me any dark looks, and Butch had smiled rather than looked on me with pity, so I assumed (I hoped?) the call had nothing to do with my mother.

Mom breezed in shortly before five, looking very "Grace Kelly on the Riviera" with yellow ballet flats, giant sunglasses, hair tied back in a Hermès scarf, tailored black capris, yellow summer-weight sweater, and restrained gold jewelry.

The sparkle had returned to her eye, and I decided I would not think about the last time I'd seen her: heading off to the lounge with George, manager. "Now," she said, after greeting me with a peck on the cheek, "let me see this apartment. I can't believe you actually live in a lighthouse. Above a library. If you're short of funds, dear . . ."

"I love it," I said, leading the way upstairs as Charles ran on ahead. The members of my family are not cat people; we'd had dogs when I was growing up. At first Mom ignored Charles; then she tried pushing him gently away, and then less gently. Charles wound around her ankles and rubbed up against her legs. I hid a smile. Nothing Charles liked better than to torment non–cat lovers. When we were admiring my tiny kitchen (me admiring, Mom horror-struck), Charles jumped onto the counter and threw himself at her. Mom shrieked and leapt back as the cat clung to her shirt and peered into her face. I plucked him off and held him tightly for the rest of the inspection, while Mom attempted to remove strands of long tan hair from her clothes.

Louise Jane had arrived while we were upstairs. She stood by the desk, chatting with Charlene. Inspired by the success of the Jane Austen exhibit, Louise Jane was determined to have a haunted Outer Banks display at the library in the fall. Organized by herself, of course. Her arms were piled high with books on the paranormal history of North Carolina. As soon as she heard our footsteps on the stairs, she dropped the books onto the circulation desk and hurried over to greet my mom. "Mrs. Richardson. Welcome to the Lighthouse Library. I'm Louise Jane McKaughnan, one of the library's biggest boosters. I fill in here now and again when the workload gets too much for the *regular* staff to manage. Isn't that right, Lucy?"

"Uh, right." *What else could I say?*

"I'm sorry we didn't get a chance to chat at book club. Have you been having the grand tour? My family's lived on the Outer Banks since the seventeen hundreds, so if there's anything you want to know, anything an *outsider* like Lucy wouldn't, then I'd be awful happy to help."

"My mom's family's as old as yours, Louise Jane," I pointed out.

"Yes, honey, but you aren't. What do you think of our library, Mrs. Richardson?"

"It's lovely," Mom said. "Lucy's apartment is simply darling. It's small, but adequate for temporary accommodation."

At the word *temporary*, Louise Jane's eyes lit up as if the first-order Fresnel lens had been switched on inside her head. "You're staying at the Ocean Side, are you?"

"Yes."

"That hotel has a fascinating history. Are you interested in history, Mrs. Richardson?"

As if anyone could say no.

"Yes," Mom said.

"Will you look at the time?" I said. "Let's go, Mom."

"I just happen to have tomorrow afternoon free," Louise Jane said. "If you don't have previous plans, how about I drop by the the hotel, say at three? We can have a nice chat and I can give you a private tour of some of the interesting historical aspects of the hotel, Mrs. Richardson. May I call you Suzanne?"

"Please do," Mom said.

"Great. Three o'clock in the lobby." Louise Jane bolted for the door. Mom blinked. It's not often my mom was outmaneuvered. About the last thing in life she's interested in is the history of the Outer Banks, and the haunted history at that. If it had been anyone but Louise Jane, I'd have chortled. Instead I wondered what she was plotting now.

Theodore Kowalski was next to arrive, his hair blowing in the wind stirred up by the exit of Hurricane Louise Jane. "Where's Louise Jane off to in such a hurry?"

"I have no idea," I said, imagining potions, cauldrons, and black cats.

"Nice to see you again, Suzanne," he said. "We didn't get much of a chance to chat the other night. Lucy runs a tight ship in her book club." He waved his finger at me. "No frivolity allowed."

"Speaking of that night," I said. "You didn't hang around outside by any chance, did you?"

"How I wish I had. Perhaps I could have been of assistance to poor Karen. Awful business. Gang of drunken college punks, people are saying."

"Are they?" That was news to me. "Did you see these . . . uh, punks?"

"I've spoken to Detective Watson. He's been questioning everyone who was at the book club that night.

They were also asking about some beach bag. I don't know what that has to do with—"

"From England, are you?" Mom said.

Theodore beamed. He was, in fact, from Nags Head, North Carolina. He liked to pretend he was an English scholar.

"Lucy," Bertie called. "Can I have a minute?"

I left my mom telling Theodore how much she loved London.

Bertie had a form for me to sign, and I did so. When I got back to Mom, Theodore was asking her where she was staying. She managed to gasp out, "The Ocean Side" as I dragged her away.

"Why did Theodore want to know what hotel you're at?" I asked, once we were in the SLK and speeding down the highway.

"No reason."

Oh dear.

My mom and I weren't all that close; we never had been. We'd certainly never been *friends*. I was surprised at the amount of time she wanted to spend with me on this trip. Was she lonely at the hotel without my dad or any of her girlfriends, or was it that she didn't want to appear to be alone? She still hadn't said anything about going home, which had become a moot point since Watson ordered her not to leave Dare County. I didn't exactly have a packed social life myself, but I did enjoy getting together with Josie and her friends, or just having time on my own to read and daydream and explore the Outer Banks.

"About that necklace," I said now.

"There is nothing to discuss. I've never seen the thing before, and I have no idea how it got into my bag. As if I'd be interested in anything so tasteless in any event. I doubt very much it was stolen. Rather than admit she'd lost it, some old broad with early-onset Alzheimer's played the prima donna. Either that or a malicious housemaid took it and hid it in my bag to get revenge for some supposed slight."

"I thought you and Karen made up," I said.

"Did I mention Karen? I did not."

"Oh, come on, Mom. I know that's who you meant."

"We made up, as in I decided to apologize for my rudeness, yes. And I will admit I was rude to her. Does that make you feel better?"

"It's not up to me to feel one way or another."

She turned her head to give me one of her patented glares. The car veered into the passing lane and I shrieked.

"Control yourself, Lucille," Mom said, deftly returning to her own lane, as an SUV gave us a blast from its horn. "I see North Carolina drivers are no politer than when I was a girl out for a day's outing with my parents."

I ground my teeth. My feet pressed harder into the foot well.

"You needn't help me with the brakes; I can drive all by myself. To return to the subject at hand. I told your police friends that the sequence of events is perfectly obvious. Karen stole the necklace. She was a maid in that hotel, wasn't she? She then snuck into my room and put it in my bag as a way of getting it out of the hotel. I assume the staff are checked closely to ensure nothing, shall we say, accidentally finds its way into their pockets. She would have naturally assumed I'd be coming to your charming little book club, and schemed to retrieve the item then. Why she didn't is up to the police to determine. Not me. Overcome by guilt, I suspect. I assume her accomplice—don't they call such a person a post?"

"Fence."

"Whatever. The fence arranged to meet her at the library, and when she didn't have the necklace, he killed her."

I wanted to believe her. Truly, I did. But I didn't think it was so simple. If Karen had hidden the item in Mom's bag, wouldn't she have been anxious about it all evening? Karen had rarely had much to say at our meetings. I didn't think she'd even read the assigned books. She would tell us she'd wanted to, but she had been so busy, time had gotten away from her. I suspected that she came to the club for the companionship and the bakery treats more than any great love of literature. I didn't mind that. Everyone has their reasons, and at the Lighthouse Library our goal is to create a community as much as to lend out books or help with research.

I couldn't remember what everyone was doing all the time at the last book club meeting, but I hadn't noticed Karen being particularly agitated. She'd pointedly ignored my mother the entire time. So pointedly, it could have been a pretense. "You might be onto something, Mom." I pressed my right foot into the empty space on my side of the car as we tore through a yellow light turning red. Mom drove like she lived life—with total abandon, in full expectation that everyone else would get out of her way.

Was that what my dad had first seen in her? Was that why he'd fallen in love with an Outer Banks high school girl, shocking his bluest-of-blue-blood Boston Brahmin parents to the core?

They'd met when my dad was vacationing on the

Outer Banks. She'd been seventeen, about to begin her senior year of high school, spending the summer waitressing in a restaurant that's no longer in business. He'd been in law school, the only son of a prominent Boston family, his future in the firm founded by his grandfather laid out before him.

She'd been a breathtaking beauty (she still was, in her late fifties). A picture taken that summer of my tanned, sun-kissed, bathing-suit-clad parents laughing on the beach might have been of two young movie stars relaxing in Malibu. His parents had been appalled when he announced he was going to marry the waitress, so young she hadn't even finished high school yet, whose mother worked in a shop and whose father *fished* for a living. Oh, Mom never put it quite like that. She told her children that the Richardsons had been wary but eventually were won over when they realized how deeply in love the couple were.

In lust, more likely. My oldest brother was born five months after their wedding. Two more boys came at a more sedate pace, followed last of all by me.

We pulled into the parking lot of Jake's Seafood Bar, careening across two lanes of traffic with milliseconds to spare.

"Josie's young man seemed very sweet," Mom said, bringing the car to a neck-straining stop. "I thought it would be nice to have our drink here, help support his business. Have they set a date for the wedding?"

"No. I don't think they're formally engaged, Mom."

"I love weddings. I've been the mother of the groom three times, but not yet mother of the bride. It's such an honored position. I'd hate to see Ellen get there before me."

I got out of the SLK, grateful not to have to reply to

that last comment. Mom had parked in her usual fashion — taking up two spots.

Once we were seated on the outside deck, Mom excused herself. I leaned back in my chair and enjoyed the view over the sound. At first glance, Mom's theory sounded pretty far-fetched. But maybe there was something to it. Oh, not about Karen smuggling the necklace out of the hotel and murderous accomplices lying in wait, but the fact of the necklace being in Mom's bag. What had Karen said when she and Mom had their altercation in the lobby? Something about Mom being a common thief? If that had been the rumor when they were back in school, so what? It was a long time ago. Mom wouldn't care. She'd so totally put her Outer Banks life behind her, I wondered sometimes if she believed she'd lived her whole life in Boston.

Had Karen decided to get revenge for Mom's slight by making it look as though Mom was still a thief? Karen, a hotel maid, was in a position to steal jewelry from a guest's room and then to get into Mom's room. Had she dropped the necklace into Mom's bag, not to get it out of the hotel to recover later, but in hopes that Mom would be found with it?

Even I had to admit that my theory was a stretch. All Mom had had to do was look into her bag, see the necklace, wonder where it had come from, and tell the desk she had it if anyone was searching for it.

I knew that's what my mother would do. No reason Karen would, though.

All of which had absolutely nothing to do with Karen being murdered outside the Lighthouse Library.

The two incidents appeared to have nothing at all in common. But they had to be related somehow.

I watched Mom make her way through the room toward our table. A man seated at the bar by himself said something to her. She gave him a radiant smile, and a shake of her head. Once he was behind her, and she saw me watching, she stuck out her tongue. My mother could be infuriating at times, but I loved her so very much.

The problem was, I could see only one thing that joined the theft of the necklace and the murder of Karen. My mother.

I would have to do everything I possibly could to ensure the police didn't take that thread to that conclusion.

Chapter 11

In the interest of protecting the reputation of the library, Bertie had asked us to not talk about the death of Karen, but if we had to, to imply she was found in the marsh, rather than in the shadow of the lighthouse wall. I suspected Bertie might have had a hand in placing that impression into the news reports.

Unfortunately Diane Uppiton had no intention of protecting the reputation of the library.

Once the news was out, the knowledge that we were the site of a "brutal murder" seemed only to increase our custom. The police had finished their work; the tape was taken down; the crime scene tidied up. The parking lot soon filled with people pretending to be going bird-watching in the marsh, but most of them had neglected to bring binoculars and wear suitable footwear. They walked a couple of yards through the grass, and then circled around to come out beside the lighthouse. As there was no sign saying "Murder happened here," many of them popped into the library to ask.

Fortunately for me, this morning I wasn't downstairs to answer their questions, but was upstairs gazing out the window, watching cars come and go and people tiptoeing through the marsh. I had the day off work, and luxuriated in a quiet morning of sitting in the window alcove in my pajamas, drinking coffee and reading *Maddy Clare*. It was another beautiful day, and I wondered if it was possible to get tired of this view. I considered myself to be very brave, reading that ghost story here in my apartment. According to Louise Jane, not exactly a reliable source, the lighthouse was haunted by the ghost of a woman brought here as a young bride by a cruel old man, who'd locked her in this very room until she'd taken the only way out and had leapt through the window to her death on the hard ground below.

I hadn't believed a word of it, but nevertheless I'd snuck a peek at some of the haunted-history books among the library's collection. I found plenty of ghosts, but no mention of the tragic bride, who Louise Jane said was known as *the Lady*.

Just in case, this morning I kept Charles upstairs with me rather than allowing him to go down to the library.

Eventually hunger got the better of me, and I put the book aside. I pulled my bathing suit on under shorts and a T-shirt, tossed a towel, sunscreen, a bottle of water, and the book into my beach bag, and headed out the door. Charles dashed on ahead.

The library was busy, but I didn't slow my pace as I waved at Ronald behind the circulation desk. I needed one more thing before I hit the beach.

Lunch.

I headed for Josie's to pick up a sandwich. As I drove into Nags Head, I tried to smother a little niggle of guilt about Mom. I hadn't told her I wasn't working today. Selfishly, I wanted to do what I wanted to do, and that was to go to the beach. Alone. I loved nothing more than setting up my folding chair at the edge of the water, letting the waves play with my toes, and enveloping myself in a book the way one can only when one is alone.

I'd never before had to give a thought to entertaining my mother. But on this trip, she almost seemed needy. Needy of my time and my attention. I thought back to the day of her arrival. I'd wondered if something was wrong. Was she becoming conscious of the passage of time, and wanting to connect with her only daughter? Or just hoping to wear away my objections and convince me to quit the Lighthouse Library and return to Boston? With the commotion over the death of Karen Kivas and the discovery of the necklace in Mom's beach bag, I'd put most of that out of mind.

It was reasonably quiet at Josie's before the lunch rush. I placed an order for roast beef with caramelized onions and red peppers on a baguette and asked the clerk if my cousin was in. She bellowed over her shoulder and Josie came out, wiping floury hands on her bibbed apron.

"Morning, sweetie," she said, eyeing my shorts and flip-flops. "Day off?"

"Yup. Beach day."

"Lucky you," she said. "I'd skip work and join you, but I have a function to cater tonight."

I reached across the counter and took my bagged lunch from the sandwich maker, a skinny young man with long bleached dreadlocks.

"I'm making something new," Josie said. "Let me get you one and you can tell me what you think."

"I shouldn't . . . ," I said, but Josie ran off.

Two men came up to the counter. They were in their early fifties with short gray hair, which was lightly gelled, and they were dressed in summer business clothes of open-necked dress shirts. The taller one studied the menu printed on the blackboard on the back wall, while the other said, "Mornin', Alison."

"I'm so sorry for your loss," the woman at the cash register said. "Please accept my condolences."

I edged away, not wanting to look as though I was hovering.

"Thank you," the man said. "We're still in shock. The family can't come to grips with it yet."

"Darn disgrace, that's what it is," his companion said. "I'll have the Reuben sandwich and a pecan tart. And a bottle of that iced tea. Doug?"

"Sounds good. Same for me, but just water."

"Never mind the tragedy to Doug's family," the second man said, "but it's also bad for Nags Head, bad for businesses like this one. We don't want word getting out that this isn't a safe place to bring your family."

"Stuff happens." Alison rang up the charge while the dreadlocked man began making the sandwiches. I wondered what was keeping Josie.

"Stuff doesn't happen," Doug said. "People make things happen. And other people can put a stop to it. If they're allowed to."

Okay, now I got it. This must be Doug Whiteside, Karen's brother. Hadn't Connor told me Doug was going to run for mayor? As if he'd picked up my thoughts, he turned toward me. "I hope you're not worried, miss. The killer will be long gone, and I'm going to do everything in my power to make sure none of their like come here again." He thrust out his hand. "Doug Whiteside."

I took his hand in mine. His grip was firm, so firm I wondered if he was intending to crush every bone I had.

"You can rest assured that the Outer Banks will remain the perfect place for your vacation."

"I live here," I said.

His eyes lit up. "Is that a fact? How could I possibly not have run into you before? I would have remembered if I had. Billy?"

His companion handed me a fridge magnet. It didn't say anything about his running for mayor. It didn't have to. It featured a picture of Doug Whiteside, all polished teeth, sprayed and styled hair, with the words FOR NAGS HEAD, a phone number, and a URL: www.doug fornagshead.com.

"You might have heard about that murder over in the marshes the other night," Doug said.

"I did."

"My sister, Karen."

"I'm sorry."

"Thank you. I've been saying for a long time that we need a new administration in this town. A mayor that's going to work with the chief of police, not put obstacles in his way at every turn. Let the police do their jobs, and keep the scum of the cities away from our town and our families. Don't you agree, Miss . . . ?"

"Lucy Richardson." This was the first I'd heard about the mayor being at odds with the police chief. I was under the impression they got on quite well. Like every town department, including the library, the police wanted more money. The mayor and the town council tried to balance everyone's interests with what they could afford to spend.

Where on earth was that Josie?

"Folks are clamoring for Doug here to run for mayor," Billy said.

Doug Whiteside shrugged modestly. "I haven't de-

cided yet. A political campaign is tough on the family."
*So undecided he'd had fridge magnets and a Web page
made up already.*

"You're right, Doug." Billy placed a firm, supporting
hand on Doug's manly shoulder. "But nothing can be as
tough on a family as a death. Particularly a senseless
murder. Isn't your duty to Karen now?"

"I'll take one of those things," the sandwich maker,
who'd been listening to the entire conversation, said.
Billy handed him a magnet. Then he slapped one onto
the metallic trim of the display case. "We have to be going, Doug. Can't be late for that meeting."

"Duty calls. It was nice meeting you, Lucy. I'm sure I'll
see you around." He gave me a megawatt smile, and
walked away.

Billy pulled a notebook out of his shirt pocket. "Let
me take down your name and phone number, Lucy. If
Doug does decide to run for office, we'd like you on our
team."

I held up the fridge magnet. "Why don't I call you?"

His smile froze in place. "That'd be great. Just great.
You too, buddy," he said to the sandwich clerk. He swept
their order off the counter and left.

"Is it safe to come out?" Josie whispered from the back.

"You rat," I said.

"I'd heard that Doug's milking Karen's death for all
it's worth. And don't you even think of voting for him,
Kyle Bradshaw." She glared at the sandwich clerk.

"Just listenin' to what the man had to say," Kyle said.

Josie snatched the magnet off the display case. She
thrust a plate toward me. "Here, try this. It's an old recipe
of our grandmother's. She called it Dream Cake. Nuts

and coconut in a filling of brown sugar and eggs on a rich shortbread base. Did your mother ever make it for you?"

I looked at her.

"Oh, sorry. I forgot," Josie said with a grin. "The only thing your mother makes is reservations. I tweaked it a bit, made a few updates, and have been wanting to give it a try. What do you think?"

"I think I don't need cake for lunch. But anything to help you out." I took a bite. Deee-licious. "Wow, this is great." I finished the treat and licked my fingers.

As we talked—and I ate—we walked to the door. Josie tossed the fridge magnet into the trash. "Doug's business must have been working around the clock last night."

"What do you mean?"

"Karen's death is tailor-made for him. He'll be handing those magnets out by the truckload."

"That's a bit harsh, isn't it? She was his sister."

"Doug and Karen were estranged for a long time," Josie said. "I don't know why, but as a guess, I'd say because one was as manipulative as the other. Karen got her way by playing the poor-little-me card, and Doug gets his way by pretending he has to be talked into doing what he wants to do in the first place. He's been planning a run for mayor for months. Now he'll humbly say he's been forced into it by his sister's murder. Although he never cared about her when she was alive. He never gave her a penny or so much as offered to help her out. She said she didn't want his charity, but it's not charity when it's from your own brother, is it?"

"He looks prosperous enough. What does he do?"

"He owns a sign company. Doug's Signs and Labels.

They make signs for businesses, and labels to put on bottles and cans. And now, I guess, they make fridge magnets. He's going to use Karen's death to claw his way into the mayor's office. Tough on crime, and all that blather. I heard him bad-mouthing Connor. Who, by the way, has the full support of the chief. Mark my words, Lucy: Karen's picture will start appearing on his promotional literature."

"Won't that backfire? Won't people see it for the opportunism it is?"

"Some will. But those people aren't likely to vote for Doug Whiteside in any event." She spun around to look at the chalkboard on the wall. "Do you think I should add Grandma's Dream Cake to the menu?"

"Absolutely."

She gave me a hug that smelled of flour and coconut. "Have fun at the beach."

I tried to have fun at the beach, but for once, my book, no matter how good it was, couldn't keep my attention.

I watched two young kids in brightly colored bathing suits chase sandpipers through the surf under the watchful eyes of their parents. Another family was occupied in constructing a sand castle that, judging by the intensity of the father, might be on the way to becoming one of the wonders of the world. The children, for whom this was supposedly a fun activity, lost interest and wandered away. Dad continued digging trenches to hold back the sea and constructing ramparts.

I thought about Doug Whiteside and his challenge to Connor. But most of all, I thought about my mom, meeting with Louise Jane at three.

At a quarter to three, I decided I was getting chilly. Dad was building dykes to keep the incoming tide away from his castle. His family had gone back to their hotel. He hadn't seemed to notice their departure.

I figured he had as much chance of saving his empire from the sea as I had from keeping Louise Jane from plotting with my mom.

But, like the frantically bailing man in front of me, I had to try.

I arrived at the hotel to find Louise Jane waiting in the lobby. She did not appear to be thrilled to see me.

"Oh," I said, "I totally forgot. Today's the day you and my mom are getting together, isn't it?"

She looked as though she didn't believe me. "I called her room. She'll be right down. You're not at work?"

"Day off."

"What a nice surprise." Mom greeted me with a peck on the cheek. "I wasn't expecting to see you this afternoon, dear." She studied my outfit. "Don't you have to be at work?"

"Day off."

"How nice. I'm sure you don't mind, Mary Jane, if my daughter joins us."

"Louise Jane," my archenemy corrected her.

"I had a lovely, relaxing morning and enjoyed a light lunch. Now I'm positively starving again. I do believe it's cocktail time." Mom headed for the lobby bar.

Louise Jane, looking somewhat nonplussed, scurried to catch up. "But I thought we were going to tour the hotel, Suzanne. I was going to show you some of the historic places they don't tell the ordinary tourists about."

The word "ordinary" might have been what caught my mom's attention. She stopped. "Oh, right. History."

"Sounds fascinating. Lead on, Louise Jane," I said.

She gave me her circling-barracuda smile. "The most . . .

intense ... ghostly activity is at the lighthouse, Suzanne. In Lucy's own apartment, as a matter of fact. People have been driven to leap from her window by the force of the haunted presence."

"What?" Mom said, her bored, yet polite, disinterest disappearing with the speed of a barracuda snatching up a minnow.

"Nonsense," I said. "That story you told me about someone killing themselves back in the nineties? Bertie says no such thing ever happened."

"Bertie would, wouldn't she?" Louise Jane put a hand on Mom's arm. "No need to worry about Lucy, Suzanne. My mother and grandmother have a lifelong interest in the spiritual happenings of the Outer Banks. They gave me some ... instruments to use to keep Lucy safe in her apartment." Her voice trailed off. "Of course, spells lose their strength over time. But that shouldn't matter. As long as she doesn't stay too long."

Wasn't that a direct hit? Mom was nodding in agreement. She might not believe in ghosts or in talismans against them, but she did like the sound of me not staying too long. Shortly after my arrival, Louise Jane had laid a row of herbs that she called her grandmother's spells across my door. I don't know whether they got rid of any spooks, but they'd proved highly ineffective when I was attacked by a mad killer in the lighthouse and had to defend myself with the help of Charles the cat and a classic work of literature.

Louise Jane held the door to the deck open. Simultaneously the three of us reached into our bags and pulled out sunglasses. Children splashed and shouted in the pool while parents relaxed under sun umbrellas with colorful drinks at their side. The wooden boardwalk, gray with age and covered with windblown sand, curved through the sea oats and beach grass, over the dunes and to the beach. The pool area was surrounded by a tall fence, but as we were standing on the steps, I could see over it to a line of parked cars. As I watched, a woman dressed in the hotel's house-keeping uniform, climbed out of a rusty Impala.

"First stop," Louie Jane said, lowering her voice. Mom leaned closer to hear. Despite myself, I did also. "The swimming pool was built over a graveyard."

I snorted.

"Did you know, Suzanne," Louise Jane said, "that this coast is called the Graveyard of the Atlantic?"

Of course Mom knew that. She'd been raised on the Outer Banks. Her father had been a fisherman, for heaven's sake. Louise Jane didn't wait for a reply. "Because of the number of shipwrecks. Many went down near here." She lifted a hand and pointed out to sea. I was reminded of the Ghost of Christmas Yet to Come pointing Ebenezer Scrooge toward his doom. "So many bodies washed up over the centuries. So many of them nameless and unclaimed. Many of them were buried here. When time came to build the hotel, the bones were dug up and the pool was put in that very spot."

"I didn't read that in the hotel information brochure," Mom said.

"My grandmother tells me that spirits usually move with their bones. But some do not. They're bound to the place in which they were laid to rest. In some cases"— Louise Jane lowered her voice still further—"they may have been laid to rest without actually being dead."

"Surely not," Mom said.

"Prolonged immersion in cold water can lead to a state that appears like death. An unknown body and a quick burial, all during a time of few doctors and no advanced medical equipment." Louise Jane shivered in delight. "I can't imagine a worse fate than to be buried alive. When they awoke, the unfortunate souls would have tried to claw their way out. Even now, centuries later, they are still trying to get out."

Louise Jane was good—I had to give her that. In the brilliant sunshine and the damp heat, surrounded by laughing, swimming children and sunbathing, rum-punch-swigging adults, I saw Mom shiver and rub her arms. I have to confess to feeling a sudden chill myself.

I doubted very much that I'd find this story in any of the ghost legends of the Outer Banks. Louise Jane liked to make them up—or, as she said, tell the hidden ones. I suspect she chose her subjects so as to have maximum impact on her listeners, to make it personal.

"Does your room overlook the pool, Suzanne?" she asked.

"Yes."

"Be sure to keep your balcony door closed at night."

"Or what?" I said.

Louise Jane's barracuda smile turned into her circling-shark one. "Your skepticism does you credit, Lucy. But I wouldn't want your mom to have a—shall we say—fright because you mocked my precautions."

That put me neatly in my place.

"Now, let's go back inside. What floor are you on, Suzanne?"

"The second."

"Really? That is interesting."

We trooped back into the hotel and up the steps, arriving on the second floor by the back stairs. In the stairwell, paint was peeling from the walls, the concrete was cracking from one corner to the other, and patches of rust spotted the railing. On the landing, a housekeeping cart stood abandoned, piled high with dirty laundry. I've never understood why in public buildings elevators are kept all shiny and polished, yet stairs are allowed to be dirty and unadorned. Is there a universal plot to discourage people from getting a bit of exercise?

We emerged onto the second floor. No one else was in sight. "I heard about that necklace being found in your bag," Louise Jane said.

"Who told you that?" I said.

She waved her hand. "Word gets around."

"I did not steal it," Mom said. "I explained that to the police. A minor misunderstanding."

"Exactly my point. When I heard your room's on the second floor, then everything became clear."

When she heard . . . about two minutes ago. I let that one slide.

"What became clear?" Mom said.

"We think of ghosts as Civil War soldiers or women in long dresses carrying candles through gloomy Scottish castles, but of course, unnatural death didn't end when the modern era began. Ghosts can also be our contemporaries. Case in point, a maid in this very hotel killed herself after being caught stealing from the guest rooms."

"Imagine that," I said.

"It was about twenty or so years ago. Of course the hotel hushed the whole thing up."

"Of course," I said.

"My grandmother was brought in to help, and things settled down for a while. But it's possible she's come back."

"Your grandmother's back?" I said.

Louise Jane gave me a glare that would freeze the water in the swimming pool.

"Sorry," I mumbled. I reminded myself not to openly antagonize Louise Jane. Let her have her fun.

"The maid is back. It happened like this. She was a local girl, not well educated. Some say she was simpleminded. She was seduced by a dishwasher in the restaurant. He spun her a story about needing money to pay for an operation for his mother. Only if his mother was well again, and not a burden on him, would he be free to marry."

This time it was Mom's turn to snort. "Never heard that one before."

"You are so right, Suzanne. It's a shame what awful fools some women can be." I thought Louise Jane showed amazing restraint by not looking at me as she said that. "He persuaded her to steal from the rooms. She'd be discovered eventually, of course, but the plan was that they'd be long gone by then."

"Presumably having forgotten all about the mother," Mom said.

"Exactly. As could have been predicted, once the dishwasher had the jewelry, he left, without taking the maid or his mother with him. Before the girl could be arrested, she killed herself."

"Poor thing," Mom said, her voice full of genuine sympathy.

"She walked into the sea the night of a major storm. It was three days before her body washed up."

"How awful," Mom said.

"What's that have to do with the second floor?" I said.

"She was the second-floor housemaid, of course."

"She didn't kill herself in the hotel."

"Try to follow along, Lucy, honey. She's haunted by her guilt. Her guilt at the theft, her heartbreak at having been abandoned by her lover. She haunts this hotel, attempting to undo her mistake. She wants to put the stolen items back!"

We said nothing for a few moments. The shadows in the hallway seemed to lengthen. A couple came out of a room at the far end of the corridor. They passed us with vacant smiles and dips of their chins, and went down the stairs.

"I believe," Louise Jane said, once they were gone, "she took that necklace and put it in your room, Suzanne."

Mom looked as though she wanted to believe Louise Jane.

I tried to play nicely. "Be that as it may, it's hardly a story we can take to the police. And what about Karen? Dying so soon after the necklace was stolen. I can't believe those two incidents aren't related."

"The spirit world—so my grandmother tells me—is highly connected. One to the other. That long-ago maid can't leave this hotel. She can't leave this floor. But can she communicate? She must have been furious that the necklace, which she wanted to save, was removed from the hotel. The press are saying Karen was found in the marsh, but we know that's not true, don't we, Lucy?"

"What of it?"

"You remember I told you about the workers killed when the lighthouse was being built? Crushed by tons of heavy stone. They were standing at the base of the lighthouse, weren't they? In the exact spot Karen was found. I'm not fully convinced, but my grandmother insists that it's possible those nineteenth-century workmen had been communicating, in some way, with the twentieth-century hotel maid."

"That's getting to be too much for me," Mom said.

"I thought you should know, Suzanne. The lighthouse is a highly haunted place. Your daughter's awful brave to want to continue living there."

"I'm sure it won't be for long," Mom said. "Now, how about we forget all about ghosts and hauntings and death and have a drink?"

I returned from the ladies' room to find Louise Jane telling Mom that she was prepared to step into the empty position at the library the moment I left. Mom smiled at me as I pulled up my chair. "Isn't that nice, dear, to know you don't have to worry about leaving your colleagues in the lurch?"

Mom had ordered a glass of Pinot Grigio. I was having a hot tea, and Louise Jane had an Outer Banks Brewing Station Ale. No matter how much Louise Jane and Mom might conspire to get me to leave the Outer Banks, I had no intention of going anywhere, so I shouldn't have minded their scheming. But I did, and so I stubbornly insisted on staying to have a drink with them.

"If you're interested in the paranormal history of this area," Louise Jane said to my mom, who had never before in her entire life shown the least bit of interest in history, paranormal or otherwise, "I'd love to tell you some of my ideas for the haunted exhibit the library's putting on in the fall."

"Thinking of perhaps putting on. Maybe," I said pettily. "How's Dad, by the way?"

"I assume your father is well," Mom replied, an answer that meant absolutely nothing.

"Good afternoon, ladies." A booming voice sounded

behind me as George, manager, arrived at our table. "I hope you had a pleasant day."

"Very nice, thank you," Mom said.

"Why, you have nothing to go with your drinks." He snapped his fingers and a waiter appeared in a puff of smoke. "A bowl of mixed nuts and a couple plates of whatever's good in the kitchen. Put it on my account."

The waiter scurried to do the boss's bidding.

"That's very kind of you, George," Mom said.

Uninvited, he plopped down in the vacant fourth chair. "Nothing's too much for an old friend." He beamed at Mom. She smiled back.

My head spun.

"Louise Jane was giving Lucy and me a tour of the hotel."

George blinked in confusion. "If you wanted a tour, Sue, I would've been happy to show you around."

"Louise Jane's tour was highly individual. Fascinating, too, wasn't it, dear?"

"Fascinating."

"Gotta run." Louise Jane swallowed the last of her beer in one gulp. She jumped to her feet. "Are you working tomorrow, Lucy?"

"Yes."

"That's too bad. You won't be able to come with us. See you tomorrow, Suzanne." She dashed away before the hotel manager realized she was trying to scare the life out of his guests with stories of undead housemaids lurking on the second floor.

The idea of Louise Jane spending more time with my mom was scaring the life out of me.

"Tomorrow?" I said to Mom. "You're meeting her again?"

"First I've heard of it," she replied.

The waiter arrived, loaded down with plates piled with appetizers.

I snagged a slice of bruschetta. "I'm off, too. If you, ahem, have to be here longer than you'd planned, why don't you call Dad and ask him to come down?"

"Your father's much too busy."

"Tell him to make the time. One of his army of lackeys can take his cases. They usually do."

"I don't want to worry him."

"Whatever you say, Mom." I finished off the bruschetta and decided to take a spring roll with me.

Maybe two spring rolls. They were stuffed full of vegetables, weren't they?

As I was crossing the lobby, nibbling on a roll and wondering if I should call my dad myself, I passed the Gray Woman, the one who been hanging around the library. "Hi," I said.

She raised one eyebrow.

"Lucy Richardson, from the library?" I didn't offer to shake hands. They were, after all, sticky with the remnants of finger foods. Instead I wiped my fingers on a napkin I was still carrying.

"Oh, yes," the woman said. "I enjoyed spending time at your library. Very unusual setting, isn't it? In that lighthouse. From the outside, it hardly looks like you could fit a library in there."

"Amazing what can be done with nooks and crannies and careful attention."

"Someone told me you live there. In a private apartment."

"Small but cozy," I said.

"Seems a waste. Wouldn't it be put to better use to expand the collection?"

"That wouldn't be realistic. The apartment's on the fourth level. Too much of a climb for many people. No such thing as an elevator." Mrs. Fitzgerald, for example, had to be assisted to the third floor for book club. If patrons needed access to volumes kept on the upper levels but didn't have the mobility, we lugged the books all the way down for them.

"Storage, then. Or the director's office. Free up room for books." She had a way of leaning in when she spoke, as if she were about to impart a confidence. Her eyes were very intense.

This woman had too much time on her hands. She was here on vacation and seemed to have decided to redesign our library rather than go to the beach like everyone else.

"Where are you visiting from?" I asked.

"Iowa."

"Oh." I've never been to Iowa. Unlikely I ever will.

She walked away with strong, determined steps, heading for the elevators that accessed the guest rooms on the upper floors.

I realized she'd never told me her name.

Weird.

"It's a crying shame," Ronald was saying as I came through the front door of the library.

"What is?" I asked. I'd arrived minutes after closing, and my colleagues were gathered around the circulation desk, talking over the day.

"Karen Kivas always brought her grandchildren to

Friday afternoon story circle. She never missed a day. They didn't come today."

"Karen did just pass away," Bertie said.

"All the more reason they should have come. The kids have to deal with the death of their grandmother; that's tough. They need the support of familiar routine."

"Maybe they were busy with something else. Visitation, relatives arriving," Bertie said.

"I called their mom, Janice, this morning, to say I'd pick the kids up if they needed a lift. Janice works at a shop in Kill Devil Hills, and Fridays were always Karen's day off, so Karen looked after the children and brought them to the library. Janice said her dad was minding the kids today and he'd be bringing them. Norm might not realize the library's important to the girls."

"Do you know where Norm lives?" I asked, as an idea began to form in the back of my mind.

"He's back in Karen's house, Janice said."

"That was quick," I said. "Look, why don't we go around and talk to him? Explain the importance of the routine to the kids."

"I doubt he'd accept any advice from me," Ronald said.

"Worth a try," I said. "I'll even drive you. Your car's still in the shop, isn't it? I'll drop you off at home later, save Nora coming out to get you."

"You sure you don't mind?" Ronald asked.

"Not at all. We can go right now."

"That's kind of you, Lucy," Bertie said.

I accepted the praise without mentioning that I had an ulterior motive. Three days had passed since the death of Karen Kivas, and as far as I could tell, the police were going in circles. Someone needed to shake things up, and it might as well be me. As the ex-husband, Norm

Kivas had to be the prime suspect, particularly as he was apparently making himself comfortable back in the matrimonial home.

"Thanks, Lucy. Do you have the SLK by any chance?" he asked, trying to pretend he wasn't almost drooling at the thought of a ride in Mom's car.

"Sorry—beggars can't be choosers. It's the Yaris or nothing."

Ronald tried not to look too disappointed.

Karen and Norm Kivas lived in a small, nondescript house on a road of similar dwellings. Mailboxes at the end of many of the driveways indicated that this was a street of full-time residents, not holiday rentals. Their lawn wasn't more than a patch of sand with a few tough plants struggling to survive, and the house had seen far better days. A rusty pickup was parked in a driveway that was more weeds than gravel. A red tricycle and a deflating soccer ball sat on the front porch.

"You can wait in the car, if you like," Ronald said.

"Way too hot. My mom taught me never to leave a car engine idling. Bad for the environment." I leapt out and followed Ronald to the door.

He rang the bell, and the door swung open.

"Ronald! Ronald's here. Yeah!" A bright-faced little girl with brilliant blue eyes jumped up and down in excitement. "Grandpa, Ronald's here." A younger girl, the front of her T-shirt smeared with what looked like peanut butter and jam, joined her in screeching with delight. I couldn't see the TV, but I could hear it. It was set to a children's program. High-pitched voices and bouncy music.

Ronald beamed. "Jasmine, Savannah, I missed you at story time today."

"We missed you, too, Ronald," the older girl yelled.

Norm Kivas came out from the back room. He was dressed in a pair of beige shorts that needed a wash and a faded Atlanta Braves T-shirt. He hadn't shaved today. His eyes passed over me. He didn't seem to recognize me from the other night at Jake's, which I thought just as well.

"What's all the fuss?" he said.

"Mr. Kivas. I'm Ronald Burkowski from the library. My condolences on your loss. Jasmine and Savannah didn't come to reading group today, so I wanted to stop by and see if everything's all right."

"Come in, Ronald," the older girl said. "Want a glass of lemonade? We have lemonade, right, Grandpa?" Norm Kivas made no move to get out of our way. Ronald extended his hand. A long, awkward pause hung in the air before Norm took it.

"I don't go to the library," he said.

"Karen brought the girls every Friday. In the summer holidays we have reading group at three."

"Kids are on school vacation."

"Yes, I know. That's why the library's important. Keep their minds active when school's closed. As they missed today, why don't you bring them around tomorrow? I'm sure we can find time to give you girls an extra story."

"Yeah," the older one cheered. As little sisters do, the younger one cheered also. "Can we have lemonade?"

"I don't see why not," Ronald said.

"I don't think so," Norm said.

"Name the time, then." Ronald's smile was beginning to look strained. I took a deep breath and sniffed the air. I was relieved to smell peanut butter and not alcohol on Norm's breath.

"My wife just died. I have arrangements to make."

"I understand. Why don't I come around and pick up the girls myself, if you're busy?"

"Why would you do that?"

Ronald was momentarily at a loss for words. "Karen knew the library was important to the girls. I'll do it because she would have wanted me to."

There was another awkward silence as Norm examined Ronald, paying particular attention to the tie, featuring the starship *Enterprise* (original version) streaking across a star-studded background. The girls stopped chirping. Finally Norm said, "What kind of a man works at a library, anyway? You think I'd allow my precious little ones to be alone with the likes of you? I don't think so."

I stepped forward, smile plastered on my face, hand outstretched. "I'm Lucy Richardson, Mr. Kivas. I run the book club at the library. Karen was a member of our group. I'm sorry for your loss. I can assure you that Ronald runs the best children's library in the state, but if it would make you more comfortable, I can collect the girls."

He didn't take my hand, and I pulled it back and rubbed my palm against my shorts.

"I recognize you. You were at the seafood place the other night, with that interfering Josie O'Malley."

My face was beginning to hurt from all this smiling. The girls were watching us through wide blue eyes. The youngest one put her thumb in her mouth.

"I don't have any truck with libraries," Norm said. "Waste of hardworking taxpayers' money."

"Do you include yourself in that group, Mr. Kivas?" Ronald said.

It took me a moment to realize that kind, laid-back, charming Ronald had insulted Norm Kivas. Norm himself didn't seem to understand. "Darn straight. Folks want to read books, they can darn well go out and buy them. Don't ask me to pay for them."

"Some people can't afford—" I began.

Ronald put his hand on my arm. "Mr. Kivas has made his point, Lucy. Sorry to bother you, sir. Again, my condolences on your loss." He turned and walked away.

"Where's Ronald going?" the older girl said. "We have lemonade, Ronald. Grandpa, tell Ronald we have lemonade."

"I'll ask you to consider changing your mind," I said. "Your granddaughters are obviously very fond of Ronald, and they enjoy the library program. Lots of children their age come to it. Come yourself. You're welcome to sit in. Then you'd see the value—"

"Don't know what kinda man does a woman's job." The door shut in my face.

When I got behind the wheel of the Yaris, Ronald was in the passenger seat, his face tight with anger. "Jerk," I said.

I backed out of the driveway. As I swung into the road, I snuck a glance at the house. The two girls were standing at the window. The older one waved and the younger continued sucking her thumb.

"At least he wasn't drinking," I said.

"Give him time—it's still early. Those girls need the library now more than ever. Jasmine's reading above her grade level, but she told me there are no books in their house. I can't bear to think of them sitting around watching TV all day when school's out."

"You know their mother. Why not speak to her and offer to pick the girls up? I'll help."

"Thanks, Lucy. I'll give Janice a call this evening. I

don't know her except to speak to on the phone, but she'll probably agree. To get the kids out of her hair if nothing else. Although right about now, I'd imagine Norm Kivas is explaining to Jasmine and Savannah that book reading is for sissies and wimps."

I hadn't had the chance to ask Norm what he knew about Karen's death, but the trip hadn't been wasted. Now I knew that as well as taking financial advantage of the death of his ex-wife, Norm Kivas was a sexist jerk who thought libraries were a waste of money. He had moved to the top of my suspect list.

Chapter 12

"I won't be surprised if they decide they might as well go ahead and open a branch office here," Charlene grumbled. "We can hang a sign on the wall beside the original. *Body's Island Lighthouse and Police Station.*"

She stood at the window, peering into the parking lot. I left the circulation desk and came up behind her. At the entrance to the lighthouse tower, a plaque had been set into the wall with the date of the lighthouse's construction, and the original name of this area: "Body's Island." It was called this, not (as Louise Jane wanted me to believe) because of the number of bodies washed up over the years, but after the original settlers, the Body family. In fact, the area wasn't even an island anymore. The shifting sands and driving currents had reconfigured the landscape and attached it to the mainland as a peninsula.

Charlene was referring to the police car that had pulled up out front. Butch was driving, with Sam Watson in the passenger seat.

Following the police, a gray Toyota Corolla drove slowly down the lane. It didn't stop, but made a circle in the loop and headed back to the highway. Lost tourists, I assumed. Watson and Butch got out of the cruiser.

Charlene scurried up the spiral iron stairs, and I plopped myself down behind the circulation desk. When the door opened and the police officers walked in, I was busily checking in returned books. I pasted a look of surprise on my face. "Detective Watson. Officer Greenblatt. What brings you here today? News about the case, I hope."

"What case might that be, Lucy?" Watson asked.

I decided I would not be intimidated. "The case of the dead person found outside our library doors, that's what."

"And why do you think I'd bring you news, if I had any?"

"I . . ." Intimidated, I glanced at Butch. He gave me a slight shake of the head.

"I want to speak to you about the events of the other morning," Watson said.

"I've told you all I know."

"Perhaps. Perhaps not. We'll use the break room."

"I'll need to get someone to staff the desk. You never know who might sneak in to pilfer the new James Patterson in my absence." I waved the book I happened to be holding in the air. Neither Watson nor Butch laughed.

I picked up the phone and pushed the button for the extension in Charlene's office. No one answered, but I said, "Charlene, can you fill in for me for a couple of minutes? The police are here." I hung up, and turned to Watson with a smile. "She'll be right down." I counted to ten and then heard her footsteps clattering on the stairs. I knew full well Charlene had been lurking on the landing, listening.

One more time, I led the cops to the back. Bertie was out, at a meeting with the town's budget chief. I decided not to offer my guests anything to drink. This was not a social call. The moment we walked into the room, I said, "Can I get you anything? Water, a glass of tea? I can put the coffee on?" Southern manners must be inbred.

Before Watson could refuse, Butch said, "Water would be nice." I busied myself finding a clean glass, rummaging in the freezer for ice, then pouring the water, while Watson drummed his fingers on the tabletop.

Finally, I ran out of things to do, and sat down.

"Has your mother," Watson began, "ever been in trouble with the police?"

"Certainly not! The idea's preposterous." I didn't have to try to look offended. "I can't believe you haven't accessed police records. If you did, you might have found a speeding ticket or two, nothing more."

"Considerably more than two speeding tickets, I might point out, but that's not my concern. Any trouble the police don't officially know about, maybe? Your father's a mighty prominent lawyer. Big firm, lots of hungry young lawyers."

"If you're asking if my mother has broken the law and been protected by my father's influence, the answer is absolutely not."

"Bit of shoplifting maybe, taking a small but valuable item after a dinner party? The sort of minor incident that can be hushed up with influence and restitution?"

"No," I said firmly. "Anyway, you're talking to the wrong person. My mother is . . . well, she's my mother. She's hardly going to confide in me. I bet you don't tell your kids all your naughty secrets. Mom could be an ax murderer, and I wouldn't know."

Jeez, was that ever a bad choice of words. I clamped my lips shut. Watson had a way of getting me to blurt out the most awful things. I suppose that was why he was such a good detective. He stared into my face. I forced myself to keep my mouth shut. Butch hadn't taken a seat, but was leaning against the wall. He was not smiling.

"I'll grant you that point, Lucy," Watson said after a long, painful silence. "We rarely know our parents' secrets."

"But we know their character. My mom would never hurt anyone." At least this time, I knew not to add that Mom could gleefully spread the worst sort of gossip disguised as concern, and had been known to cut people dead for the most minor of social infractions. But she behaved that way only to people of her own income level and social circle. The idea that she might murder poor Karen Kivas, or steal a piece of jewelry, truly was preposterous. I had to remember that, no matter what Watson might try to get me to say.

"There was some trouble years ago, back in school, I hear," he said.

"Trouble? School?" For a moment I almost confessed to that time in eleventh grade when I bought an essay on the Lewis and Clark expedition off the Internet. It was terrible, but I'd been desperate. I'd talked Mom into letting me go skiing in Vermont for the weekend, planning to work on the essay in the evenings. But the lure of après-ski beside the roaring fire and mugs of spicy scented mulled wine won out over working alone in my room. And when I did make it back to my room—alone, I might add—I collapsed face-first onto the bed. Of course, I was found out. The essay was nothing like my own style of writing and unfortunately Mr. Wrenhauster, our formidable American history teacher, had spotted it for sale himself. I got an F on that paper, and a call was placed to my mom.

There were no more skiing weekends in Vermont that year, and I never bought an essay again.

I realized that Watson wasn't asking about my failed attempt at plagiarism. "Now you're really stretching, Detective. I wasn't even born when my mother was in school."

"True. But stories have a way of living on in families, don't they? I wasn't much more than a grade-schooler myself when your mother was in high school, but Bankers—some of them, anyway—have long memories. I've been told that your mother, before she moved away, was believed to have been a thief."

"Told by who?"

"You don't expect me to tell you that, do you? It seems as though your mother is remembered by some people of her age group. And not always fondly."

"Jealousy, probably. My mom's done well for herself. Some people might think she didn't deserve what she has."

"People like Karen Kivas?" he said.

"Karen might have expressed some resentment, yes. But they smoothed that over. Karen and Mom departed friends. I told you that."

"Yes, Lucy, you did. Although no one else seems to agree. Your mother and Karen Kivas were observed by a substantial number of people arguing at the Ocean Side the day before Karen died. The atmosphere between them the following night here, at the library, has been described to me as excessively chilly."

"But they made up! They did! They hugged and everything."

Watson said nothing. I glanced at Butch for support. He only shrugged. Butch had been at the book club. He was a smart, observant man. He couldn't have helped but notice that Mom and Karen not only kept themselves well apart, but pointedly stared at anything but the other woman and didn't address the other during the conversation about *Pride and Prejudice*. Heck, everyone else in the room, including Detective Watson's own wife, would have been able to tell what was going on. The air was so thick you would have needed an icebreaker to cut through it.

And when Karen and my mom did make up, only one other person had been there: me.

"They did," I repeated, my protest sounding weak in my own ears.

"You see, Lucy," Watson said, "this necklace is bothering me a great deal. The necklace connects the Ocean Side Hotel to the library. It connects a hotel maid to a well-off guest."

"A lot of people visit both the hotel and the library," I pointed out.

"True. But at the time in question, this one guest publicly insulted the maid; the maid was heard to promise to retaliate; the women were observed by several witnesses to be hostile to each other. One of them ended up dead, and the other was the last person to see her alive."

"Other," I said, "than the person who killed her."

"The question I have," Watson said, "is who stole the necklace. Mrs. Richardson, who has a history of theft—"

"That's gossip and hearsay. I bet it's not even true, and if it is, it was a long time ago."

"—or Mrs. Kivas, who might have planted it in Mrs. Richardson's bag in retaliation for the earlier insults. Realizing what had happened, did Mrs. Richardson lash out at Mrs. Kivas after everyone had left book club and the library was dark, the grounds empty?"

I found a hole in his logic. "Mom didn't know the necklace was in her bag. She left the bag behind."

"Is your mother normally an absentminded woman? The sort who forgets her belongings?"

I had, very reluctantly, to admit that she was anything but absentminded. I tried to explain that Mom did seem preoccupied this visit and I suspected something was bothering her, so she might have forgotten the bag.

"Bothering her?" Watson said. "You mean like having killed someone?"

"Hey! My mother did not kill anyone. And you can't keep going around saying that she did." I threw down my dad card. "My father won't stand for it."

"Threats, Lucy?"

"Only making a statement." My heart was pounding so hard, I feared Watson might hear it. I feared that Charlene and everyone else in the main room would hear it.

"I'm not saying anything, as you put it," Watson replied. "I am merely speculating out loud." He rose to his feet in one quick movement. "Thank you for your time, Lucy. I can find my way out."

"Wait," I said. "There are other suspects. What about Karen's husband, Norm. Now, there's a sleazy piece of work. Did you know that they'd recently divorced? She's the one who told him the marriage was over. I bet he wasn't happy about that. I went around there yesterday, and he's back in their house. Her death has benefited him. There might even be insurance money in it, as well as the house."

"Why were you at the Kivas home?"

"Library business. And I have to mention that he wasn't at all friendly to Ronald and me. He shut the door in my face. Then there's Doug Whiteside, Karen's brother. They were estranged for a long time. Did you know that?"

"Yes, Lucy. I did know that. As I know that Norm Kivas has been observed acting as though he's about to come into more money than he's used to having. As for her brother, I shouldn't have to point out, but I will, that when people are estranged for a long time, it's unlikely that one person will suddenly decide to get rid of the other."

"And I am simply pointing out to you that you should be following other avenues of investigation."

"I appreciate all your help." Watson headed for the door. Butch stepped aside. Watson turned and, as though he'd learned his interrogation techniques by watching the old TV show *Columbo*, said, "One more thing, Lucy. If you are keeping anything from me out of loyalty to your mother, I will find out. You can tell your father that also."

He left. Butch didn't follow.

"You going to be okay?" he said.

"It is true. My mom and Karen Kivas departed as friends."

"I believe you, Lucy. But I can understand why Watson doesn't. Your loyalty to your mother's admirable."

"It's not loyalty. It's the truth."

"Your mom was the last person, as far as we know, who saw Karen before she died."

"You know the time of death?"

"The autopsy says between eight and eleven. Book club broke up at nine, as usual, and we all went our separate ways."

"Mom and Karen stayed to help me clean up. That took about fifteen, twenty minutes, so they left sometime after quarter past nine."

"Is it possible," he asked, "that Karen left, but came back for some reason?"

That would be the ideal situation, wouldn't it? If Karen had started for home, but turned around and then been attacked by person or persons unknown. Nothing to do with Mom. Nothing to do with the library. I forced myself to be honest. "I've been trying to come up with a reason why she might have done that. But I can't. If she'd forgotten something, she'd know I'd be upstairs. Not to mention that she didn't forget anything. You didn't find anything of hers, did you?"

"No. But suppose she had planted the necklace on your mom. And then she had a change of heart, and when she noticed your mom hadn't taken the bag with her, she came back for it."

"She could hardly drag me out of bed to hand over my mother's tote bag." Here I was, arguing against proof of my mom's innocence. "You're not playing good cop, are you?" I said. "To Watson's bad cop?"

Butch gave me a smile and the gold specks in his eyes shone in the harsh lights of the break room. He did have lovely hazel eyes. "Watson's not playing bad cop, Lucy. He's not playing anything. He's trying to find a killer."

I sighed. "I know that. I just wish he wasn't looking so closely at my mother."

"He's looking at everyone. Try to remember that. I have to go, or Watson will leave me to find my own way back to town. You'll take care, won't you, Lucy? There's a killer out there."

"I know." Feeling a tiny bit better, I gave him a smile, and we walked out of the break room together. If Butch was telling me to be on my guard, then he had to believe the killer was *not* my own mother.

Chapter 13

Charlene and I were once again standing at the window, trying not to be seen as we watched the police cruiser pull away. "Everything okay?" Charlene asked me. Her bright blue earbuds were draped around her neck, running to the iPhone she kept in her pocket.

"As okay as can be. Watson is sure interested in my mother's behavior." Despite what Butch said, I was still worried that Watson wasn't focusing hard enough on other suspects.

"You're worrying for nothing, Lucy," she said. "He's asking you about your mother because you're in a position to know. He's not going to ask you about people you don't know, now, is he?"

"No, but . . ."

"No buts. Here, listen to this. I downloaded this new album this morning. Take a listen—you're going to love it."

Before I could protest, she was pushing buttons on the phone and stuffing the earbuds into my ears. I was hit by a blast of noise I didn't like to call music and a man chanting hideous poetry in a repetitive monotone.

"Uh," I said.

She pressed the phone into my hand. "Keep it for a while. I've been doing some research for a couple of California grad students on shipping along this coast during the early eighteenth century, and need to give them a call. You have to get down and dirty and *into* the music to appreciate it. A couple of bars don't give the full effect. If you like it, I'll include it in the bunch of CDs I'm putting together for your mom."

She walked away, her shoulders and hips bopping to the memory of the tune. I waited until she disappeared before whipping the earbuds out of my ears. The full effect, I did not need. Her taste in music was dreadful, but her love of it so infectious I would pretend I'd listened to it.

Ronald had warned me that Charlene gave everyone rap CDs for Christmas. And then she spent the month of January asking which track they'd liked best. Fortunately, rap singers rarely gave concerts in the Outer Banks, and we could usually come up with an excuse not to accompany her to Raleigh for a performance.

I realized I was smiling. This was why I loved this library so much.

I stopped smiling as the door slammed open and Bertie marched in with a face that would frighten small children.

"Problem?" I asked, probably redundantly.

In answer she tossed a copy of the local newspaper onto my desk. It was folded open to the third page, to the op-eds.

PROMINENT LOCAL BUSINESSMAN CALLS FOR CLOSING OF LIGHTHOUSE LIBRARY, screamed the headline.

Heart in my mouth, I scanned the page.

Once again, tragedy has struck at the Bodie Island Lighthouse Library, this time taking the life of beloved Outer Banks native, mother, and grandmother Karen Whiteside Kivas. When will the mayor and townspeople realize that, aside from being a waste of hardworking taxpayers' money in these difficult times, the remote location of the lighthouse is a danger to innocent women working and visiting there, particularly at night? Although we might wish that only well-meaning vacationers came to enjoy the benefits of our spectacular coast and beaches, in these lawless times the dregs of the city can also be found among us. As a library, the spectacular historic lighthouse is nothing but a drain on the funds of this town. If it were turned into an income-generating tourist attraction, not only could everyone enjoy its historic beauty, rather than members of a select special-interest group, but funds could be raised to install perimeter lighting, hire guards, and implement other safety measures to protect the women and children who would enjoy visiting in complete safety.

The horrible piece was signed *Douglas Whiteside*.

I looked up. Bertie's face was beet red and a vein pulsed in her throat. For a moment, I thought she might be about to have a heart attack.

"Rather harsh," I said.

"Harsh! I cannot believe Doug Whiteside has turned the death of his own sister into a political campaign attack ad. His concern for the safety of *innocent women* is pure bunk. Note the campaign slogans slipped in: *hard-*

working taxpayers, *special interest groups*, *income gener-ating*." She was so angry I thought she might spit. "As if *readers* are a special interest group. As if we insist that anyone who wants to come in and tour the lighthouse has a library card!"

"He doesn't say anything about running for mayor."

"Of course not, this is the opening salvo. He's found his issue to run against Connor with. Everyone knows Connor's a big supporter of the library."

"People won't vote for Doug because of this, will they? We're popular with tourists as well as locals. We're always busy." I glanced around the empty room. "Well, except for today."

"You meet the people who use the library, Lucy. Our patrons and our friends. Yes, we have plenty of friends. But there are some people who don't see the value in libraries. Particularly not one like this that could be turned into something *income generating*."

I thought of Norm Kivas, who saw no need to take his grandchildren to the library reading group.

"The death of Karen has opened a whole world of pos-sibilities for Doug Whiteside and his supporters. Now he can hit the campaign trail insisting that the library is not only a waste of money but out-and-out dangerous." The indignation dropped from her voice. "You don't feel un-safe here, do you, Lucy? If you don't want to continue . . ."

"No! Not for a moment. I'm safer here than I was in my apartment in Boston. My place is four flights up in a building with four-foot-thick stone walls, with one door and one iron-barred ground-floor window." I didn't bother to mention Louise Jane's hints at things that could move through walls, for whom lack of doors and windows was not an obstacle.

"If I was a nasty-minded person," Bertie said, "I might think Doug Whiteside had murdered his own sister to further his political ambitions." She stormed off down the hallway to her office, her long, colorful skirt swirling around her ankles.

She'd left the newspaper on my desk. Maybe I was a nasty-minded person, but I was thinking precisely that.

Two of our regular patrons came in, staggering under the weight of the books they were here to return. They plopped the volumes down on the desk. These women were lifelong friends, but they never exchanged their reading material. Ann Atkinson loved science fiction, the more military-focused the better. The top of her pile was a Tanya Huff, the cover illustrated with hard-bodied men and equally hard-bodied women bristling with weaponry. Brenda Morrison adored cozy mysteries. She'd taken out the full set of Erika Chase books: Siamese cats, glasses of sweet tea, and stately white verandas.

Brenda saw the newspaper on the desk, still open to the op-ed page. "That Doug Whiteside's a fool. As if this town couldn't get on without this library."

"I'm glad to hear you say that," I said. "I hope you'll remember that at election time."

"I heard rumors Doug's going to run for mayor," Ann said. "I've no worries. Connor will whip his butt."

"Wouldn't mind whipping Connor McNeil's butt myself," Brenda, who had to be at least seventy, said.

Her friend roared with laughter and they went to select more books.

I felt color rise in my cheeks and gratefully answered the ringing phone. "Bodie Island Lighthouse Library. Lucy speaking."

"Time for drinkies!"

"Hi, Mom."

"What time do you finish work?"

"We close at five on Saturdays."

"Is today Saturday?"

"Yes. What's up, Mom?"

"Your delightful friend Theodore is coming by for drinkies later. I thought you might like to join us."

"Theodore is neither delightful nor my friend."

"Time you made friends, then, dear. See you at six." She hung up. I had not agreed to go. About the last thing I felt like was *drinkies* with Mom and Theodore. And since when did my mother use words like "drinkies," anyway? I debated phoning her back to say I had other plans. Then I reconsidered: I hadn't had a chance to speak to Theodore since the night Karen died. He'd been at book club. He was observant, what nasty-minded people would call "nosy." He might have noticed something. Something the police hadn't thought to ask. I decided one drink at the hotel couldn't hurt.

The phone rang again.

"Bodie Island—"

"Hi, Lucy."

"Connor. We were . . . uh"—I glanced at Ann and Brenda, each trying to convince the other to, just this once, try a different type of book—"talking about you." Despite myself, I blushed. "If you want to talk to Bertie, she's in her office."

"I saw her at the meeting earlier. It's you I want to talk to, Lucy. Are you free for dinner tonight?"

"That'd be nice."

"Can I pick you up? Say around six thirty?"

"I'm supposed to be having a drink with my mom after work. Why don't you join us? You can meet my mother." My hand shot up to my mouth as soon as I realized what I'd just said. "I don't mean that you need to meet my mother, I mean—"

"I'd like that, Lucy."

"Can you make it quarter to six?"

"Sure. See you then."

I put down the phone. When I looked up again, Ann and Brenda were grinning at me from over the tops of their piles of books. "Now," said Brenda with a laugh, "I wonder who that might have been."

"He of the nice butt, perhaps," Ann said.

My face burned.

Chapter 14

As the clock crawled toward closing time, I began to worry that I'd made a mistake asking Connor to join me for a drink with Mom. I didn't quite know what my relationship with our handsome mayor was. He liked me; I liked him. Were we dating? We'd gone out a couple of times. We'd exchanged good-night kisses. But nothing more. I'd also gone out with Butch. Nothing more there, either. I'd been with Ricky for as long as I could remember. At the ripe old age of thirty, I was new to this dating thing, and found it quite confusing.

Although, I thought, as Connor smiled at me across the threshold of the library, I could get used to it.

I'd decided to wear the dress I'd discarded the night we'd had dinner at Jake's. It was a cheerful yellow with short sleeves, a deep neckline, and a soft skirt that flowed around my knees. When I'd been in college, my roommate's birthday gift to me was to have my colors done at a fashionable dress shop. I'd been told that with my black hair and a complexion that tans well, I'm a winter and thus yellow is "my" color.

Charles watched from the bed. I held up a necklace in

one hand, a soft black scarf in the other. "You choose," I said. He tilted his head to the right.

The necklace it would be. Charles had excellent taste.

Last of all I slipped on my best shoes. Black sandals, with straps the thickness of dental floss and heels so high it should be illegal to wear them. I hated them. I could barely stand upright in them, and by the end of the evening my feet are on fire. I wear them because they're Jimmy Choos, cost me five hundred bucks (I must have been out of my mind), and make me look as though I have long, sexy legs.

"How do I look?" I asked the cat.

He washed his whiskers.

I'd left my phone on the window ledge, where it sometimes got a weak signal. As I picked it up to slip into my purse, it beeped with an incoming text.

Josie: I'm escaping the oven! Beach tomorrow?

Me: You can count on me!

During the day, Charles wanders the library, greeting patrons and accepting compliments. When I go out in the evening, I leave him in my apartment, with a clean litter box and a full food bowl. Tonight, as soon as I opened the door, he dashed between my ankles and was downstairs before I could stop him.

I teetered carefully after him.

He was at his post on the shelf closest to the door as a knock sounded.

I took a deep breath and opened the door. Connor's eyes lit up as he saw me standing there, and I was pleased I'd gone to the trouble to dress up. He looked suitable for meeting his date's mother, in crisply ironed gray slacks and an open-necked blue shirt.

Charles meowed. Connor gave him a scratch behind the ears in return.

I'd come to realize that Charles was a superb judge of character. He clearly liked Connor. Then again, he liked Butch, too. No help there.

The night air was warm and the sky clear, but the wind was rising. "Storm coming," Connor said as we drove to the hotel.

We stopped at a red light, and Connor turned to look at me. "You remember the ball on Thursday?"

"Yup," I said, frantically mentally flicking through my wardrobe. Did I have anything suitable to wear to a ball? And would it be a real ball, like something out of *Pride and Prejudice*, or just a fancy name for a cocktail party?

The car behind us honked to tell us the light had changed.

Mom and Theodore were seated in the hotel's lobby bar when Connor and I arrived. Mom's manners were always impeccable, so I was the only one who noticed that she wasn't at all happy that I'd brought a guest of my own.

Theodore was in his full eccentric book-collector garb of belted Harris Tweed jacket and large spectacles. He leapt to his feet and said, in his proper English accent, "Connor. Delighted you could join us. Lucy, now I know from where you get your radiant beauty."

Mom preened.

The waitress bustled over and asked what we'd like to drink. Mom chose a glass of Sauvignon Blanc. Theodore asked for a pint of Guinness. Connor ordered an orange juice, explaining that he was driving, so would save himself for wine with dinner. I followed Mom's lead and also asked for a white wine.

"Did you see Louise Jane today?" I asked Mom, sounding perfectly nonchalant.

"She phoned this morning. She seemed to have had

some idea we had an appointment, and apologized for canceling."

"That's good." I leaned back in my chair.

"So we arranged to get together Monday afternoon."

"I—"

Mom changed the subject. She was good at that. "Theodore has this wonderful idea—"

"Now, now, Suzanne. Let's not bore the young people," Teddy, who was only slightly older than me, said.

"I don't think book collecting is boring," Mom said.

"I read something quite scandalous in today's paper," Theodore said. "Connor, you must have seen Doug White-side's letter. What's your take?"

I eyed my mother. Book collecting? Since when did Mom have the slightest interest in books? She had served on the library board in our town and was still with the Friends of the Library group. More because it was socially required for a woman of her position, I always thought, than because she cared about the library. Although she did read a fair amount. Bodice-ripper time-traveling romances when no one was looking, historical tomes when they were.

And why was Theodore not only not talking about his favorite subject but actively turning the conversation away? A nasty feeling began to creep through my bones.

"I've no comment," Connor said. "Doug Whiteside is welcome to his opinion."

"You don't think it's gauche of him to tie his political ambitions to his sister's death?" Theodore asked.

The edges of Connor's mouth turned up. "I'll admit that it's obvious someone else wrote that letter for him. I've never known good old Doug to use such formal language."

"You mean like a campaign manager or press person

or something?" I said. "That would mean he's pretty much committed to throwing his hat into the ring."

"Why are we talking politics?" Mom said. "Nothing drearier than politics. Particularly for the council of some insignificant small town in the back of nowhere."

"I quite agree, Mrs. Richardson," Connor said.

"Connor here is our mayor," Theodore said. "Didn't you know that, Suzanne? I should have introduced you properly."

The waitress chose that moment to arrive with the drinks. We gratefully began rearranging napkins and cutlery. Mom's eyes flickered between Connor and me. "The mayor," she said once the waitress had departed. "How . . . nice."

Theodore plunged into a discussion (lecture?) about the police investigation (incompetent), the composition of the library board (inept), the general state of literature in the modern world (tragic). Everything, in fact, except book collecting.

Mom drank wine and watched Connor. Connor tried to look fascinated by Theodore's ramblings. I downed my own drink in record time. "Where has the time gone?" I said when I could get a word in. "We'd better be off. Thanks for the drinks, Mom. I'll call you tomorrow." I made a show of gathering up my purse. Connor pushed his chair back. "It was nice to meet you, Mrs. Richardson."

"Shall we have another round, Suzanne?" Theodore said. He began to get to his feet. "I'll fetch it. Oh, I keep forgetting. In America, the waiter comes to the table." As if he hadn't been born and raised in Nags Head and gone to UNC. He plopped back down.

"Don't be in such a hurry, Lucille," Mom said. "Why don't—"

"Evening, folks." George, manager, appeared at our table. "Everything being taken care of here?"

"Yes," we chorused.

George smiled at Mom. "Glad to hear it. I'm going off duty now, and wanted to make sure you're happy, Sue, before I head off for my dinner."

"Dinner," Mom said, leaping to her feet. "What a delightful idea. Won't you join us, George? You've met my daughter, Lucy. And her . . . uh . . . friend."

"Mr. Mayor," George said.

"George," Connor said.

Neither of them was rude enough to mention that the last time they'd spoken was when my mother had created a scene with Karen Kivas in the hotel lobby.

"The restaurant here is superb," Mom said. "No need for us to go out. Table for five?"

George, manager, looked as though he'd just had a visit from the tooth fairy. "It would be my pleasure to dine with you nice folks."

"I'm not sure," Theodore said. "I might . . . uh . . . have an appointment."

Mom linked her arm through George's. "Come along, everyone. Dinner's my treat."

"I've remembered," Theodore said. "That appointment is tomorrow night."

"Theodore, why don't you escort Lucy through to dinner? Oh, dear. We seem to be unbalanced in terms of gender. Can't be helped. Come along, everyone."

Theodore held out his arm. I glanced at Connor. He threw me a quick wink. *Mothers!* it seemed to say.

The Ocean Side Restaurant is all starched white linens, polished silver, sparkling glassware, and soft candlelight. The low lighting went a long way toward hiding the chipped baseboards, peeling plaster, and tattered rugs. The room looked full to me, but at one word from his boss, the maître d' whisked us to a large round table by a window. George beamed from ear to ear. He couldn't take his eyes off Mom, as if he was amazed that this woman was on his arm. Mom looked pretty good in high-heeled silver sandals, a shimmering silver sheath with matching jacket, diamonds in her ears, and a long silver chain around her neck.

Theodore and I followed Mom and George, and Connor brought up the rear. I felt as if I were in a George Bernard Shaw play, the understudy thrust onto the stage at the last minute, who'd forgotten who she was supposed to be.

"Your mom's very nice," Theodore said in something resembling his own North Carolina accent.

"Why are you here?" I asked.

"Having dinner," he said.

"I mean meeting with my mother. I can't think that you have anything in common."

"Over there, isn't that Bertie waving at us?"

I looked. The woman trying to catch the waiter's attention was about twenty years old and looked as much like Bertie as I did.

When we arrived at the table, Mom directed everyone to their seats. She insisted that I take the best view, out the wide French doors overlooking the softly lit boardwalk that led through swaying ocean grasses toward the beach. Theodore was told to sit on my right. Mom took the chair at my left, placing herself between Connor and me. George sat across from me.

As we unfurled our napkins and accepted menus, George told us that the hotel would be having a memorial service for Karen tomorrow. "Not everyone can take the time off to attend the funeral, so I thought something small and intimate here, for her hotel family, would be appropriate."

"That is so thoughtful of you, George," Mom said. She gave him her full-voltage smile. I wondered if he would melt under the strength of it. "Lucy, why don't you come with me?"

"I don't—"

"Theodore will be coming, of course. He can pick you up and bring you."

"What?" Theodore pulled himself out of his inspection of the menu.

"We're not part of Karen's hotel family," I said.

Mom waved that inconsequential detail away. "We'll have a bottle of red wine. George, why don't you select something? I'm partial to an Oregon Pinot Noir."

The meal dragged endlessly on. The food varied between delicious (the lamb shanks) and barely edible (the overboiled frozen vegetables). Mom turned to Connor and kept up a stream of mindless chatter. Any good dinner party hostess would know to lean back in her chair so as to not block the people on either side of her with her body. Mom seemed to have forgotten that rule tonight. I was left to talk to Theodore and George.

I was annoyed, but I understood why Mom wanted to separate me from Connor. If I was dating Connor, I'd be less likely to return to Boston and the hypothetically waiting arms of Ricky. But I could not comprehend why on earth she seemed to be trying to shove me in Theodore's direction. Unless he had convinced her he was a man of money and influence. I didn't see him doing that. Teddy might enjoy playing the distinguished scholar, but that was as far as his pretense went. He never pretended to have money he didn't. I knew he'd recently had to sell a much-loved set of first-edition James Bonds because he was short of funds.

The penny dropped. I interrupted him in midsentence. "Do you have your eye on any new books?"

"As a matter of fact I do." He lowered his voice. "I'm sure you remember that unfortunate incident with the Ian Flemings."

He was referring to the time I had accused him, in front of a prospective buyer, of stealing several Jane Austen first editions. Nice of him not to mention that. "Yes."

"They're on the market again. At a reduced price. The gentleman who purchased them from me has found himself temporarily embarrassed, financially speaking." His eyes drifted over my shoulder. They settled on my mom, laughing at some pearl of wisdom from George, manager. "I'm raising the funds to buy them back."

Funds. My mother.

Okay, that explained what Theodore was doing here. It didn't explain why Mom would let him believe for a second that she'd lend him money to buy rare books. At that moment she turned to me with a beaming smile. "Enjoying yourself, dear?"

I couldn't say no, now, could I? "This lamb is beautiful."

"Our chef sources everything locally," George said, glad to be allowed the chance to say something. "We're very lucky to have her."

"I'm sure," Mom said, "luck had nothing to do with it. Good management is never a matter of luck." She lifted her wineglass in a private toast.

I refrained from saying that those vegetables might have been local, but if they were, they'd been shipped halfway across the country to a factory, then processed and returned as a frozen lump.

George beamed. Yup, the tooth fairy was smiling on George, manager, tonight.

A heck of a lot more was going on at this table than I could follow.

At last the endless meal was finished. I refused dessert, hoping to get the heck out of there. But Theodore indulged himself with a towering slice of four-layer chocolate cake, meaning the rest of us had to wait until he'd finished. Then mom ordered cappuccinos for everyone. She was getting around to asking if we wanted liqueurs, when I pushed my chair back. "That was great. Thanks, Mom. Shall we go, Connor?"

"Why don't you let Theodore drive you home, dear? No need to take Connor out of his way."

Theodore broke away from his examination of the port and whiskey menu. "What?" He also lived in Nags Head. The lighthouse was as much out of his way as Connor's.

"Be a dear and drive Lucy home, won't you? You don't mind, do you, Connor?"

What could Connor say? He threw me a confused look. "No. I don't mind."

Between them, George and Mom had finished off two bottles of wine. I'd had one glass. Connor had ordered a single beer to accompany his appetizer of calamari. Teddy had kept to his original pint of Guinness, sipping slowly. I suspected he didn't like the thick, dark beer much, but as he considered it part of his persona, he endured it.

Reluctantly Theodore put down the drinks menu. Poor guy, he'd been looking forward to a glass of postprandial port throughout the entire meal. I wondered if he liked port any more than he liked Guinness. "Shall we?" he said to me, graciously.

Connor stood up also. "Good night, Mrs. Richardson. Thank you very much for the evening. Most enjoyable."

Mom smirked. "Lovely meeting you."

I left the restaurant between my two escorts, feeling like Lizzy Bennet, with a mother as manipulative as Mrs. Bennet. Unfortunately I had no idea what she was trying to manipulate me to do.

As we walked through the lobby, a figure rose from one of the slightly worn wingback chairs. It was the woman who kept hanging around the library by herself. The one I had come to think of as the Gray Woman. She looked from Connor to Theodore to me. Back to Connor.

"Hi," I said.

She walked away.

"I keep seeing that woman," I said. "Here and at the library. I'm starting to get the feeling she's watching me. Do you know who she is?"

"A tourist," Theodore said, without much interest.

"No," Connor said. "I'll see what I can find out."

We hesitated on the hotel steps.

"I'm sorry," I said to Connor.

He laughed. "Don't apologize. I liked your mother very much. She's a woman who knows her own mind and ensures everyone else knows it, too."

I shuddered. "Oh, gosh. What did she say?"

"She told me your fiancé is pining away back in Boston."

"In her dreams. Not in his." I'd told Connor about Ricky, and why I'd left Boston and my job at Harvard so suddenly.

"That," he said, "I'm glad to hear. Night, Teddy."

"Night, Mr. Mayor."

Chapter 15

On the way back to the lighthouse, Theodore didn't bring up the subject of the Ian Flemings. He was smart enough to know I might not approve if I thought he'd approached my mom for money. Instead he told me that *Tess of the D'Urbervilles* wasn't his favorite Thomas Hardy and he'd been disappointed when it was chosen at book club, but he didn't like to overrule the less literary among us. How about a rip-roaring adventure yarn next? He suggested *Kidnapped* by Robert Louis Stevenson.

Outside Nags Head, Highway 12 runs along the shore and through the Hatteras National Seashore. It's a long way to the next town, tiny, picturesque Rodanthe. At night the road's dark and quiet. A single vehicle passed us, throwing light into the interior of our car. I glanced at Theodore. His eyes were fixed on the road ahead, his hands firm in the acceptable ten-and-two position on the steering wheel. If my mom, for some completely unknown reason, was intent on setting me up with Theodore, the poor guy didn't know any more about it than I did.

He didn't get out of the car to see me to my door, but watched until I was safely inside. Charles greeted me with an indignant hiss. He seemed to be objecting to having been locked out of the apartment without any dinner.

"Your fault," I said, following him upstairs.

Once I'd taken care of Charles's culinary needs and prepared myself for bed, I powered up my iPad to check for messages. I was surprised to see the screen fill with e-mails from the members of my book club. The subject line on them all was "Karen." Louise Jane seemed to have started the thread. I opened the message. In Louise Jane's abrupt style it said:

> I want to meet to discuss the death of Karen after last week's book club. Clearly the police aren't up to the job. Monday noon at the library. Third floor.

Aside from the fact that Louise Jane had no business taking over the meeting room without checking with us to see if it was available, I wasn't pleased. What was she up to now?

The rest of the e-mails were some variation of "I'll be there."

Which reminded me that nothing more had been said about the memorial service at the hotel tomorrow. I didn't intend to go. I wanted to go to Karen's funeral, which hadn't been announced yet, but I was hardly a member of her "hotel family." I remembered that George had been about to fire Karen on the steps of the hotel after her altercation with Mom. Some family.

I closed the iPad and climbed into bed. I was in the middle of the Simone St. James book. I glanced around my apartment, looking into the dark corners. Not that it had any corners, since it was a round room. Charles kneaded at the quilt, preparing to settle down.

I opened the book and began to read.

I put it down.

Books. Theodore. He'd seemed quite sure he'd be able to recover the set of first editions he'd had to sell recently. That had to mean he'd come into some money. It made no sense to me that Mom would offer to help him out. Unless . . . unless it was part of a business deal.

You bring my daughter back to Boston and I'll buy your books for you.

If so, she must have explained his part of the deal pretty obliquely. Teddy had scarcely been attempting to charm me. Tonight, he'd shown as much interest in my life as he usually did. Meaning absolutely none. He wasn't a stupid man; in fact he was very intelligent. Just socially awkward and obsessed with books. And inclined to have sticky fingers around other people's collections on occasion.

Not that anything's wrong with being obsessed with books. I've been accused of that myself.

Not the sticky fingers part, though.

Then again, when carried to extremes, obsession does have a way of overcoming scruples and values. How much did Theodore want those James Bonds back? It must have hurt him enormously to have to sell them. To see them passing into other hands. And then to hear they were back on the market only a short time later?

How far would he go to recover them?

Would he steal?

Would he kill?

I thought back to book club night. Theodore had been sitting beside Aunt Ellen. Ellen sat next to Mom. He was close enough to Mom's beach bag, particularly before the meeting, when everyone was getting drinks and pastries, or when they were preparing to leave. Had Theodore stolen the necklace and slipped it into Mom's bag, intending to get it out of the hotel that way and later recover it at book club?

No, that wouldn't work. Theodore wouldn't have been searched leaving the hotel. If he'd had the necklace on him, he could've simply walked out with it.

Had it happened the other way around? Had Theodore taken the necklace and brought it, concealed on his person, to book club? Did Karen Kivas see him take it? Did she confront him and tell him what she knew? Did she convince him to slip it into Mom's bag so it would be discovered and returned to its owner?

My heart almost stopped beating.

Did Theodore tell Karen he was going to return the necklace? And then kill her because of what she knew?

If that was what had happened, then he'd killed Karen for nothing. He didn't have the necklace. But other than the aforementioned sticky fingers, he was no experienced criminal. He would have acted in panic, and then seen the prize slip between his fingers.

I clutched the quilt to my chest. Theodore had driven me home. He'd sat in his car in the parking lot when I let myself into the building. I hadn't checked to see if he'd driven away.

Was he out there now, in the dark, watching my window? Waiting until the light went out?

Something moved behind my head. I screeched. Charles's tan face and dark brown ears appeared.

Okay, maybe tonight wasn't the best night to read a ghost story.

I switched out my light. Charles's warm bulk curled up against my side and he purred.

Chapter 16

I love Sundays! The library's closed and I have nothing to do all day except relax, read, and indulge myself. I slept late and then enjoyed a long, luxurious morning in bed with coffee, a toasted bagel laden with cream cheese, smoked salmon, and capers and my book. I pushed aside the internal voice telling me to be a good daughter and call my mom. Mom, I reminded myself, was more than capable of entertaining herself. The storm Connor had predicted had not arrived; instead sunlight poured through my window. The book I'd been afraid of in the quiet and the dark was nothing but a good, satisfying read in the warmth of a sunny day.

Josie didn't often take a day off, so I'd been pleased when she contacted me yesterday to suggest we go to the beach. I struggled out of bed at eleven and threw my beach things together. I was ready and waiting when Josie arrived to pick me up. I was happy to see that our friend Grace was with her.

It being a Sunday in July, the beach was busy, but it never gets too crowded and we found a quiet spot to lay out our towels. Grace pounded an umbrella into the sand.

Then the three of us stripped off shorts and T-shirts, kicked our flip-flops into the air, and ran, screeching with delight, into the waves. When we came out of the water, Josie and I arranged our towels in the sun. Grace, her Irish ancestry plainly written in her red hair, freckles, and pale skin, crawled into the shade of the umbrella. Grace opened the cooler and pulled out bottles of tea, bags of chips, and sandwiches from Josie's Cozy Bakery.

"It's nice," I said, selecting a ham and cheese on a croissant, "that you could take the day off." I dug my toes into the sand and my teeth into the sandwich. It had been made yesterday but was still delicious.

"I'm trying to tell myself that I can't be at the shop all the time," Josie said. "Not if I want some kind of a life. Not if I'm ever going to have kids. But it's tough to let someone else take over. I guess I'm a control freak."

"The Wyatt women are."

My cousin smiled at me. "Some of us are. Not you, though."

"These days, I'm incapable of having control over my own life. Speaking of kids, any news on the wedding front?"

"Ha!" Grace shouted.

"If there is, you two will be the first to know," Josie said. "Between Jake's new restaurant and the bakery, I don't know that we can even find a day when we're both free so we can have a wedding."

"Is everything okay?" I asked.

"It's all good. You know me—I like to grumble."

"You can say that again," Grace said. She wiped her hands on a napkin, arranged her towel under her head, lay back, and closed her eyes.

"No comments from the peanut gallery," Josie said.

"Despite the occasional grumble, we're happy, Jake and me. We're making our life our way. We're chasing our dreams, and we know some sacrifices have to be made. The bakery's booming, the restaurant's getting great reviews, and business has been good. We're concentrating on making money now, and in the winter we'll have time to sit back and make long-term plans."

North Carolina is too far north to be a year-round beach destination, and the tourist trade dries up over the winter months. A welcome break for some, but it can be hard to make a year-round living.

"Have you put Grandma's Dream Cake on the menu yet?" I asked, as I popped the last piece of my sandwich into my mouth.

"Yes, and it's been a huge success. We sold out yesterday, or I would have brought some leftovers. I have triple-chocolate brownies, though. Want one?" She started to get up.

"Sit down," I ordered. "I'm perfectly capable of getting myself a brownie. You do need to stop working sometimes."

She laughed. "So my mother keeps telling me." She dug in her bag for her book. I wasn't at all surprised to see that it was a cookbook: *Baking with Chocolate*. Yum. I forced myself to remain where I was. No triple-chocolate brownies for me.

Maybe one wouldn't hurt.

I crawled across the hot sand to the shelter of the umbrella and dug in the cooler. Grace rolled over. She was sound asleep. "Want one?" I asked my cousin.

"No, thanks."

Too lazy to stand up, I sort of crab-crawled back to my towel on one arm, holding the rich dessert aloft.

When it was finished, I lay back. I'd slathered myself with sunscreen, and now I pulled a Red Sox ball cap down over my eyes. I started to drift off.

I sat up. "Josie?"

"Yes?"

"Does your mother ever talk about when she was young? In high school, say?"

"Once in a while. She's still friends with some of the girls she knew back then. The high school had a big reunion last year for its fiftieth anniversary. Mom was disappointed that your mom didn't come."

"She wouldn't. She's not exactly proud of her Outer Banks childhood."

"Her loss," Josie said. I agreed with her. The Outer Banks back in the sixties and seventies must have been a wonderful place to grow up, and my grandparents hadn't exactly been poor. Just solid, respectable, hardworking people. "Why are you asking, sweetie?"

"I don't even know if I know. Mom didn't kill Karen. She hadn't seen Karen for more than thirty years until this week, and then the next day jewels are stolen, Karen's killed, and Mom's accused of both those things? I'm thinking that whatever did happen might have roots in their past. Did your mother ever say anything about any trouble my mom was in when they were young?"

Josie lowered her sunglasses. She focused her intense cornflower blue eyes on me. "You're thinking about that necklace, right? The one that was stolen and found in your mother's possession."

"Not in her possession, in her bag. Where anyone could have put it."

"Everyone who was at the library that night was questioned by the police. Sam Watson came to the bakery the day you found Karen, not long after you left. I told him what I knew, which wasn't much. Another detective came around later to ask me about your mom's bag. Questions like, if I'd seen anyone paying attention to it, moving it, that sort of thing. I said no. At the time, I didn't know why they were interested in that bag, but word got around pretty fast. Stolen diamonds make delicious gossip."

"Do people think Mom took it?"

"Local gossip says that Karen stole it and was killed by one of her criminal contacts. No one seems to know who that might be or why. A double cross maybe. Gossip doesn't have to make sense."

"And that's all this meeting of the book club that Louise Jane has called for tomorrow is going to be," Grace said in a voice thick with sleep. "A rehash of the worst of the gossip. She's read too many mystery novels."

"More like too many old Westerns," Josie said. "Louise Jane wants to seem important. She'll probably suggest we deputize her to help the police. I won't be surprised if she has a tin star to fasten to her scrawny chest."

"Well, I for one am positive your mom didn't kill anyone or steal any necklace, Lucy," Grace said. "I thought she was very nice. I told Detective Watson that."

"Thanks," I said.

"I don't know how you two can sit in that sun. I'd be broiled to a crisp. I'm going for a swim. Anyone coming?"

Josie stood up, and I followed. "Sweetie," my cousin said. "If you want to know about your mom's past, why not ask my mom?"

We ran into the water, sending a flock of sandpipers scurrying to get out of our way.

We packed up and headed home around four. After

Grace and Josie dropped me off at my front door, I took a long shower, washing away the salt and sand. Then I put on a pair of jeans and a plain white T-shirt and headed back out.

Josie had suggested I speak to Aunt Ellen. It was time to do precisely that.

I drove past the colorful beach houses set into patches of drifting sand and tough vegetation that lined either side of Virginia Dare Trail until I reached a small yellow home. The house backed onto the dunes protecting the beach, and was built in typical Outer Banks style: tall and thin, with outdoor staircases and balconies on every level, including the roof, to give sea views.

Aunt Ellen's car was in the driveway.

She answered the door, wiping her hands on her apron. "Lucy, this is a surprise, although a very nice one. Come in. Your mother's coming to supper. You're more than welcome to stay. I apologize for not inviting you. I thought you'd enjoy a break. Was I wrong?"

"Not at all. It's because of my mom that I'm here. Do you have a moment? I can come back another time."

"I'm just putting the chicken in the oven, and then we can sit down and have a chat. I have a fresh pitcher of sun tea. Why don't you pour us each a glass, and take a seat outside?"

I followed her into the big, welcoming open-plan kitchen on the second level. A fat white chicken, coated in a thick layer of herbs and spices, lay on the table, beside a pile of yet-unpeeled potatoes. A baked pie, probably from Josie's Cozy Bakery, rested on the counter. I breathed in traces of apple and cinnamon. I pulled down two tall glasses and poured the tea. Leaving Aunt Ellen to pop the bird into the oven, I carried the drinks outside. Soft blue-and-yellow cushions had been laid out on the chairs, and the table set for three. I stood at the balcony railing for a moment, watching the end-of-the-day activity on the beach.

"There," Aunt Ellen said. "Dinner's in the oven and I can sit for a while. You don't mind if I peel potatoes while we talk?" She put two plastic bowls on the table and sat down.

"Of course not." I turned away from the view but did not take a seat.

"What's bothering you, honey?" Aunt Ellen asked.

"Why do you think something's bothering me?"

"Because I saw you take your first breath, and I can read that pretty face like a book. Now spill." Her hands moved deftly to strip the peel off the potatoes.

I smiled at my beloved aunt. Sometimes she seemed as much a mother to me as my own mom. The happiest times in my life had been long summer vacations on the Outer Banks, in Ellen and Amos's chaotic house, surrounded by my cousins and love and life and laughter. Ellen had been the one at my mother's side when I was born. My dad couldn't make it—some incredibly important business trip that couldn't be postponed.

"I think something's bothering Mom, but she won't say anything."

"Sounds like your mother to me. She's an intensely private person. You must be used to that."

"Yes, but this time, with all that's going on, I'm worried. This awful business with the death of Karen, and then being accused of stealing, has to be upsetting her. But there's something else, something underneath. Something deeper worrying her. Do you have any idea, Aunt Ellen, what it might be?"

My aunt peeled potatoes. "Comes a time in a woman's life she feels the years catching up to her. Catching up, and then passing her by. Happens to men, too. They go out and buy themselves fast cars and sometimes take up with young girlfriends. Heavens, look at Norm Kivas the other night, acting like cock-of-the-walk with that young woman. Looking like an old fool, more likely. For women? I love my sister, Lucy. She's a wonderful person. But she did get through life on her looks and it can't be easy to start losing that."

"She's not losing her looks. She's still fabulous."

"But she's not twenty, honey. Or even thirty, and soon her fifties'll be in the rearview mirror, too. It's gonna be hard."

I studied my aunt as her strong, competent hands stripped skin from the potatoes. Ellen's fingernails were unadorned, the nails neat but not painted. Her gray hair was loosely pulled into a knot at the back of her head, tiny lines spread out from the corners of her eyes and mouth, and the delicate skin under her eyes fell in soft folds the color of a distant storm. She wore no makeup and her only jewelry was small gold earrings.

"Do you think she's had plastic surgery?" I asked.

Aunt Ellen popped a naked potato into a bowl of water. "That I can't say, honey. If she did, they did a very good job. You won't remember our uncle Gus."

"I've heard of him."

"Our mother's older brother. He died in a boating accident when you were a baby. He was a wild one, for sure. Anyway, Gus always said Sue was the pretty one and I was the brainy one."

I laughed, but Ellen gave me a look. "Honey, you cannot imagine how much that hurt. Imagine telling a young girl she wasn't pretty. Being smart didn't exactly make up for it." She smiled at me. "Now, you, Lucy, have the brains *and* the looks."

I felt my mouth twist. "Yeah, right."

"Gus thought he was being witty. I doubt he intended to be mean, but he didn't do Susan any favors, either. She could have done fine at school, gone on to college if she wanted, but as soon as she reached puberty, she decided she wanted to get out of the Outer Banks and the way to do that was to play on her looks. She took singing and acting lessons. Our dad encouraged her, although Mom thought it a waste of money. Poor Sue had no talent whatsoever. Did you know she was planning to go to New York after high school, try out for a model?"

I shook my head.

"Unlikely that would have worked out. She's lovely to be sure, but not tall enough. You know the story. She met your dad and that was that."

I took a deep breath. Ellen and I had never talked about Mom before. Not like this. "Do you think she married him only because he was rich?"

She put down her potato peeler. "Honey, your mom loved that man like crazy. In all my life, I don't think I've ever seen a girl so in love. My mama was dead set against the marriage at first, thought they were too young. Course, she came around mighty fast, and we all knew why when your brother was born. Your dad absolutely adored Sue and she loved him completely. Would she have loved him as much if his daddy wasn't rich? That I can't say."

I thought of my parents, sitting at far ends of the dining room table, Mom chattering about her social circle and her round of activities while my dad grunted, almost rude in his obvious lack of interest in whatever Mom was talking about. When dinner was finished, she'd put aside her cutlery and tap her lips with her napkin, and he'd push back his chair and head off to his study.

I wondered when they'd stopped loving each other.

"Was Mom popular in school?" I asked, thinking of George and Karen, who both remembered her all these years later.

"She sure was, honey. She was one of the in girls, the pretty and popular crowd. Me, I was the brainy one, remember? I belonged to the chess club."

"Do you remember a guy named George Marwick? He's the manager of the Ocean Side now and he dated Mom back in school. That is, he says they dated. She says they didn't."

The potatoes had all been peeled and were resting in a cold-water bath. Ellen leaned back and sipped at her tea. "Your mom had a lot of boyfriends. Even then I thought she went with them mostly because that was what popular girls were expected to do. She was a real heartbreaker. Uncle Gus approved of that, too. He told me once that it didn't matter that I wasn't pretty. I could get a good job as a secretary and help support my husband."

Aunt Ellen had a wonderful life: marriage to a man she clearly still adored, who adored her in return; a comfortable home in the Outer Banks; great kids; friends and community. But even all these years later, I could tell that good old Uncle Gus's casual insults had hurt her deeply.

"I vaguely remember some boy named George, and some rather mean gossip about him having ambitions above his station."

"What station?"

"I'm sure you remember what high school can be like, Lucy. The social structure of the court of Louis XIV couldn't have been stricter. George wasn't a football player or from a family with money. If he wanted to date one of the popular girls, according to the 'rules'"—Aunt Ellen made quotation marks with her fingers—"he didn't have a chance. But rules or not, Sue never got serious about any one boy, and I don't think she led anyone on. She didn't need to. The boys followed her like dogs follow a man eating a hot dog, hoping something will fall their way. No, your mom wasn't going to get trapped into a life as wife of a garage mechanic or fisherman."

"Karen Kivas said something to Mom when we ran into her at the hotel. About being a thief. Do you know what she meant, Aunt Ellen?"

Ellen studied me for a long time. A seagull swooped low over the balcony, and then turned and headed out to sea. "Our family was never anything more than solidly middle-class. Mama and Daddy worked hard and provided for us well. We had a nice home, a car, but not a lot of extras. We didn't go on fancy vacations or have expensive clothes. Sometimes my mother shopped at the secondhand store. Sue, well, you have to remember that according to Uncle Gus, Sue was special. Heck, even my daddy would buy her bits of jewelry or a pretty blouse if he had some extra money. At Christmas and birthdays Sue got fancy things. I got books. I remember one year in particular. I was about to graduate high school, and Mama and Daddy were saving every cent they had to send me to college. Never for a minute was there a question that I wouldn't go, so money was tight at home. Sue had an after-school job, but she didn't make much. The big end-of-year dance was coming up and she wanted a new dress. She couldn't afford the one she liked, and went into a screaming fit about how hard done by she was.

"The night of the dance, she came down wearing the dress. Daddy fussed about how beautiful she looked, but I could tell Mama wasn't happy. A few days earlier, one of the girls at school had reported that her purse had been stolen and a lot of money taken."

"You think Mom stole it?"

"Yes, honey, I do. And so did a lot of other people. Rumors swirled like mad. Now that I think of it, it was around that time that your mom and Karen Whiteside, later Kivas, fell out. Karen never came to our house again. I suspected at the time she'd been eagerly helping to spread the rumors. Anyway, if your mom had been less popular, she might have been accused, maybe even the police called in. You know what high schools are like. The girl who'd been robbed was one of those who are always on the outside, wanting to be allowed in. Her family was reasonably well-off, but she was overweight, badly dressed, and socially awkward.

"Your mom didn't have a good time at the dance. She came home early and went straight upstairs to bed. I figured at the time she'd had a fight with whatever boy she'd gone with, but later I understood that she was plain guilt-stricken. It was a few months before she met your dad, and after that dance she seemed quieter, more serious. She even started being friendly with the girl who'd been robbed. I know why you asked me all this, Lucy, honey, and I can tell you that if something was stolen from a room at the Ocean Side Hotel, it was more likely to have been a creature from outer space than Suzanne Wyatt Richardson."

Chapter 17

Bertie was not pleased, to say the least, when I told her that the Bodie Island Lighthouse Library Classic Novel Reading Club was having an impromptu meeting to discuss the murder of one of the group's members.

"Here?"

"Here. Noon. Third floor."

"I don't suppose I can forbid it."

"Probably not," Ronald said.

"You can tell them the room's booked," Charlene said.

"That would be a lie," Ronald pointed out. He was, after all, a children's librarian.

"Not that I mind lying in a good cause," Bertie said. "But they'd find me out easily enough. Oh, well. So be it. It's nine o'clock now. Time to open up."

The morning was busy. Connor had been a day off in his weather prediction. A storm had moved in last night, bringing strong winds and cold, lashing rain. Not a day to be at the beach. Instead, parents brought their children to the library. Ronald had a program at eleven for preteens on the history of the Outer Banks, and one at three for younger kids on the flora and fauna they might see exploring the beach and the dunes. Charlene showed interested parents our collection of historical maps and rare books, and answered questions about the history of this area.

I checked out books and answered questions about where to go for lunch (Josie's Cozy Bakery, of course) or dinner (Jake's Seafood Bar). I kept an eye on the spiral iron stairs leading up through the lighthouse tower. Adults were allowed to go there—the view from the top was magnificent—but unaccompanied children were not permitted past the second floor.

Mrs. Peterson came in, practically dragging a sullen ten-year-old. "Straighten up and put a smile on your face, Dallas. You're lucky to be able to have this opportunity." Seeing me watching, she pasted what was probably supposed to be a smile on her face. "Off you go now, honeybunch, and have fun! I'll be up later to talk to Ronald about that list of books."

Dallas slouched away. She might have had an iron ball attached to her leg, judging by the way she climbed the stairs.

"Problem?" I asked.

"Of course not," Mrs. Peterson laughed. "How silly of you to think that. Dallas is such a good reader, you know, that the entire summer reading list Ronald provided her is far below her capabilities."

I interpreted that to mean that Dallas refused to spend her summer sitting in the house reading under her mother's watchful eye. No one is more a proponent of getting children reading and involved in the public library than I am, but even I had to think that sometimes Mrs. Peterson went overboard with her girls. Dallas had probably arranged something with friends for today—it was school holidays after all—but her mother insisted on bringing her to the library. It wasn't as if the entire Peterson brood didn't almost live here. Mrs. Peterson treated Ronald like a member of her private staff. Unfortunately, Mr. Peterson had squandered what little money they'd had on poor investments, and thus his wife had to get by with no staff at all, never mind the exclusive services of a children's librarian.

When Dallas's leaden footsteps had fallen quiet, Mrs. Peterson leaned over the desk, all ready to impart a confidence.

Charles always seemed to know when a non–cat lover was in the building. He left the children's library and came downstairs. He leapt onto the circulation desk and rubbed himself against the jacket of Mrs. Peterson's peach suit. She screeched and leapt back. "That cat is a nuisance. I don't know if I can continue bringing my children here if he's allowed to remain. When I think of Phoebe's allergies."

Phoebe Peterson had never so much as sniffled in Charles's presence. In fact, she seemed particularly fond of him, and I'd once overheard her telling Ronald, sadly, that their mother didn't approve of animals in the house.

Charles gave me a smirk and jumped off the desk. He walked away with his tail high and a wiggle to his hips.

Mrs. Peterson dusted cat hairs off her jacket, and continued in a huff, "I can't believe I was interrogated by the police!"

"They were talking to everyone who was here last Tuesday night."

"I can only thank my lucky stars that my sweet Charity and Primrose hadn't come to book club that particular night. They're at such a delicate age, you know."

I thought of Charity in particular, a hefty, muscular teenager more interested in sticks and pucks and mitts and balls than in books. Nothing wrong with kids who preferred playing sports to reading, but Mrs. Peterson was definitely pretending (to herself most of all) that Charity was a delicate flower of Southern womanhood.

"Although," she said with a deep sigh, "it's unfortunate I had to leave so promptly that evening, without staying to help you tidy up." Mrs. Peterson always fled before anyone could have the audacity to ask her to put away a chair or throw a napkin in the trash. Tidying up was for the hired help. "I'm a keen observer of human nature, you know, Lucy. I might have been able to tell the police something that more . . . shall we say, self-concerned people would have missed."

I hid a smile. I would never call Mrs. Peterson self-concerned. But if it didn't affect one of her five daughters, it simply didn't exist.

"Poor Christine, struck down in the prime of life."

"Christine? Oh, you mean Karen."

She waved her hand in the air. "Yes, of course. They're saying it was a falling-out among thieves."

"I think we should leave speculation up to the police, don't you?"

"Of course. I would never presume to repeat gossip. Why, there's Lennie Saunderson. I hear her Jeremy failed his exams. And her wanting him to go to med school. I know some excellent private tutors. I'm sure she'd like to hear about them." And Mrs. Peterson bustled off to delight the hapless Lennie with words of advice.

At a few minutes before noon, the Gray Woman walked in.

"Good morning," I said.

She nodded. A drop of rain fell off the tip of her prominent nose.

"Can I help you with something?"

"No." She disappeared behind MORRISON–PROULX. This was starting to get seriously weird, but I didn't have time to think about her before the book club began arriving. Louise Jane was first, accompanying Mrs. Fitzgerald.

"Josie can't make it," Louise Jane announced, shaking water off her plastic poncho. "She's working, of course."

"Did you mention this to Butch?" I asked.

"No," she said. "And I didn't invite CeeCee Watson, either, in case she tells her husband. The less the cops know, the better. Same for the mayor. But Connor wasn't here that night anyway."

Grace looked charming in a pink-and-yellow raincoat and matching rubber boots. She gave me an exaggerated wink. At least someone thought this was funny. My mother was next through the doors, followed by George, manager. He fumbled to close his umbrella, managing to deposit a considerable amount of rainwater on the floor.

"What are you doing here?" I asked my mom.

"Louise Jane phoned the hotel. A message was waiting for me after dinner last night. She correctly assumed that I'd be interested in going over the events of the other night. George kindly agreed to give me a lift."

Mom smiled as the next book club member arrived. "And here's Theodore. How nice." He carried a small black umbrella, wet but neatly furled. He turned to George, still struggling with his. "Need some help with that, old chap?"

"Perhaps you, Lucy, and Theodore might put your heads together and go over the events of that night," Mom said. "One of you might remember something."

I refrained from rolling my eyes. This was probably not the time nor the place to mention that I had my suspicions about our book collector himself.

Mrs. Peterson joined us. "I was telling Lily here—"

"Lucy."

"Whatever—that I regret not staying the other night. I would have loved to be able to help the police with their inquiries."

Mrs. Peterson read nothing but parental-advice books. She was probably not aware that in the British detective novels, "helping the police with their inquiries" referred to a character who was under suspicion.

Our library's very small, and gets crowded quickly. Which it was now with the book club, various hangers-on such as George, the parents and kids lingering after the children's group, as well as regular patrons, everyone dripping rainwater onto the black-and-white marble floor.

Bertie came out of the back hall. "What on earth?"

"Bodie Island Lighthouse Library Classic Novel Reading Club and Detective Agency at your service," Mrs. Fitzgerald said with a giggle.

"This isn't a laughing matter, Eunice," Bertie said. "A woman died."

"We know that," Louise Jane said. "And we intend to do something about it."

The non–book clubbers had stopped whatever they were doing to stand and watch. The Gray Woman stuck her head out from behind the stacks. Charlene and Ronald appeared on the stairs.

"Can I be a detective, too?" a cute little girl, all freckles and pigtails, asked.

"Don't be ridiculous," Louise Jane huffed. "Come on, everyone, let's go upstairs." The crowd surged forward. "I mean everyone I've invited!"

"Not so fast," said a deep voice from the door.

As one, we all turned. Detective Watson filled the entrance, his legs apart and his hands on his hips. "What's going on here?"

"An impromptu meeting of our book club," Louise Jane said. "None of your concern."

"I'll decide what's my concern. Any reason Officer Greenblatt wasn't invited to this impromptu meeting? He's a member of the club, I believe."

"I assumed," Louise Jane said, "he'd be at work."

"A correct assumption. Officer Greenblatt is, in fact, at work. Outside right now, as it happens, in his cruiser. Ready to take anyone interfering in a police investigation downtown."

Grace whispered into my ear, "Maybe you could interfere and get to spend some quality time with Butch."

"Shush," I said, my cheeks blazing.

"Time for Dallas's violin lesson." Mrs. Peterson dragged the girl, who was for once showing some interest in her surroundings, out the door.

"I'm only here to get a book," Mrs. Fitzgerald lied.

"I have no idea why I'm here," Theodore said. "I was told Lucy needed me."

"What?" I glared at my mother. She smiled innocently in return.

"Lucy, honey, do you have that new Threadville Mystery in yet?" Mrs. Fitzgerald, who was totally up-to-date on her cozy reading, asked. "I've been waiting for ages."

"Let me check," I said, knowing full well the new book wouldn't be out for another month yet. I bent over the computer.

"If anyone has anything new to reveal about the death of Karen Kivas," Watson said in a voice that would have reached the back rows of the Metropolitan Opera, "they may tell me about it. Otherwise, leave it alone. The police have the matter in hand."

"Do you?" Louise Jane protested. "After the death of Jonathan Uppiton, I advised you to bring in a medium. Someone to communicate with the other residents of this building. But you wouldn't hear of it, Mr. Skeptic. Mr. New York Detective. You refused. And now look what's happened."

"Jonathan Uppiton's murder was solved," Watson reminded her. "Nothing supernatural about it."

"My point exactly!" Louise Jane shouted, although I didn't see that Watson had said anything to support her argument. "We have another mysterious death in the library. Another chance to ask the spirits what's going on."

People began murmuring. I heard words like "murder," "death," "ghosts." A couple of parents grabbed their children by the arm and pulled them, protesting loudly, out of the library.

"That's enough." Bertie pushed herself through the crowd. "There has not been another death in this library. The unfortunate incident to which you are referring, Louise Jane, happened outside."

Louise Jane turned to Bertie. "A technicality. You can't tell me it hasn't occurred to you that this spate of murders"—another group of parents bolted for the exit, wide-eyed children in tow—"isn't related to the arrival of Lucy."

"Hey!" I said.

"What?" my mother said.

For once Bertie was speechless. Detective Watson, however, was not. "That's enough. Anyone who isn't here on library business, leave now." He focused his steely gray eyes on Mrs. Fitzgerald.

"Oh, dear," she said, "I do think I left the coffeepot on the stove. Getting quite forgetful in my old age. Louise Jane, take me home."

"I'm not ready—"

"Yes, you are," Mrs. Fitzgerald said. "I'll see you folks next week. At the regular meeting." She clamped her hand onto Louise Jane's arm and pulled the other woman out the door with considerably more strength than her small frame hinted at. "Suzanne," Louise Jane called over her shoulder, "don't forget we're having drinks tomorrow at six."

In all the excitement and the mass of people, I hadn't seen Diane Uppiton come in. I spotted her now as the crowd began to thin out. A highly unpleasant smile was on her red lips. She caught my eye and smirked. Then she plastered on her fake smile and strode across the room, heels tapping on the marble floor. "Bertie, honey. What an unfortunate scene. I sure hope this doesn't damage the reputation of the library. That'd be a real tragedy."

Diane couldn't help herself turning her head toward the stacks as she said that. A glance passed between her and the Gray Woman. I shivered.

Gradually the library emptied out. Book clubbers left, pretending they weren't at all disappointed in the ruination of their attempts at playing Sherlock. Grace gave me another exaggerated wink. The remaining patrons returned to the stacks.

"That was odd," my mom said.

"What are you doing being friendly with Louise Jane?" I asked.

"I like her."

"I don't want you to like her. My welfare is not her primary concern."

"Everything I do isn't about you, Lucille. Come along, George. Clearly we are no longer needed here."

I was gobsmacked. But I didn't have the luxury of time to reflect on what on earth Mom was up to now. Watson stepped in front of her. He lifted one hand in the universal *stop* gesture. "Mrs. Richardson. Nice to see you're still in the area."

"I'm enjoying my vacation. And having a pleasant visit with my daughter. Good afternoon, Detective."

"Now that you're here, I have a couple more questions about the other night."

Mom hesitated. "Must I call Amos?"

"That's up to you."

George pushed himself between Watson and my mom. "I won't have the police harassing Mrs. Richardson like this."

Oh, dear. Watson had kept his voice down. George, on the other hand, was getting indignant. No doubt enjoying the opportunity to rush to the rescue. St. George slaying the dragon that was the Nags Head PD. Heads were once again beginning to turn, Diane Uppiton's among them.

"I'm not harassing anyone," Watson said calmly. "Come to think of it, you were here that night, weren't you, Mr. Marwick? Do you have anything you'd like to add to your original statement?"

George sputtered.

Mom simply walked out of the building. George Marwick scurried after her. Watson made no move to follow. Instead he came over to the circulation desk. He kept his voice low. "No more impromptu book club meetings, Lucy. Leave the detecting to us."

"I didn't call it."

"I know that." He left.

I didn't need the help of Sherlock Holmes to figure out how Detective Watson knew what the book club was up to. Someone on the e-mail distribution list must have noticed that CeeCee had not been included and helpfully passed it on. And she'd told her husband.

I was more concerned at what had brought Diane Uppiton here at exactly the right time. Diane, as well as the Gray Woman. My first thought was Louise Jane, causing mischief. But that couldn't be it. Louise Jane seemed to have called this meeting in all seriousness, not simply grabbing another chance to stir the pot. And hope I fell out of it. All the way back to Boston.

Speaking of which . . . Mom and Louise Jane were meeting again. Mom was getting quite chummy with George, manager. Mom was throwing Theodore at me.

My mother was still under suspicion of murder.

My head hurt.

It was still hurting at five o'clock when we announced that the library was closing. The rain hadn't let up once, and Ronald, Charlene, and I were on mop duty all day. Parents with small children might have fled at word of a murder on the premises, but suspense and thriller lovers beat a path to our doors. The mystery shelf was looking somewhat depleted by midafternoon.

Once the last of the stragglers had left, I flipped the sign to CLOSED. Before locking the door, I stuck my head out to check if it was still raining. It was. I heard the rumble of engines and, through the mist and driving rain, saw a small convoy of cars coming down the lane.

A gleaming black Cadillac Escalade was in the front, followed by two sedans, and then a battered old pickup truck. A van blazoned with the logo of the local TV station brought up the rear.

"Bertie," I bellowed. "You'd better get out here."

"This," Ronald said over my shoulder, "cannot be good."

"Oh, no," Bertie said.

"What are we going to do?" I asked.

"As Bertie pointed out earlier," Ronald said, "the lighthouse is on public property. Nothing we can do."

The cars pulled into the parking lot. A man leapt out of the passenger seat of the Escalade before it had fully come to a stop. He popped open a golf umbrella and held it aloft to provide shelter as a woman climbed out of the back. She was dressed in a crimson suit, a white blouse, and red patent leather pumps. A button was pinned to her suit jacket. Doug Whiteside emerged from the driver's seat, unfurling his own umbrella. Two men in somber suits got out of the second vehicle. A sloppily dressed fellow emerged from the third car. He was a reporter with the local paper. The TV van disgorged a middle-aged woman done up like a high school girl on prom night and a man who hefted a camera onto his shoulder. The reporter opened a pink umbrella. The camera was draped in plastic. As I'd suspected, the pickup was driven by Norm Kivas, who was accompanied by Sandy, his date from the other night.

Bertie dashed out, heedless of the rain. Ronald, Charlene, and I followed.

Doug Whiteside's broad smile didn't reach his eyes as he held out his hand to Bertie. She ignored it. "What's going on here?"

"Sorry we're late," the woman with him said. "The newspaper guy got tied up."

"Late for what?" Bertie said.

Late for a full house at the library, no doubt.

A police cruiser pulled into the parking lot, and Butch joined our sodden little group.

"Don't worry, Ms. James," Billy, who'd been with Doug at Josie's the other day, said. He held a big bouquet of wilting red roses, wrapped in supermarket cellophane. "Nothing's wrong. We've asked the police to provide some crowd control." I counted a crowd of less than ten.

"Can we hurry this up?" the TV woman said. "I'm freezing here."

Billy led the way, still carrying the flowers. Doug took what I assumed was his wife's arm (she looked suitably politican's-wife-ish), while the man holding the umbrella aloft slipped and slid in the mud. The party stepped off the path and rounded the lighthouse. We followed. The women's heels sank into the sodden muck. The TV reporter swore a blue streak. One of the men matched her curses as his leather-clad foot found a hole in the grass. Mrs. Whiteside threw her husband a glare that was not found in the good-politician's-spouse handbook as mud flowed over the top of her shiny shoe.

Norm Kivas followed, looking as if he didn't quite know what was going on. He had not dressed for the occasion, whatever the occasion was, and was in clean but well-used jeans and a Steelers T-shirt that was so new it almost shone. A FOR NAGS HEAD button was pinned to the shirt. His woman friend had a similar button attached to her tight T-shirt. She was wearing skinny jeans above four-inch heels. "Norm, honey," she said, "you didn't tell me we'd be *hiking*."

Rain dripped down my nose. My hair was plastered to my head.

The last of the police tape had been taken away. Nothing remained to mark the place where Karen had died. Doug obviously didn't know where it was. He looked around, momentarily confused. "Over here, Mr.

Whiteside," Billy said, gesturing to a patch of muddy earth against the round walls. He was about ten feet off. I didn't bother to point that out. The location had been chosen because it had a nice backdrop of the open field to the marsh.

Everyone took their positions. "Mrs. Whiteside," Billy said. "If you'll step over here." She tiptoed through the grass as though she were keeping an eye out for evidence of a passing dog. The color of the campaign button fastened to her jacket clashed with her red suit. She and Doug held hands. They didn't bother to look at each other. Billy passed her the spray of flowers and she cradled it awkwardly in her free arm. The newspaper guy pulled out a digital recorder and the camera guy checked his angles. Sandy smiled at the TV reporter. The TV reporter ignored her.

I glanced at Bertie. Her mouth was set into a tight line of disapproval. Butch came to stand beside me. He gave me a smile of hello and a shrug of what-can-you-do.

"Is that on?" Doug asked.

"When you're ready," the cameraman said.

Doug checked his tie was straight. He composed his face into serious lines. "One week ago, my beloved sister, Karen, was brutally murdered on this very spot." Mrs. Whiteside wiped a tear away, barely avoiding sticking a rose petal into her eye. Doug gestured to the expanse of land and sky behind him. "This is a beautiful spot. One of the many wonders of nature to be found on the Outer Banks. Sadly, it is not a place where women can feel free to come and go at night. It is not a place for a library. I'd like to see this wonderful lighthouse and the grounds returned to the people of the Outer Banks, whether visitors or residents. A place where people can relax in safety and comfort." He paused to wipe at his eye. Bertie huffed. I hoped the microphones would pick that up.

"For the past year, people have been telling me that they want me—no, they need me—to run for mayor. They need someone with a firm hand on the tiller of our community. A firm eye on the hardworking taxpayers' hard-earned money. For the past year, I've resisted. My family, I always said, has to come first." Doug turned to his wife. He gazed adoringly at her. Billy jerked his head. Mrs. White-side suddenly realized she should be gazing adoringly back. She did so, and Doug went on. "But in light of what happened to Karen, Trixie has convinced me that I have another duty. A duty to the memory of Karen, and to all the families of our town." Trixie smiled bravely.

"Therefore," Doug went on, "I am here today, at the spot that shall forever be sacred to my family, to announce my candidacy for mayor." The small group around us broke into applause, making up with enthusiasm what they lacked in numbers. Noticeably, the camera did not turn to pan across the crowd. Doug lifted his wife's hand. He kissed it and then released it. "I have the pleasure of letting you all know that I have the support of my brother-in-law, Norman Kivas. Let's do this for Karen, Norm." Doug stepped to one side, his hand held out. Norm came forward, blinking rapidly. Sandy made to follow. Billy's arm shot out and caught her at the level of her campaign button. Norm shook Doug's hand. Then Doug said, "Trixie." Trixie bent awkwardly—her skirt was too tight—and laid the flowers against the lighthouse wall.

"I will now take questions," Doug said. "Yes, Miss Lancaster?"

The TV woman held out her microphone. "My condolences on your loss. Are the police any closer to making an arrest in the murder of your sister?"

"I am, of course, only a concerned citizen, the same as the rest of you. I'm not privy to the police investigation, but I can assure your viewers that if they honor me by electing me mayor, I'll conduct a thorough review of police procedures. Unlike our current administration, I believe in working with law enforcement agencies from all over the area." Trixie looked adoring. Norm churned up mud beneath his big boots. Norm's girlfriend pouted.

"Do you plan an increase in the police budget, then?" the TV reporter asked.

Doug laughed. "Unlike the current administration, gouging more money from the hardworking taxpayers isn't my solution to everything. I've already identified places in the police department where we can find efficiencies."

"Pardon me," Bertie said. "I have to go and throw up."

"Do you want me to ask him a question?" Ronald said. "I can point out the popularity of the library."

"Save your breath," Bertie said. "These are his tame reporters. They don't care what you say."

"You don't think he has a chance at winning, do you?" Charlene asked.

"I certainly hope not."

"So do I," Butch said. "All this talk about efficiencies? Just a fancy word for cutting the police budget by laying off cops."

"I'm outa here," Charlene said. "Night, all."

Ronald walked with her to their cars. Bertie went back inside, emerging a few minutes later with her purse. She also drove away. I stayed with Butch, thinking that Connor would want to know what had happened here.

The TV woman turned to face the camera full-on,

while Doug spoke to the newspaper guy. Billy had his hands full keeping Norm's girlfriend away from the reporters. It wouldn't do the grieving-husband image any good if the public got a look at her. Trixie wandered around, bored. One of the men held the umbrella over her head and led her back to the car. She gave Butch an approving appraisal as she passed us. Me, she ignored.

Then it was over. The reporters rushed to pack up their equipment and bolted back to their cars. Doug, Norm, Sandy, and the entourage followed. No one was smiling anymore.

Billy spotted me and approached, hand outstretched. "Hi, there. Nice to see you again. Doug, you remember Miss . . ."

"Richardson."

"Of course."

"How ya doin'?" Doug also gave my hand an enthusiastic pump. "Billy, give this lovely lady a button from me."

Billy pulled a FOR NAGS HEAD button out of his pocket. I snatched it away before he could pin it to my chest.

"Lovely spot here, isn't it?" Doug said. "Don't you worry for a moment about that killing, Miss Richardson. The police are about to make an arrest. Strictly a personal affair, I understand. Isn't that right, Officer? I'm a strong supporter of the police. Get rid of political interference and let our heroes in blue, such as this fine fellow here, do their jobs, right? I plan to turn this whole area into an attractive spot so visitors like you can enjoy it in complete safety."

As if I were standing here, in the driving rain, without an umbrella, dressed in a cotton blouse, a plain skirt, and one-inch pumps, because I was about to head off for a nature hike. "Safe," I said. "Like Disney World or a zoo."

Doug beamed. "Got it in one!"

Billy seemed to be more on the ball than his boss. "If the library's closed to make room for tourist facilities, Doug'll make sure everyone who works here finds other jobs, won't you, Doug?"

"Huh? Oh, right. Jobs. Yup, we need jobs. Good jobs. I've a plan—"

"I need gas money," Norm Kivas said.

Billy swung on his heels. "Let me walk you to your car, Norm, Sandy. Mrs. Whiteside's waiting, Doug. We have the ladies' tea next. Can't be late."

"I'm glad I have your vote," Doug said to Butch and me. "For Nags Head."

I didn't fail to notice Billy reaching into his pocket and pressing something into Norm's hand. Norm's girlfriend turned and ran toward us before Billy could stop her.

"Hey," she said. "Nice to see you again. Remember me? I'm Sandy Sechrest."

"Lucy."

"Speaking of jobs, do you have any openings here? I mean, like, at the library?"

"Didn't I just hear that your pal Doug wants to close the library? That would mean no jobs. For anyone."

"Oh, heck. It's all talk. He hasn't got a chance of winning anyway. I never vote, but I might this time. That Mayor McNeil's kinda cute."

Nice to see Connor had the fluffy-headed-bimbo voting bloc locked up.

I studied Sandy. On closer inspection I could see that beneath the excessive makeup, her eyes contained a glimmer of intelligence. "If you're ever hiring, I'd appreciate a heads-up. I'm not a librarian, but I'm a darn hard worker." Her smile was genuine.

"I'll bear that in mind. Why not stop by sometime, have a look around, see what we're all about here? This is not your grandmother's library."

"Thanks. I'd like that. Gotta run. I was kinda hoping to get myself on TV. I guess that's not gonna happen. See you around."

Butch and I stood in silence, watching them drive away.

"Rather convenient for good old Doug. Having his sister die that way." I spoke through chattering teeth.

"You're absolutely drenched, Lucy," Butch said. "Let's get inside."

"I'm fine." I rubbed my arms in a feeble attempt to generate some warmth.

The library was deliciously warm, dry, and cozy. I grabbed a shawl from the back of the circulation desk chair. Butch smiled at me. "You do look like a drowned rat."

Charles shuddered in sympathy and rubbed against my ankles, bringing some circulation back to my legs.

"Not much worse than you," I said to Butch.

"No, but my job often involves standing in the rain. You better get upstairs and dry off before you catch your death."

"Don't worry about me. I never get sick. Are you going to tell Watson what I said? About Doug benefiting from Karen's death?"

"Yes."

Charles leapt up onto the desk. He rubbed his head against Butch's arm, asking for a scratch.

Butch obliged.

"And not only the whole grieving-brother thing, either," I said. "The flowers were a nice touch. Do you think Mrs. Whiteside is on something? She sure looked out of it to me."

"Bored to death, most likely. As was everyone else."

"Family relationships are important in political campaigns. Particularly in close-knit communities like this one. Doug and Karen were, so I've been told, seriously at odds for a long time. I've also been told that Karen had a mean streak, and wasn't one to let bygones be bygones. I wonder if she would have done something to sabotage her brother's campaign. A few well-placed words about family secrets, skeletons in the closet."

"I don't know, and neither do you, Lucy."

"No, but I can speculate to my heart's content. Doug had two reasons to want his sister dead."

"Doesn't mean he did it." Charles purred as Butch's big fingers scratched all his favorite spots.

"As for Norm, he's also benefiting by Karen's death. For one thing, he's back in their house, and has a cute young girlfriend. Doug's paying him to traipse around after him and look suitably grief-stricken. I hope you and Watson haven't forgotten that Norm was seen the day after Karen's death dining at an expensive restaurant with that girl, Sandy."

"We haven't forgotten, Lucy."

"In fact," I went on, as the cold seeped through my light blouse and into my bones, "about the only one who has no reason to have wanted Karen dead is my mother."

"Lucy, I can't talk about that with you. Except to say that Watson's keeping an open mind. Look, you're shivering all over. You need to get upstairs and have a hot shower."

"Okay."

"Can I see you up?" His hazel eyes twinkled. "I can scrub your back."

"No, you cannot. I have to lock the door after you."

"You can always lock up first."

If I'd been Josie, I would have tossed my hair and laughed delightfully and punched him playfully in the arm. But I'm not Josie and blood rushed to my head and my laugh was so strangled I wouldn't have been surprised if he'd begun to perform the Heimlich maneuver.

Charles chose that moment to jump to the floor. Butch leapt back as a mass of tan fur passed in front of his face. "Whoa, I get the hint, buddy."

This time my laugh was real.

"Come on," Butch said. "Walk me to the door." He held out his hand. I took it in mine. It felt warm and solid and safe, very safe. He bent down and gave me a kiss on the cheek. A kiss as light as a drifting feather.

Then he stepped back. "I'll wait right here, until the door's closed and I hear the lock turn."

"Yes, Officer Greenblatt," I said. "Whatever you say, Officer Greenblatt."

Butch left and I did as I'd been ordered.

Charles jumped onto the iron railing and escorted me upstairs. I eyed the big cat. Had Charles attempted, like an Austen chaperone, to protect my honor?

Did I want, like an Austen heroine, to have my honor protected?

An image of Connor's smiling face and sparkling blue eyes popped unbidden into my head.

Who knew life in a library on the Outer Banks could be so interesting?

Chapter 18

I stood under the shower for a long time, letting the steaming water bring some heat back to my body and some clarity to my mind. My body responded as desired, but my mind did not. The suspects in the murder of Karen were mounting. The only thing I could be positive about was my mother's innocence.

Norm Kivas and Doug Whiteside. And those were only the people I knew about. What other enemies might Karen have had?

With a sudden shock, I realized I was forgetting someone.

The Gray Woman.

Watching me, watching everything. Saying nothing.

The Gray Woman wasn't just snooping around the library. Every time I turned around in the Ocean Side Hotel, she seemed to be there. She'd witnessed that altercation between Karen and Mom.

Was it possible that, for reasons unknown, the Gray Woman had followed Karen (or Mom, or even me) to book club, then lurked silently on the grounds as night fell and we drank tea, nibbled on pastries, and discussed

Pride and Prejudice? Had the Gray Woman slipped up behind Karen as she unlocked her car, and whispered that they had to talk?

Let's step over here. Around the corner. Where no one can see us.

Had the Gray Woman and Karen known each other?

Had the Gray Woman been Karen's fence in the theft of the necklace? Mom had speculated that Karen had been killed by the person waiting to receive the necklace, and I'd dismissed that as improbable. But what if it was true? What if the Gray Woman had been at the hotel to meet with Karen? Maybe between them, they arranged for Karen to steal the necklace from the guest room, and the plan was to smuggle the jewels out of the hotel in Mom's bag. Maybe the Gray Woman was going to do a snatch-and-grab when Mom got back to the hotel. But, seeing that she didn't have her bag with her, the Gray Woman then came to the lighthouse to meet Karen. They argued, and . . .

Surely, in that case, the Gray Woman would have left town abruptly, not hung around? But what did I know about the criminal mind? She might be working with other hotel staff, planning another heist.

Why was she spending so much time in the library? Our library, like all public libraries, was a very busy place. People came and went all day long, and no one spared a moment's thought for a total stranger strolling in and making herself comfortable.

Was she waiting for her next contact to make a drop?

I was onto something; I knew it. I should call Butch or Detective Watson with this information. But I didn't even have a name for the Gray Woman, and nothing at all substantial to report. I could hardly say she gave me a creepy feeling.

Then I remembered. Connor had said he'd see what he could find out. I checked my watch. It was coming up to six o'clock. He might still be in the office. I pulled up his number on my cell phone, and then dialed it, using the landline.

"Connor McNeil," he said in his official mayoral voice.

"Hi, Connor, it's Lucy."

"Lucy. How nice to hear from you." His voice relaxed and I was pleased that just hearing from me had that effect on him. "Is everything okay?"

"I'm fine, but I'm calling about two things, Connor. First you might want to know . . ." I explained about Doug Whiteside and his official declaration that he was running for mayor.

"Thanks for the heads-up, Lucy. The paper called me a few minutes ago, but I was in a meeting, so I didn't take it. I'm not surprised to hear Doug's in the race, but I have to say I'm disappointed that he's playing on Karen's death to score political points. But let's not talk about politics. You said there were two things?"

"At the hotel the other night, you said you'd see if you could find anything out about that woman who's always hanging around. Did you? She was here again today."

"I asked around, but didn't find much. Unfortunately, I don't have police powers," he laughed. "Her name is Irene Dawson, and she's from Iowa. She booked into the hotel for a week, and appears to be by herself. Sorry, nothing more."

"Thanks for doing that."

"And thank you for the call. Now I can be prepared when I talk to the papers."

We hung up. I tapped the receiver against my cheek.

Time to go to the hotel. Time to confront this Irene Dawson and demand to know what she was doing at the Ocean Side and at the Lighthouse Library. I wouldn't go to her room; I wasn't that stupid. I'd wait in the crowded lobby, and accost her when she walked through.

It was just after six now. She'd probably be going to dinner soon.

Set on my course of action, I dressed quickly.

Charles lay on the bed and watched me. When I sat beside him to tie on my sneakers, he gave me a long, plaintive whine. His eyes were wide and his ears up.

"Don't give me that look," I said. "I know what I'm doing." I headed for the door. "Don't wait up."

My timing was perfect. I didn't even have to get out of my car. As I pulled into the driveway of the hotel, a small gray Toyota Corolla with Iowa plates passed me, heading in the opposite direction. The Gray Woman was driving, and she was alone.

I swung my car around, and followed.

Corollas are very common cars, but as I drove, I thought there was something familiar about this one. Was it the one I'd seen the other day, following the police down the lighthouse lane before speeding up and driving away? I'd dismissed it as belonging to a lost tourist, but it now seemed as though the Gray Woman had been spying on us. It was definitely time to find out what she was up to. Even if she was not involved in the death of Karen, if she'd been creeping around the library that night, maybe she'd seen something she should have taken to the police.

I convinced myself I was doing my public duty in trying to find out what was going on here.

We headed north, farther into Nags Head. The rain had

almost stopped, but visibility was poor in the mist and the gathering dusk, and my windshield wipers were hard at work pushing aside water kicked up by cars' tires. Fortunately the weather was keeping people indoors, so the traffic wasn't bad, and the low visibility should be in my favor. She'd be less likely to realize she was being followed. We stayed on Virginia Dare Trail. She was a cautious driver, sticking to the right lane at a solid five miles per hour under the speed limit. Impatient cars pulled out and zipped past us. Some rude person even honked at me.

Before too long, the turn indicators of the car ahead began to blink. She slowed, and turned into the parking lot at the fishermen's pier. This was not a day for fishing, and the lot was mostly empty. I'd once been here with Connor and knew that the pier had a restaurant and a covered bar with a view out to sea.

The Gray Woman parked close to the entrance. She got out of her car and the lights flashed as she locked it with the remote. Then she hurried up the steps.

Should I follow?

Suppose I was completely wrong and she was here for an assignation?

It was entirely possible that was the case. Perhaps she'd told her family she was visiting friends, but in reality was here to meet her lover. That would explain why she was here on her own. Bored and lonely. Waiting until her lover got the chance to sneak out.

The image of the glance that had passed between her and Diane Uppiton flashed through my mind. They knew each other; I was sure of it. I'd forgotten about that in my speculation that she was Karen's killer.

Could Curtis Gardner, unwanted library board member and Diane Uppiton's lover, be the Gray Woman's lover also?

No. Diane was not one to hold back. If she so much as suspected the Gray Woman was involved with Curtis, she'd have torn the Gray Woman's gray hair out by its gray roots.

Killer or philanderer, she was up to no good. And I was determined to get to the bottom of it.

Hadn't I recently been thinking that life here was interesting?

I marched boldly up the steps and into the restaurant, trying to look as though I knew where I was going. About half the tables were occupied, and people sat in colorful stools along the railing, gazing out at the storm-tossed sea.

I tiptoed forward, trying to stay out of sight against the wall.

A waitress, bearing a tray overflowing with burgers, wings, and pitchers of beer, passed me. "With you in a sec, hon." No one I recognized was at the outside seating. I stuck my head around the corner. There she was! The Gray Woman was standing beside a table, looking down at the occupants. Her body hid whoever was sitting to the left side of the table, and the wall behind which I was trying to conceal myself blocked the right.

Then she pulled out a chair and sat down.

Diane Uppiton. I stuck my head farther out. Curtis Gardner.

"Are you looking for something?" I leapt out of my skin at a voice by my shoulder.

"No. Nothing. Nothing at all."

"Would you like a table?" A waiter was eyeing me

suspiciously. Probably thinking I was here on an assignation of my own.

"No. I mean, no, thank you. I'm looking for . . . my mother. I seem to have lost her."

"Perhaps—"

"Silly old Mom. She wanders off sometimes." I threw one last look at Diane, Curtis, and the Gray Woman and bolted for the exit. Wrapped in their conversation, they hadn't noticed me.

I gunned my car and tore out of the parking lot.

So, the Gray Woman was here to meet with Diane and Curtis, was she? In that case her snooping around the library wasn't an attempt to pass the time or to take possession of stolen goods. The three of them were plotting something.

I was heading toward the police station. Butch had said he was going off duty, but Watson might still be around. I only realized I'd been so deep in thought I'd let my foot off the gas pedal and was driving at a sedate twenty miles an hour when someone honked at me and made a rude gesture as he passed.

I sped up, and passed the police station in a spray of rainwater. What could I tell Watson? That I'd followed a woman to a restaurant. I'd seen her having dinner with people I didn't trust.

He'd be more likely to arrest me for being a stalker than rush out to interrogate the Gray Woman.

I wouldn't tell Watson my suspicious, not yet. But I would let Bertie know something was up with Diane and Curtis.

Chapter 19

Tuesday brought more rain and another busy day at the library as frantic parents sought some way of entertaining bored and restless children.

I'd given a lot of thought to the Gray Woman, Diane, and Curtis. In the aftermath of the shock of seeing them together, I'd been convinced that all three of them had been responsible for the theft of the necklace and the death of Karen.

But then, as I'd run over the accusatory speech I'd planned to give Detective Watson, like a sailboat becalmed, I began to run out of wind.

Diane and Curtis had not been at the hotel, as far as I knew. They were not members of my book club (another mark against them in my mind), and they hadn't seemed to know Karen.

Much as I might want to see them under arrest (and off the library board), I couldn't come up with a reason to suspect them of criminal behavior.

But they and this Irene Dawson, the Gray Woman, were up to something. And whatever it was, it wouldn't be good for the Lighthouse Library.

Unfortunately Bertie was away all day in Manteo at a meeting of the Dare County library directors, and had mentioned that she was looking forward to having dinner with friends after. I didn't think this was something I could talk to her about on the phone. It would have to wait until tomorrow.

"Rain's stopped," Ronald said as we were tidying up at the end of the day. "It's going to be a nice evening."

I harrumphed.

"Is your mother still in town?"

"I am beginning to fear she'll never leave."

"Trouble on the home front?"

"Maybe. I just don't know." I dropped into a chair. Charles jumped into my lap.

"Wanna talk about it?" Ronald said.

I rubbed Charles's ears. "She wants me to come home to Boston. I've told her and told her I have no intention of doing so. I'm happy here, and I am going to stay. If Ricky crawled all the way from Boston on his knees to beg me to come back, I wouldn't go. I just don't know what Mom's up to. She's not usually sneaky and devious. What my mom wants, she goes for. If she doesn't get it, then she decides she didn't want it after all. All this plotting is making my head hurt."

"Why don't you just ask her?"

"What?"

"Come out with it. Have a serious mother-and-daughter heart-to-heart. Tell her what you've told me. Point out to her that she can't live at the Ocean Side Hotel forever. Or maybe you could get one of your brothers to phone and tell her to come home."

"There is the unfortunate matter of her being told not to leave Dare County."

"Your mother's not exactly a hardened criminal," Ronald pointed out. "Or a member of the mob or something. She's a respectable citizen with a home and family life. Watson will let her go home if she promises to keep in touch."

I let out a long breath. "You're right. I won't go to my brothers for help, but I do need to talk to Mom." I lifted Charles off my lap and stood up. "No time like the present. I'll go over there now."

"You go, girl," Ronald said.

I gave him a big hug, and ran upstairs. Ronald was right. It was time to have a good talk with Mom. If there was one word I'd have used to describe my mom, it would be sensible. This insistence on staying on, in the face of everything I said about not going home, was highly uncharacteristic of her. Her behavior over the past week had been so abnormal I was beginning to worry that something was seriously wrong. Was she ill? She didn't look ill. She looked as good as ever, although naturally strained as the police investigation wore on. I'd try to convince her once and for all that I was not going back to Boston and I was not going to marry Ricky. If she refused to give up, I'd demand to know what was going on in her life. She and Louise Jane were supposedly meeting at the hotel this evening. It was a few minutes after six now. Rather than phoning ahead and alerting Mom to my arrival, I'd pop around and hopefully catch them in the act. The act of plotting against me, that is.

Life in the Outer Banks was proving to be interesting, all right, but also complicated. I'd never suspected anyone of plotting against me in Boston. Unless it was Ricky trying to ensure that no one told me he'd gone away for a weekend at the Cape with Marjorie Price.

Silly boy. Of course the minute Marjorie "accidentally" let it slip, all my so-called friends (more like daughters of my mother's friends) called me with the news.

I pulled on a pair of much-loved jeans, a thick, warm sweater, and sneakers, and stuffed my hair into a rough ponytail. I didn't want to be dragged into another dinner with George and anyone else Mom might round up.

Great minds think alike, or so they say, and my phone rang as I was waiting at the end of the lighthouse drive for the highway traffic to pass.

Mom got straight to the point. "If you've finished work, dear, Louise Jane's here and we're about to go for a walk. Why don't you join us? There's nothing nicer than a stroll along the beach as the sun sets, is there?"

Right about now, a root canal sounded nicer than a walk while Louise Jane and Mom schemed to get me back to Boston. I'd try to think of some way to get rid of the pesky Louise Jane so Mom and I could have that talk.

"Oh, and Detective Watson called a few minutes ago. I thought you might be interested in what he had to say. When shall we expect you?"

"Five minutes." I threw the phone onto the seat, and pulled into the traffic. Outer Banks drivers seemed dreadfully impatient today. A man leaned on his horn and waved at me in an unfriendly gesture. Must be the weather.

I parked and walked up to the hotel entrance. To my considerable dismay, whom did I see heading in the same direction but Theodore Kowalski?

"Hi, Lucy," he said, sounding genuinely surprised to see me. And, dare I say, pleased. Today's outfit was gray slacks, blue shirt, blue-and-white-striped linen jacket, accented by a white cravat with blue stripes. All he needed was a straw hat to look like he was heading for the Royal Enclosure at Ascot.

I looked into Theodore's eyes. He was eccentric all right. But did that eccentricity go any further than dress and fake accent? Was he a killer?

How the heck could I tell? What did a killer look like, anyway?

"What brings you here?" I asked.

"Your mother suggested a stroll on the beach. Perhaps an ice cream on the pier."

"And you just happened to have a suitable outfit handy?"

"Of course."

I was about to ask him straight out if my mother was giving him money to buy the Ian Flemings. But I swallowed the words. What Mom did was her affair. I'd never spared a thought to how she or my dad spent their money in the past. I wouldn't now. I had more than enough on my plate.

Theodore held out his arm. "Shall we?"

"Oh, all right." I took it, and we walked into the lobby. Mom smiled broadly at the sight of us together.

I reconsidered asking about the books.

Louise Jane also smiled. As usual she resembled a shark playfully circling a hapless fish.

I had no doubt that I was the fish.

Mom and Louise Jane had empty glasses in front of them and a book spread open on the table. I knew that book. It had come from the library. *Legends of the Outer Banks*. The page was open to a black-and-white sketch of the Bodie Island Lighthouse. It was night and wispy clouds drifted across a full moon. The light of the moon shone on a Civil War–era soldier, holding a lantern aloft against the dark.

My teeth were beginning to ache from all the gritting I'd been doing lately. "I'm tired," I said. "It's been a heck of a long day. You know that book's fiction, right, Mom?"

"Legends," Louise Jane corrected. "Myths and legends have their origins in true stories."

"Not always."

"You can't deny that strange things have been happening at the lighthouse since you arrived, Lucy. Why, you hadn't been there for a week when poor Jonathan Uppiton was killed."

"That had nothing to do with me!"

"And now Karen Kivas."

"I didn't—"

"My point exactly. You had nothing to do with either of those tragedies. But you clearly have stirred up something that had been quiet. Quiet for a very long time."

"I hope you're not proposing to come back to my apartment and spread more *protection*?"

"You mean like a spell?" Mom asked.

"Fat lot of good that did last time," I pointed out.

"You're still here, aren't you?" Louise Jane snapped.

"No thanks to—"

"This is the first I've heard," Mom said, "of any last time. Now, I'm not one for the supernatural—" That at least was true. Mom was nothing if not totally practical. "—but it does seem as though this lighthouse is not a safe place for you to be living, Lucille."

"My living arrangements are not open to discussion."

Mom got to her feet. Louise Jane closed the book and put it into her cavernous bag.

"Now, let's have that walk," Mom said. "By the time we get to the pier, it'll be dark. We can take a cab back.

Theodore, dear, you walk with Lucy and try to talk some sense into my daughter."

Mom and Louise Jane marched away, leaving me with Theodore. He was probably the last person in the world I'd take advice from.

He gave me a rueful grin. "The library always seems like a perfectly safe place to me."

"You don't really feel like a walk, do you?"

"Sure I do," he said. Acting was not his strong suit.

"Oh, come along, then." I grabbed his arm and we followed my mother.

The storm had cleared and the clouds had moved on, leaving a beautiful twilight. The beach was full of families and couples enjoying the last rays of light. Children ran here and there, searching for flotsam washed ashore by the winds and high waves. The ocean, of course, is to the east, so there isn't a spectacular sunset when the great ball drops beyond the rim of the earth, but the soft, gentle light is diffused with orange and pink, deep grays and purple. Everything looks so fresh and clean and the world seems like a peaceful, calm place. I took off my sneakers and held them in my hands. The wet sand was deliciously cool under my feet, and the surf purred as it stroked the shore. Out at sea, lights were coming on, specks of yellow and white in the blackening water and sky.

Mom and Louise Jane walked ahead of us. I snapped my head out of my appreciation of the evening as I remembered why I'd been lured on this pleasant little stroll, anyway. "Hey!" I yelled. I abandoned Teddy and ran up the beach. "You said you had something to tell me, Mom. About Detective Watson?"

"Oh, yes, him. He called earlier. Said I am free to leave."

"That's great! Did he say why?"

"No, but I immediately called Amos. He told me that the police simply have no reason to continue to restrict my movements. They had to admit that anyone could have put that necklace in my bag, and as for Karen ... even they were forced to agree that after a life of perfect respectability, the idea that I would turn into a cold-blooded murderer over a minor slight is preposterous. Amos did, I gather, convince them that if I had killed Karen, I would have confessed and thrown myself on the mercy of the court."

"Have they arrested someone?"

"Amos says the investigation continues. He added that Watson has my address and I may be called back."

"When are you going home?"

"In a couple of days."

"Why not tomorrow? Aren't you anxious to get home and put all of this behind you?"

"I've had enough walking. Let's turn back and have a drink in the bar."

She retraced her steps. Louise Jane scurried after her and they soon caught up with Theodore. My mom was cleared of the theft and the murder. I had not for the slightest moment thought she was guilty, but now that the suspicion was lifted, I wasn't feeling as happy as I should be. I'd been worried about Mom from the day she arrived. She'd been behaving so strangely. Why wasn't she taking the chance to dash off home?

I glanced down the beach. Children played in the surf and young couples held hands and kissed in the deepening twilight.

I would have liked to continue with the walk. Take some time to forget about the death of Karen Kivas and enjoy the ending of the day. I wouldn't forget Karen. But the cause of her death was no longer my concern.

I walked back to the hotel, deep in thought, following my mother's footsteps in the sand, slowly fading as the tide moved in.

I had no intention of joining them for a drink. Leave the three of them to plot all they want. When I walked through the lobby, planning to head straight for my car without even saying good-bye, Mom was standing at the reception desk. She held a piece of paper in her hand and had a puzzled look on her face.

"What's up?" I asked. "Where's Louise Jane and Theodore?"

"I told them to go ahead. The clerk called me over. She said someone left this for me. What do you make of it?"

She handed me the note. It was on hotel stationery, the type left out on tables in the alcove by the windows overlooking the dunes. A strong, rough hand had written: *I know your secret. Be in your room 8:00. Or else I make some phone calls.*

I checked my watch. "It's almost eight now. Ask them to move you to another room. Or better still, check out of the hotel altogether. You can go to Ellen's."

"I want to see what this is about."

"Some nut wanting to get you alone in your room. That's what it's about, Mom."

"Then why the warning?"

Why indeed?

"This must have something to do with Karen," she said.

"That's entirely possible. Which is why I don't want you meeting him. I'm going to phone the police."

"No. I don't like that Watson. I don't trust him."

"Butch, then. He'll come."

"I am sure he will," Mom said. "He's quite handsome, isn't he?"

"Butch? I hadn't noticed."

"If you like that overly large, manly sort." She dismissed the overly large, manly sort with a wave of well-manicured fingers. "He's obviously very fond of you."

I felt my color rising. "He's Josie's soon-to-be brother-in-law. It's just a family thing."

"I have eyes, dear. He has a way of looking at you when you aren't looking back that any fool can read. He's handsome and charming and very nice, and he clearly adores you. But you'd be making a big mistake getting involved with a policeman."

"I'm not getting involved with—"

"Their divorce rate is astronomical. The job always comes first, even though they say it won't. Before family. Before children. Not to mention the constant worry about the danger."

"But we're—"

"Now, if you must remain in the Outer Banks, dear, Theodore would be a much better choice. Such an educated and intelligent man."

"Theodore isn't interested in me, Mom."

"He's shy, dear. All he needs is some encouragement."

"Don't you dare. I don't even like . . . Hey, why are we talking about men, anyway? You have a stalker threatening you, or have you forgotten?"

"I haven't forgotten." She stuffed the note in her pocket. "I'll meet him. And you'll come with me." She walked away without waiting for me to agree. She never did; she simply assumed that any sensible person would always agree with her.

I ran to catch up. "I suppose two to one isn't bad odds. I have my phone. I'll set it so I only have to press a button to get nine-one-one. We'll keep the door open."

"You can hide."

"I'm not going to hide."

She unlocked the door. "Get in the closet." The room was neatly made up; a light breeze off the balcony stirred the curtains.

"I am not getting in the closet."

"Bathroom, then."

We froze at a sound from the hallway. Then a woman laughed, footsteps continued on, and my mother and I breathed again.

"He might not talk if you're here," Mom said.

"He'll have to."

"I intend to find out what this is about. Karen dared to malign my reputation, and I was publicly accused not only of theft but of murder and dragged off to the police station as though I were O. J. Simpson. When the police finally admitted they'd made a mistake, their apology was hardly satisfactory and not made in public. I may have to sue for damage to my reputation."

"Mom!"

"Get into the bathroom, Lucille."

She used her *Go to your room, young lady* voice. Despite myself, I did.

I made myself as comfortable as possible, meaning not very, and amused myself by checking Facebook. Nothing new out of Boston. My friends were either still dating the same guys or complaining about their husbands. I resisted posting "Hiding in hotel bathroom, waiting for killer."

I'd give this farce fifteen minutes and then take my mom to spend the night at her sister's, even if I had to tie her up in the four-hundred-thread-count sheets and wheel her out of the hotel in a housemaid's cart.

A knock on the door.

I stopped breathing.

I heard the door open. My mother said, "Who are you?"

"Norm Kivas. Karen's husband."

Chapter 20

"What do you want, Mr. Kivas?" my mother said. "Shut the door."

"The door stays open."

"Don't matter to me if the entire place hears your business," he said. "The police aren't going to charge you with the murder of my wife."

"Who told you that?"

"Never mind."

Doug Whiteside, I guessed. If Doug was taking a run for the mayor's job, he'd have tried to make friends in high (and not so high) places.

"I want twenty thousand dollars," Norm said.

To my surprise, Mom laughed. "Because I didn't kill your wife? That's a new one."

"Karen talked about you. A lot, for many years. She didn't like you much, you know. Said you were a terrible person in school. One of those stuck-up girls quick to make fun of ones not so pretty, ones without much money."

"I'll agree that your information's correct in one aspect. I was one of the pretty ones."

Don't be glib, Mom. He's serious.

"But," she said, "my family didn't have any more money than almost anyone else at our school."

"Karen kept track of you, you know, for years. I told her you weren't worth her stewing over, but she couldn't let it go. You moved to Boston, married into some big-shot family. Had kids. Brought your kids to visit your sister every summer. I thought she'd gotten over it, as the years passed. But then here you were, back again, still high-and-mighty, still lording it over us peasants."

"Mr. Kivas, that sounds nothing but sad. If Karen was jealous of me all these years, then I'm sorry for her. I truly am. And I'm glad we parted as friends. You might not believe that, but it is true."

"It wasn't fair, Karen always said. You should've paid for being a greedy, bullying cow. Instead you struck it rich."

"Mr. Kivas, this conversation is at an end. Good-bye. I'm sorry for your loss. But it has nothing to do with me." Mom had slipped into her hoity-toity Boston Brahmin accent, the one that had been fading over the last few days. I didn't think that was wise: she was only reinforcing Norm's point. I doubted she even knew how she sounded. This was her defensive posture, her fighting voice. It couldn't have been easy for a teenage girl from an Outer Banks fishing family to fit into my dad's family and social circles. She would have learned early to fight with the only weapons she had.

Speaking of fighting—if I had to, I was ready. I had one hand firmly on the bathroom doorknob and the other on my phone. I flexed my knees and bounced on the balls of my feet, prepared to move.

"Karen told me all about it," Norm said, "back in the early days when we was first married. You were a common thief, she said. You saw something you wanted, and figured you were entitled to it. Everyone in school knew it. But they wouldn't do nothin' because of your family having connections."

"My family had no influence whatsoever. On anything. That was all a long time ago, and things that may, or may not, have happened when we were in school are of no consequence now. Good-bye."

"I have proof."

"Proof of what, pray tell?"

"Melanie Harris told Karen. Told her you stole her purse. She wrote it down. Made a statement like. Karen kept it."

"That sounds like something Karen would do. She probably pulled it out from under her pillow at night and dreamt of revenge. I have absolutely no idea what the statute of limitations is regarding the theft of a hundred dollars, but it isn't thirty-five years." I realized that they were talking about the incident Ellen had related to me. Mom suspected of stealing a classmate's purse containing a hundred dollars to buy herself a dress for the dance. And how Mom had been so guilt stricken, it had changed her for the better. Poor thing.

"How'd you know it was one hundred?"

"Oh, gosh, you tricked me there, Inspector. Now go away."

"I'm not gonna take it to the cops. But there's other people'll be interested. Your daughter's living here now, isn't she? Think she wants to know what her mother's really like?"

"I doubt," Mom said, with a deep sigh, "that she even cares." At that, she sounded so sad, I almost threw open the bathroom door and declared, "I do care, Mom!"

"Think about it," Norm said. "You can afford it. I'm not askin' for nothing you don't have. I've met this girl, see. She wants me to buy her nice things. She wants to go to California for a vacation. I've never been to California."

"Didn't Karen have life insurance?" Mom asked.

Norm growled. "Stupid woman rewrote her policy after kickin' me outa the house. Our kids get it all."

"Way to go, Karen!" I would have shouted if I hadn't remembered I was hiding.

"I'll be back tomorrow," Norm said. "Have the money ready."

The door shut. Mom said, "You can come out now."

"I'm going to Detective Watson," I said.

"Don't bother," Mom said. "I'll ask for a new room, and tell the desk to keep him away." She plopped down on the bed. "I'm sorry, Lucille. Sorry you had to hear that. It's true, I'm ashamed to say. There was this girl, back in school, Melanie Harris. She was overweight and had bad skin and absolutely no fashion sense. She wanted to be my friend. Her family was better off than ours, so I told her if she wanted us to be friends, she'd have to give me money. She wouldn't. Clearly Melanie had a good deal more pride than I did. I stole her purse one day. I liked the purse and didn't think it fair that she had a better one than I did. I convinced myself that I deserved to have a nice purse. I found one hundred dollars in it. I used the money to buy a dress to wear to a dance. I told myself she shouldn't have been carrying that much money around, so she deserved to lose it."

I sat down beside my mother, and wrapped her in my arms. I didn't tell her I knew the story already.

"I found out that I wasn't as tough-minded as I thought I was. I had a horrible time at the dance, and took that dress to the charity shop the next day. I've never in all my life stolen anything since. One good thing came out of that, though. I never told Melanie I'd taken her money, but I knew she knew, and slowly we became friends."

"What's Melanie doing now?"

"You might have seen her on TV. She went to law school, married a man in her class, and they moved to the Midwest. Where she's now the senior senator. Her married name's Melanie Brackenfield."

"No kidding?" Not only a United States senator, but a rising star. There was even talk of a presidential bid.

"I'd like to say she owes it all to me," Mom said. "But that isn't true, although I do think I played some small part in convincing her she didn't have to follow along behind the in crowd, begging for scraps of attention. And I knew, not that it matters, that Melanie had told Karen about the hundred dollars."

"But it does matter, Mom. Don't you see? Norm Kivas must have killed Karen. Obviously he did it for the insurance money. And then he found out he isn't entitled to it. I bet he's splashed money on this new girlfriend, and now ... whoops ... can't tell her he doesn't have any more. Doug Whiteside might toss a few bucks his way to get Norm to support his mayoral bid, but aside from the grief factor, Norm's no benefit to any political campaign. He needs money, and he needs it now. I've suspected him all along. You can't trust a man who doesn't like libraries.

"You're not staying in this hotel one minute longer. If he killed Karen, then who knows what he'll do when you don't have the money for him?" I got to my feet. I tossed her Louis Vuitton suitcase onto the bed, marched to the closet, and began tearing clothes off hangers. "We're outa here. Now. No arguments."

She said nothing. I turned and looked at her in surprise. She was smiling, a soft, gentle, genuine smile of the sort I hadn't seen for a long time. "Mom? Do you understand what I'm saying? I'm taking you to Aunt Ellen. Uncle Amos can tell the police what's happened."

"I understand, dear. You're right. I'm glad you're here for me."

"Oh, Mom." I dropped onto the bed beside her and gave her a hug. We held each other for a long time. When I finally pulled away, Mom's eyes were wet. I felt more than a touch of moisture in my own.

"Your father's having an affair with his secretary."

"What?"

"You heard me. I might not even mind so much if it wasn't such a horrid cliché."

"Dad's sleeping with Mrs. Ferguson?" The very idea was preposterous. Mrs. Ferguson had been assigned to my dad the day he'd arrived at the firm, still wet behind the ears. I had no idea how old she was, but she'd seemed ancient when I first met her. I'd been nine, allowed to visit "the Office" for the first time, and everyone at the law firm had looked old to me. Still, she had to be at least ten years my dad's senior. She kept guard over Dad as though he were the castle and she the moat, full of dragons and sea serpents. My brothers and I were terrified of her. I sometimes thought even Mom was terrified of Mrs. Ferguson.

"Don't be ridiculous," Mom snapped. "Of course he's not sleeping with Mrs. Ferguson. Mr. Ferguson had a skiing accident over the winter. He broke a good number of bones. The old fool should have known better than to go skiing at seventy-five. Mrs. Ferguson took time off to care for him, and then decided to slip into retirement."

"I always thought she'd die in harness," I said. "I didn't even know she was married. I figured 'Mrs.' was an honorary title."

"They pulled some fluff of a thing barely out of diapers from the typing pool to take her place."

"I don't think law firms have typing pools anymore, Mom."

"And, as if in some low-budget French farce, your father began sleeping with her." The tears began to flow in earnest. "What am I saying? I care, yes, I care."

I held my mother close. "Did he tell you?"

"Evangeline did, of all people. Ricky told her. You know what these sordid affairs are like. The couple thinks they're being so discreet, but everyone in the vicinity, except the rejected wife, knows."

"What are you going to do?" I asked. This was a side of my mother I'd never seen before. Weeping, heartbroken. Vulnerable. I held her close while she cried in my arms.

"I don't know what to do. I didn't tell him that I know. I left for New York that night. I had my little shopping spree charged to the household account, not my personal one. So he'll know I'm upset about something."

"Has he called you since you've been here?"

She shook her head.

"You can't stay here forever, Mom."

"Why not?"

"Because your home's in Boston, and your grandchildren are there. Not to mention that you can't just walk away from an almost forty-year marriage without a word."

"I can if I want to."

"You don't want to. Do you want me to call him? I

didn't phone him about the death of Karen because you asked me not to, but I think I should now."

"It's so, so . . . humiliating."

"I know, Mom." And that was the crux of it. Poor Mom. Her pride was everything to her, her pride and her place in Boston society. If Ricky knew, then everyone at the club would know. There was nothing Ricky loved more than spreading gossip.

"I won't say anything about what you've told me," I said. "I'll say I'm calling for a chat and mention how much fun you and I are having. I'll see what he says and take it from there."

I didn't bother to mention that I had never in my life phoned my dad for a chat. He'd know immediately that I knew what he'd been up to.

I gave her another hug and then pulled away. "I'll call him later. Right now, let's get out of here. I'm taking you to Aunt Ellen's, and we're going to tell Uncle Amos about Norm's blackmail attempt."

She gave me a weak smile. Her eyes and nose were red and her eyeliner was smudged. "Give me a minute."

It didn't take her much longer than that to get rid of the red and reapply her makeup. She came out of the bathroom looking dewy fresh, as though she didn't have a care in the world.

How, I wondered for approximately the thousandth time, *did she do that?*

"I'll drive you," I said.

"I can drive myself."

"No. I don't want you alone. We don't know where Norm is—he might be watching the hotel. Aunt Ellen or someone can come back with me to get my car."

It was dark by the time we left the room. The registration clerk was on the phone. She held up one finger to indicate she'd be right with us.

"I'll get the car while you're waiting," I said. "Do you have the valet ticket?"

She handed it to me. The clerk was still on the phone.

"While I'm doing that," I said, "call Aunt Ellen. Tell her we're coming."

"I think my phone's out of power. With all that's going on, I forgot to charge it."

I pulled my iPhone out of my pocket, typed in the passcode, and handed it to Mom. "Use mine."

I headed outside to get the car.

"Be a few minutes," the valet said, jogging up to the kiosk. "I've a couple of others to sort out first."

"Give me the keys and I can get it myself."

"Sorry," he said, "some of the cars are blocking others."

I was impatient, anxious to get going, but there was no rush. "I'll wait," I said.

George Marwick came around the corner of the building. A gust of wind lifted the long strands of hairs stretched across his head, making him look as though he were trying to sprout wings. *Why do men not know how unattractive that is?* He gave me a huge smile. "Good night, Lucy. See you tomorrow?"

"Probably not," I said. "Mom's checking out now."

His face darkened. "Is there a problem?"

"No problem."

"Then why leave so suddenly?"

Mom had been here for over a week, not exactly a short stay. It was none of his business what she was doing. "Time to go home."

"Is she coming back?"

"Next year, probably. I . . ."

George stormed past me and almost ran up the stairs. Poor George, manager. If he'd thought he had a chance with my mom, he'd been seriously deluding himself. As the valet pulled up in a Lexus, an elderly couple came out of the lobby. The man patted his pockets, looking for a tip, while the valet waited patiently. Finally the woman had to dig in her cavernous purse. The valet threw me an apologetic smile. George had enjoyed a week of Mom's company; he should consider himself lucky. For George, the death of Karen Kivas had worked out rather well.

My heart stopped. *Cui bono?* Who benefits? That's what they ask in police procedural novels, isn't it? George, manager, had benefited. Mom had cut him dead when they first met, and pretty much ignored him at book club. Then, only a day later, she was being all charming and friendly and even inviting him for drinks or to join us at dinner. The murder of Karen, being suspected of killing Karen as well as having stolen a piece of jewelry, had put Mom in an even more fragile emotional state than when she'd arrived. I suspected that Mom had wanted to get back at my dad, even if Dad didn't know it. And the only available man was George, manager. Thus the abrupt change in her manner toward him.

Who would be in a better position to steal a valuable necklace from a guest's room than the manager of the hotel? I thought back to the night of the book club. Who'd sat beside Mom? Butch. No, wait—Butch had gotten up when George and Karen arrived and given the other man his seat. Easy enough for George to slip the necklace into Mom's bag when no one was watching.

Did Karen see what happened? Did she threaten to tell on George? He was her boss. All she'd have to do would be to hint that she wanted plum assignments, an increase in pay, maybe extra vacation time. George had left the library before Karen, but did he leave the grounds? Mom would have said if she'd seen his car, but the lane makes a loop in a patch of dense trees where the lights from the parking lot don't reach. A convenient place to park and wait for someone to come out of the library.

"Miss? Miss?"

I blinked. The valet was standing in front of me. The SLK was parked at the curb, engine purring softly.

I ran into the hotel. Other than the clerk behind the registration counter, the lobby was completely empty. Mom's brown and gold suitcase was next to the desk, but no sign of my mother.

"Where's Mrs. Richardson?" I asked the clerk. "Did she check out? I'm waiting outside with the car."

The clerk looked at me in surprise. "Are you her daughter?"

"Yes."

"Are you okay?"

"Yes. I mean, no, I'm not okay. I've lost my mother."

"You look okay."

"What the heck does it matter how I look?"

"Mr. Marwick told Mrs. Richardson there'd been an accident out front. Her daughter had been struck by a car."

"What!"

The receptionist leaned over the desk to see out the front doors. "That's funny. I don't hear any commotion."

"No one's been in an accident. Where'd they go?"

"Who?"

"Mr. Marwick and my mother!"

"I don't know."

"He told her I'd been in an accident. Then what happened?"

"You don't have to yell."

"I'll do a lot more than yell if you don't tell me what's going on."

"Mr. Marwick told Mrs. Richardson you'd been taken away in an ambulance. He said he'd drive her to the hospital. I thought that was nice of him. He doesn't usually . . . I mean—"

"Where does he park his car? What kind of car is it?"

"Employee parking's at the back of the hotel. He drives a blue Ford Focus, I think."

I headed for the door off the lobby marked EMPLOYEES ONLY.

"Hey!" the clerk yelled at me. "You can't go in there. That's private."

As soon as I stepped out of the public area, I could see what a genuinely poor state the hotel was in. Everything was aging and dilapidated. The industrial beige paint was chipped and peeling, the linoleum floor so cracked you could trace a map of Europe in it. Holes were in the walls, and ominous water stains dotted the ceiling. I stared down the long, ill-lit corridor. Several doors led off, and I had absolutely no idea which led to the outside. But I did know where the employee parking lot was. I'd seen it when Louise Jane was giving us our tour of the "haunted" swimming pool. I ran back into the lobby, shouting, "Call nine-one-one. A woman's been kidnapped," but I didn't know if the clerk would bother to make the call.

Mom might have believed what George had told her in a moment of shock, but she'd come to her senses quickly. No ambulance would have arrived that soon, and everyone would have heard the siren if it had. No one yelled for help; the valet hadn't come running in shouting for a doctor; people didn't rush outside to catch the excitement.

Other than my yelling, peace and calm lay over the hotel.

If George was giving Mom a lift, by now she must have realized what was going on and was not going willingly.

"You're going to have to move your car," the valet said as soon as he spotted me. I ignored him and sprinted down the driveway. I'd not gone more than a few yards when a blue car came charging around the corner. "Look out!" the valet yelled. I leapt out of the way, feeling the air around me move as the vehicle swept past. I fell hard onto my rear end, and pain shot through my right wrist. George was driving, and my mom sat in the passenger seat. I don't know if he even saw me, but Mom threw me a look. Her eyes were wide and her lips said, "Lucy." An iPhone in a white case flew out the driver's window. The car careened off a giant terra-cotta urn full of red and white geraniums and trailing ivy, but it kept going. And then they were gone.

The keys were in the SLK and the car was still running. I jumped into it and tore down the long driveway. George Marwick must have killed Karen Kivas and now he had my mom. Did Mom know what danger she was in, or did she think George was playing some sort of practical joke? Suzanne Wyatt Richardson was not one for enjoying practical jokes. I couldn't bear to think what might happen if . . . when Mom demanded he bring her back to the hotel.

The Focus made a left turn onto Virginia Dare Trail. It was fully dark now, but traffic was heavy with tourists returning to their hotels and rentals after dinner. I had to wait for a break in the traffic, but I shot forward as soon as I had a chance. A minivan came to a screeching halt with a blare of its horn. I dodged in and out of traffic, trying to catch up to the Focus. Ahead, all I could see in front of me was red taillights. I dug in my pocket, searching for my iPhone.

Nothing.

I'd given my phone to Mom. That must have been what I'd seen being tossed out of the car. Too late to go back for it now. Even if it was still working.

I gripped the steering wheel and cut in front of a panel van. My thoughts tumbled all over themselves. I didn't know what to do. I could stop and try to flag someone down to call the police. But if I did that, I'd lose them. George could be taking her anywhere. Should I try to force George to pull over? Or follow them and wait until they got out of the car? He was driving a Focus and I was in a Mercedes SLK. I had an almost full tank of gas. If it came to a chase, I'd be able to outrun him, no problem. But I didn't think it likely that if I tried forcing the bigger vehicle off the road, the two-seater sports car would come out ahead. I was terrified that I'd lose his rear lights among all the other cars, and end up following the wrong one. At Whalebone Junction, the majority of the vehicles carried on through, heading for the bridge to Roanoke Island. The one I thought was George turned left, going up Highway 12.

I made my decision and took a left. Traffic was much thinner now and I pressed down on the gas. I'd try to pull up beside them when I could. Let George see me. Let him know I was after him. I thought he might turn at the last road in Nags Head—perhaps he lived down that way—but he drove past without slowing. Now, nothing lay ahead of us other than the lighthouse and the beaches of the National Seashore for the twenty or so miles to Rodanthe. And nothing beyond that but the road to Hatteras and then a ferry to Ocracoke. I had no idea where George could be taking my mother.

Mom must have been thinking much the same thing, for the car ahead of me suddenly swerved, heading straight into the center of the highway. It careened back again, almost going off the shoulder. I leaned on the horn, and moved the SLK forward so I was almost on his bumper. I flashed my high beams, on and off, on and off.

The Focus ricocheted down the highway. More than once, I'd been sure it was about to go off the road, but then it was pulled back. Thank heavens no one was coming in the other direction. Several times when I'd been coming home after dark, my headlights had caught deer leaping across the road. I prayed the beautiful animals wouldn't be out tonight.

"Go, Mom, go," I yelled, pounding the steering wheel. She was fighting him now.

We reached the road to the lighthouse. The Focus turned into the lane so suddenly, without even slowing down, that I didn't have time to react and the SLK shot past. I barely slowed down before executing a U-turn. Small cars do have their advantages. Then I was tearing down the lighthouse road. I felt every bump jolting into my seat. The great first-order Fresnel lens flashed, and I could see that the Focus had come to a stop at the edge of the parking lot, one of the front wheels deep in mud. My car lights swept across the disabled vehicle. George had pulled Mom out of the car, and he was attempting to drag her across the sodden grass toward the marsh.

"Mom!" I cried, jumping out of the SLK. I didn't bother to switch off the engine and my headlights illuminated the ghastly scene. I ran after them, slipping and sliding in the mud. "George, what are you doing? Stop. I've called the police. They're on their way."

George whirled around. He gripped Mom tightly with one arm. She looked at me, and I was happy to see, not fear or despair in her eyes, but pure rage. She had lost one of her shoes, and the bottoms of her pants were thick with mud. She was wearing ballet flats. Too bad she didn't have on a good pair of stilettos. Those can make a formidable weapon when used properly.

George put his free hand around her throat.

"What seems to be the problem here, George?" I asked. I tried to keep my voice calm, to sound like someone in full control of the situation. I fear it came out like a frightened squeak.

He stepped backward, pulling Mom with him, taking them out of the reach of the headlights and into the deep darkness. It had stopped raining some time ago, but thick clouds covered the moon and stars. Mom kept an emergency flashlight in the SLK, and I cursed myself for not thinking to bring it.

"Go away, Lucy," George said. "Your mother and I are going to have a long talk."

"That sounds good," I said. "But it's awfully wet out here. Wouldn't you be better talking inside the lighthouse?" I was hoping to get us inside so I could use the phone.

George didn't have a weapon, not that I could see, and for that I was grateful. Then I remembered Karen. She hadn't been shot or stabbed, either.

"The police are on their way. If they think you're smothering my mom, they might accidentally shoot you."

"The police are not on their way, Lucy. You don't have a phone."

Mom was struggling to free herself and to speak, but the grip on her throat was too strong. I didn't want him applying any more pressure. "Calm down, Mom. George and I are good here."

I won't say she exactly calmed down, but she stopped struggling.

George and Mom were standing under the stone walls of the lighthouse. When the thousand-watt bulb flashed, it didn't cast enough light on them to be useful. But over George's shoulder I saw the darkness stir. A shadow moved away from the thick walls, separating from the deep black of the old building. It moved in total silence, hovering inches above the ground. The body of the shadow was the size and shape of a person, but the head had no definition. Veils of mist drifted around its legs.

The Lady.

If I hadn't been so frightened for my mom, I would have run, screaming in terror.

A cry of warning died on my lips. Maybe, just maybe, the Lady had come to save us. Louise Jane's stories said that she was not evil, or even malicious. She wanted to help those she thought were trapped in the lighthouse. Trapped as she had been. But she didn't realize that exiting by a window a hundred feet above the ground wasn't good for living things.

If she was here to help, I wished she'd move a bit faster.

"What do you want, George?" I asked. I tore my eyes away from the Lady. George had seen me looking over his shoulder, seen the shock written on my face. But he didn't turn around. He probably thought he was too clever to fall for that old trick.

The light died and all was dark again.

"What do I want?" George said. "What I've always wanted. My Sue."

"My mom's married, George. My dad won't give her a divorce. He's very religious."

"Then we'll run away, won't we, Sue?"

For a moment all was quiet; then he screamed, "I said, won't we, Sue?"

Mom managed a slight nod.

"We'll start a new life together. I have nothing to stay here for. That cursed hotel's a wreck. They gave me a year to turn it around, to start making a profit. But how can I do that when the luxury guests stop coming, and there's no money for a decent chef or to hire enough staff to clean properly?"

"Must be tough," I agreed.

The shadow drifted closer. A shape of darkness against the dark of the night.

"When Karen started giving me lip, I'd just about had enough. I was going to throw it all in. Then you arrived, Sue, and I knew everything would be all right. You weren't very nice to me when we first met. But I didn't mind. I knew I could win you over. Just like I did all those years ago."

Mom's eyes rolled. She lifted her left hand, and stroked the one George had around her throat. No, not a stroke, just a slow gentle moving of her fingers. I flexed my knees and got ready to run. We might die out here waiting for the Lady to make her move.

Bad choice of words.

I tried to control my breathing. I could not give in to fear and the instinct to panic.

"Did you take the necklace as a gift for Mom?" I asked. What could I do, except to keep talking and hope George would eventually let go of Mom, or we would be saved by a ghost that was nothing more than a shadow darker than the night?

"That worked out even better than I'd planned," George said. "I knew Sue would be confused and frightened at being suspected of stealing it, so she'd rely on good old George to help her out. Just like she did back when we were in school. Do you remember the time those boys were calling you names, Sue? I stood up to them and chased them away. You were so grateful."

I didn't ask him about Karen. This didn't seem like a good time to remind him that he was capable of killing a woman.

"Your gratitude didn't last, did it, Sue?" he said, his voice turning harsh. "Oh, no. You decided you wanted something better than George Marwick. But now, after all these years, you finally understand that I'm the only one who can take care of you. Don't you, Sue?"

Mom made a strangled noise he took as assent.

"That meddling Karen was going to ruin everything. If she told you that I'd taken that necklace, you would have been angry at me, wouldn't you, Sue? Karen would have made it sound like something tawdry, like I was a common thief. I couldn't let that happen, so I had to get rid of Karen. Now everything's going to be okay. Get back in your car, Lucy, and go away. I'll let Sue write to you when we're settled."

The Lady was almost on them. She was nothing but a dark shape, black on deeper black. The light from the Fresnel lens flashed, but it served only to throw her deeper into shadow.

My mom moved. She raked her fingernails down George's arm and screamed as she tried to twist away. I saw the fond reminiscence leave his face, to be replaced by pure thwarted rage. He screamed, put both his hands on her neck, began to twist.

"No!" I yelled. I ran forward, but I wouldn't be able to reach them before he broke my mother's neck.

At that moment, the light went into its 22.5-second dormancy. I heard a high-pitched, unworldly howl and then George screamed, not in rage but in pain, followed by the solid thud of a heavy weight falling to the ground.

I ran forward blindly. A brilliant light came on, and for a moment I thought the thousand-watt bulb had fallen at my feet. Pain shot through my eyes, and I threw my hands up to cover my face. The light moved away, although it did not go out.

I opened my fingers and peered out. My mother was standing in the field, stock-still, staring at her feet. There lay George, manager, face-first in a mud puddle. He groaned, and tried to turn over. A foot pressed down on his neck and a voice growled, "Don't even twitch."

I had not expected the Lady to have a deep, gravelly voice.

The light moved again and gradually I could see. The Lady was dressed, not in a cloak and gown, but in a long baggy sweater and a calf-length skirt above bony ankles and black boots. The hood of the sweater was thrown back and I could see a face. A real, live, human face.

The Gray Woman.

"You watch him," she said to me, pulling a phone out of her sweater pocket, "while I call the cops."

Chapter 21

Between the Gray Woman, Mom, and me, we were able to keep George facedown in the mud. Soon we heard the wonderful and so welcome scream of sirens heading our way, and red and blue lights washed the lane and the parking lot. Women and men in uniform ran toward us and we stepped back. The spluttering, complaining George was hauled to his feet.

"Sue," he said, "I only wanted us to be together. You belong to me. I would never hurt you. Tell them!"

"This man kidnapped my mother," I yelled. "He was about to kill her. He killed Karen Kivas."

"Let's go, buddy," one of the officers said.

"I wouldn't kill her. Not my Sue. Tell them, Sue, tell them!" George screamed as they led him away.

"Detective Watson's on his way," an officer told us. "He said you're to stay here."

The moment the police had arrived, my mother and I had fallen into each other's arms, weeping. Mom was the first to recover. "I'm not standing out here in the dark and cold."

"You can wait in my car. I'll turn the heat up," the officer said.

"We'll go into the library," I said. "I have a key."

"I guess that's okay."

I led our small group into the lighthouse. As soon as I opened the door and switched on the light, Charles leapt into my arms. I gave him a giant hug. The poor creature must have been watching the whole thing out the window, and been distressed at his inability to come to our aid. I flexed my wrist. It was sore, but nothing seemed to be damaged.

"You both wait here," I said. "I'll put the kettle on."

I carried Charles into the break room. I was still carrying him when I came back out. It had been difficult to fill the kettle, get down mugs, and lay out milk and sugar with the cat in my arms, all with a sore wrist, but he wasn't letting go, and neither was I.

The Gray Woman was arranging the shawl from the circulation desk chair over my mother's shoulders. As she fussed, she chatted as though she were trying to comfort a fractious three-year-old. Any other time, I would have expected Mom to swat her away, but tonight she let herself be fussed over.

Officer Franklin was standing at the door, arms crossed. She was smiling.

"Okay," I said to the Gray Woman. "Not that I'm not grateful or anything, but first things first. Who the heck are you?"

She took a seat, folded her sweater around her. "My name's Irene Dawson. I'm a time and motion consultant, specializing in libraries."

"And you're here because . . ."

"My firm was hired by concerned individuals to investigate what some members of the community considered to be improper organizational procedures."

"Which means you were hired by Diane Uppiton and Curtis Gardner."

"I am not at liberty to reveal the specific names of our clients."

I wondered where Diane and Curtis had found the money. Raided the library budget, probably, disguising it as something else.

"In the short time before we're all dragged off to be questioned by the police, what are your conclusions?" I asked.

"That you run a highly unorthodox library. Regular police visits, book club members being murdered. Talk of ghosts and spirits. Even a cat free to wander about at will."

I bristled. "The children love Charles, and it's hardly our fault that—"

She held up one hand. The edges of her mouth turned up in a surprisingly warm smile. "Highly unorthodox. But extremely efficient and wildly popular with both local residents and visitors, even under difficult conditions that are out of your control. My recommendation to my clients will be that Ms. James be allowed to continue to run her library as she sees fit."

"Thanks," I said, exhaling a huge sigh of relief.

"Yes, yes," Mom said. "Whatever. But what were you doing tonight? Outside, prowling around in the dark."

"A regular nighttime security check."

"This is a lighthouse," I said. "No one can get in once the door's locked."

"It's a standard part of our service," Irene Dawson said.

That settled to my satisfaction, I turned to my mom. "What did George mean when he said something about saving you like he did the other time?"

Mom shook her head. She looked genuinely sad. "I find it hard to believe that he's obsessed over that trivial incident all these years. We were at a football game at another school. A couple of boys catcalled my girlfriends and me. George Marwick rushed up, full of indignation, and told them not to be rude. I said thanks. It was nothing at all, but I made a joke about him defending my honor. For the next several months, George followed me around like a lost puppy dog. He never asked me out on a date. I suspected he didn't have the nerve, which was just as well as I didn't want to hurt his feelings. Really, Lucy, I had no idea he was so infatuated with me that it lasted almost forty years. Although," she touched her hair, "I shouldn't be surprised. He was a strange boy."

"Who grew up to be a strange man," Irene said.

"So you weren't almost engaged?" I asked. "Like he said when we first ran into him?"

Mom rolled her eyes. "In all our school years, we never exchanged more than half a dozen sentences. Until tonight, I've never been alone with George Marwick in my entire life. And believe me—that one experience was more than enough."

As we talked, we could see vehicles coming and going and watch people moving about the grounds.

Sam Watson came in, followed by Butch Greenblatt and Connor McNeil. All three men were dressed in sneakers, shorts, and sweat-stained T-shirts.

"George Marwick?" Watson said.

I nodded. "He kidnapped Mom. He would have killed

her without the intervention of Ms. Dawson here. I'm positive he murdered Karen."

"I'm all ears," Watson said. "Lucy, you do the talking."

I glanced at Butch and Connor. "Why are you two here?"

"Our regular Tuesday night pickup basketball game," Connor said. "Sam got a call, and headed out of the gym double-quick."

"So I followed him," Butch said.

"And I followed Butch," said Connor. "As soon as I heard the word 'lighthouse,' I thought I'd better come."

"You do have a way, Lucy, of being at the center of any incident," Butch said.

I hid a smile. They'd rushed to the rescue. My two knights in shining armor. I looked at Irene, the Gray Woman. Tonight, she'd been my knight. In more ways than one, it seemed.

Mom glanced between Connor and Butch. She looked at me. She smiled.

Charles also smiled. Then he jumped off my lap and took his place on the returns cart to hear the story.

Watson allowed me to serve the hot tea, and then I told him everything that had happened. Irene and Mom added bits and pieces of their own.

"Marwick told you he'd stolen that necklace?" Watson asked me.

"Yes. He also said he killed Karen because she knew he'd stolen it."

"He told the officer who drove him to the station that he didn't mean to kill her. It was supposed to be a tap on the head, a warning."

I shivered. "She was a heavy smoker. There's no smoking in the library, of course, so she must have stopped for a cigarette after leaving that night. George was probably waiting behind the trees in the loop. Saw she was alone and took his chance."

"In the initial search of the area, we found a half-smoked cigarette on the ground next to her car," Watson said. "We didn't know if she'd smoked it in the car on the way to the library and put it out when she got here, or had lit it after book club."

"I'm very tired," Mom said. "May I go now?"

"Of course," Watson said. "I'd like to talk to you again tomorrow, to get some details straight. Officer Greenblatt will drive you back to the hotel."

"I'm never stepping foot in that place again. I'd like to go to my sister's. Oh, dear. I never did tell her we were coming, Lucy."

I got to my feet. "I'll call her."

"You go with your mother, Lucy," Watson said. "You shouldn't be here alone tonight."

"No," I said firmly. "This is my home. I am safe and comfortable here. And that is that." I waited for them to object. No one did. "But I have another call to make, as well. Would you gentlemen and Irene mind waiting outside for a few minutes? This is private."

Connor and Butch threw me concerned glances, but they followed Sam Watson out the door. Irene Dawson went with them.

I used the library phone to call Aunt Ellen. I told her briefly what had happened and that Mom couldn't return to the hotel. She said she'd send Amos to the hotel for Mom's bags and have the guest room ready.

I put down the receiver and turned to my mother. "You ready?"

She nodded. She stood close beside me, and I dialed.

When the phone was picked up at the other end, I said, "Hi, Dad."

"Lucy!" his deep voice boomed down the line. "I called you earlier, but your phone seems to be out of service."

I thought of it lying in the Ocean Side Hotel parking lot. "It had a small accident."

"I'm starting to get worried."

I threw Mom a glance. My dad's normal speaking voice was so loud, she had no trouble hearing him.

"Worried about what, Dad?" After the evening I'd just had, talking to my father didn't have me quaking in my boots.

"Have you, uh, spoken to your mother in the last week or so?"

"Why?"

"She left the house abruptly last week. You know your mother—she likes her little 'me time' on occasion, so I thought nothing of it. But it's been a week and no one's heard from her. Not me, not your brothers."

"Did you call Aunt Ellen?"

"You know Ellen and I don't get on all that well."

Yeah, I knew. My aunt couldn't stand him.

"Suzanne took her car, packed a suitcase, and told Maria she'd be away for a few days and couldn't say when she'd be back. Some . . . uh . . . shopping was delivered to the house the other day. A rather excessive amount, actually. That's normal behavior for your mother, but I am starting to get worried, Lucy. I'm beginning to think I should call the police."

Mom's eyebrows rose.

"Has she seemed upset about anything lately?" I was touched by the concern in his voice, but I wasn't going to come straight out and tell him she was standing right beside me. Let him wiggle around on the hook for a while, draw it out.

"There's been some ... uh ... changes at the office, and I've been preoccupied. If you're talking to your mother, please tell her that Mrs. Ferguson's replacement didn't prove to be suitable for the job. We found her another position on the fourth floor." I was relieved to hear that he hadn't done like aristocrats and executives of old and simply thrown the discarded mistress onto the street. That was nice of him. Then again, this was the twenty-first century; she might have threatened to sue him.

Mom held out her hand. I put the receiver into it.

"I'm here, dear. I'm safe. I'm enjoying my daughter's company. Is there any particular reason I should come home?"

I walked out of the library and left them alone.

Chapter 22

The morning news on the radio reported that George Marwick had been arrested and charged with the murder of Karen Kivas. It said nothing about the attempted kidnapping of my mom and the confrontation under the walls of the lighthouse.

I was grateful for that. Crowds of eager crime-scene tourists would not be descending on our library to ask for directions to the exact spot.

By the time Bertie, Ronald, and Charlene arrived the next morning, the police had gone, leaving no evidence of their presence behind. Before turning the sign on the door to OPEN, I told my coworkers what had happened and asked them to keep it to themselves.

"And people think librarians' lives are dull," Charlene said. "Speaking of which, I downloaded this new album last night. Y'all are going to love it. Who wants to borrow my iPhone first?"

"No time," Bertie said, fleeing for her office.

"Kids' program to prepare," Ronald said, dashing for the stairs.

As I was the last to respond, the phone and earbuds were shoved into my hand.

And so a typical day at the Bodie Island Lighthouse Library began.

Mom and Aunt Ellen arrived around ten. Last night, I'd stood outside for a long time, watching the police go about their business and waiting until Mom finished her phone call and joined me. She said nothing about what had transpired between her and Dad, and I didn't ask. She gave me a hug, and let Butch lead her to his car.

"I'm going home, darling," she said to me now.

"Home as in Boston, or home as in our house?" I said.

"The house. Your father and I have a lot of work to do on our marriage."

I gave her a big hug. Aunt Ellen was smiling. She might not like my dad, but more than anything, she wanted her sister to be happy.

"Next week we're going to Paris," Mom said.

"Paris? You mean you and Dad?"

"Paris first, then Rome and Madrid, and a few days in Mallorca."

"Does Dad even have a passport?"

"He needed one for that trip to Toronto for the convention last year."

"Oh, right." My parents had never, as long I could remember, had a holiday together. I figured time spent in some of the world's most romantic cities would do them a lot of good.

"Believe it or not," Aunt Ellen said, "the trip was your father's idea."

"Send postcards," I said.

"Thank you, Lucy," Mom said. "For everything."

"Before you go, I have one question. Are you financ-

ing Theodore to buy a collection of first-edition Ian
Flemings?"

"Whatever gave you that idea?"

"You seemed to be very chummy, never mind plotting
something together. I was just wondering."

"I might have hinted that you were single, and that
your father and I are not short of funds. Theodore did
not seem to be getting the hint, I must say."

"Why would you do that? I'm not attracted to him in
the least."

"Perhaps I was hoping that if Theodore expressed an
interest in you, you'd flee back home. I was wrong, Lucy.
I've been wrong about a lot of things. You are obviously
very happy here. I'm nothing but delighted for you. Perhaps I can meet your Butch and Connor again another
time."

"They're not my Butch and Connor," I said.

She merely smiled, and we hugged once more.

Charlene came running down the stairs. "Thank heavens I caught you before you left." She stuffed a plastic
bag into Mom's hand. I hid a grin. The bag was full of
CDs. "This will help you enjoy the drive home. Be sure
and write and tell me which ones you liked best, and
then I can make some more recommendations."

"Thank you," Mom said in all innocence.

I stood at the door waving as Mom and Aunt Ellen
climbed into their cars. Aunt Ellen drove off first, and
then the SLK pulled away in a spray of gravel and an
enthusiastic tooting of the horn.

Our next visitor was Irene Dawson, the Gray Woman.
She was dressed in her habitual color, but she gave me a
warm smile as she came in. She carried a briefcase. Gray,
of course.

"Good morning, Lucy. Is Ms. James in?"

"She's in her office."

"I've brought her a copy of my report. The names of my clients will, of course, remain confidential, but the contents are not."

I showed Irene into the back. She came out a few minutes later, accompanied by Bertie, said good-bye to us, and left. Bertie's smile faded.

"When I get my hands on Diane Uppiton," she said, "I won't be responsible for my actions."

"Did Irene tell you Diane commissioned that study?" I asked.

"No, but who else? I can't believe she was prepared to waste library funds in such a desperate attempt to get rid of me."

"Don't forget to breathe," I said, folding my hands into my chest. *"Namaste."*

Bertie growled and went back to her office.

"You had some excitement last night, I heard," Theodore said, rubbing his hands together in glee.

"More excitement than I like," I said.

"Louise Jane and I wondered where you two had gotten to. We had one drink and then left. I must say, Louise Jane's conversation can be rather single-minded. Your mother's all right?"

"Perfectly. She's gone home to Boston." I eyed him. "Are you okay with that?"

"Why shouldn't I be? Your mother's very nice, but I didn't expect her to stay any longer."

"I guess I was thinking . . . about the Ian Flemings."

His smile stretched from ear to ear. "You heard? Isn't it wonderful?"

"What's wonderful?"

"I bought them back. I'm absolutely delighted, my dear, delighted."

"That's great. But how . . . ?"

"As you know, my collection is heavy on the classic works of mystery and suspense. Fleming, Hammett, Mickey Spillane—that's the sort of book I prefer. However, like any serious collector, I occasionally branch out into other fields. A few years ago I bought a first-edition signed children's book. Not my first choice, but it was the original British edition, and going cheap."

"And?"

"The book was by a woman named Rowling. She went on to achieve some degree of fame. Only recently did I realize that I own the first in that series."

It took a minute for the light to dawn. "You mean J. K. Rowling? *Harry Potter*?"

"The very same."

"Teddy, how could you, a serious book collector, not have known that J. K. Rowling's Harry Potter books are the literary equivalent of the invention of sliced bread?"

He looked down his long nose at me. "Children's books are not my field of interest."

"Don't you ever go to the movies?"

Judging by his expression, the answer was no.

"The sale of that one book was enough to permit me to raise enough to get back the Flemings."

"That's wonderful, Teddy."

"I prefer to be called Theodore."

"Oh, right. Sorry."

"Why did you think your mother was interested? Is she a book collector? She never said. I tried to avoid the subject when we had drinks and then dinner, as I've been told that on rare occasions I can talk too much about books. Was I mistaken?"

"No, Theodore, you were not mistaken in the least."

When he left, still smiling, it was getting on to lunchtime. I debated the merits of going to Josie's Cozy Bakery and having a roast beef and caramelized onion on a baguette versus nipping upstairs to heat a can of soup. The sandwich would be a lot better, but the soup would give me a chance to finish my book. I didn't make up my mind fast enough, and Louise Jane caught me at the desk. Unlike Theodore, she was not smiling.

"What's this I hear about your mother leaving?"

"Yup. Gone home."

"Are you, uh . . . ?"

"Also leaving? Nope."

She carried a stack of books in her arms. I read the spines. All ghost stories.

"I was going to lend these to her," Louise Jane said. "She seemed interested in the paranormal history of this area."

"Well, she isn't. Right now, she's interested in planning a trip to Paris."

Louise Jane shook her head as she drifted away, clearly confused as to why anyone would go to Paris rather than spend his or her time listening to her talk about ghosts and the efficacy of her grandmother's spells against them. I hadn't said anything to anyone about mistaking the Gray Woman for the Lady last night, and I had no intention of ever doing so. If I did, by lunchtime tomorrow, word would be all over the Outer Banks that the ghostly lady of the Bodie Island Lighthouse had saved Lucy Richardson.

I decided to open that can of soup for lunch.

When I was coming down the stairs an hour later, two little girls, all bouncing hair and bright gap-toothed smiles, ran into the library.

"Ronald! We're here for story time!" the older girl yelled.

"Story time!" her sister cheered.

Ronald passed me on the stairs at a rapid clip. "Jasmine, Savannah, it is so great to see you. Thank you, Mr. Kivas."

Norm Kivas's clothes were well-worn but clean and his hair neatly combed. "Karen loved this library," he said. "So do the girls. I thought I'd better check it out for myself." He avoided looking at my face.

"Story time begins in half an hour," Ronald said. "While we're waiting for the other kids, I'll help Jasmine and Savannah select books to take home with them. You're welcome to sit in, Mr. Kivas. See what we do here."

"I'd like that." Norm watched his granddaughters disappear up the curving iron stairs, tripping over each other in their excitement. "I'll be right there."

When Ronald and the children had disappeared, Norm turned to me. "I hear you're the one who caught that man. The one who killed Karen."

"Not me. But I was there."

He shifted uncomfortably. "If you're talking to your mom, tell her I'm sorry, will you? I acted badly toward her. I don't know what I was thinking. The booze thinking, more likely. My daughter told me straight up that without Karen around she needs me to help her with the kids. I'm going to an AA meeting tonight. They say apologies are a good start."

"I'll tell her," I said.

He held out his hand. I took it in mine. Just for something to say, I asked. "How's Sandy?"

His mouth turned down. "Last night I told her I wasn't going to inherit anything and instead of going to Jake's for dinner, I'd throw some sausages on the grill. She walked out of the house without a word."

Overhead children laughed. Norm smiled, and I said, "Children's library is on the second floor."

Chapter 23

After work that evening I had to go down to the police station to make a formal statement about the events of last night. It didn't take long, and when I left the detectives' office, Butch was standing at the reception desk.

"Everything okay?" he asked.

"Yes. I'm so glad it's over. George made a full confession. Karen saw him put the necklace in Mom's bag. She didn't say anything at the time, but once book club ended and everyone had left, she phoned George and told him that she knew what he'd done. He asked what she wanted, and she said she'd wait where she was and they'd talk about it. So he turned around and went back to the lighthouse to meet her. Talking went wrong, and he killed her. Not that it matters, but Detective Watson thinks it was probably an accident."

"Pretty stupid of her." Butch and I turned at a voice behind us. Connor had come out of the chief's office. "To meet him in a remote place, all alone, after dark."

"Karen, I'm sorry to say, was stupid," I said. "Anger and greed made her stupid. She didn't take George seriously. Mom made that mistake also."

"We can be thankful your mom had a better outcome than Karen," Butch said.

"Yeah. I gotta run. Charlene has talked me into coming around to her place for dinner tonight. I shudder to think what the musical selection is going to be."

"Good night," the two men said in unison. "I'll pick you up tomorrow at seven, Lucy."

I waved over my shoulder as I headed for the door. Then I froze. My heart sank into my stomach.

Tomorrow. Seven o'clock.

The Mayor's Ball.

The grand opening of Jake's Seafood Bar.

I had two dates for the exact same time.

Read on for a sneak peek at the next
delightfully puzzling mystery in the
Lighthouse Library series by Eva Gates,

READING UP A STORM

Coming in April 2016 from Obsidian.

It was a dark and stormy night.

I've always wanted to say that.

Tonight was the perfect opportunity to do so: a ferocious storm was fast heading our way. It wasn't going to be a hurricane, I was glad to hear, but since I live this close to the ocean, even a small storm can be a terrifying thing.

Fortunately, the full strength of the tempest wasn't due to arrive for a couple of hours yet, so we were able to continue with our carefully laid nefarious plan.

The big clock over the circulation desk struck six, announcing closing time at the Bodie Island Lighthouse Library on a Monday. Charlene, our academic librarian, wasn't working today, but she'd come in a few minutes ago on a made-up pretext to keep our boss, Bertie James, in her office. I peered out the window. Night had arrived early, as thick clouds heralded the approach of bad weather. A steady line of headlights flashed between the rows of tall red pines on either side of the driveway, and cars were pulling into our parking lot. Fortunately, Bertie's office was in the back of the building, where she didn't have a view of the road.

"Coast clear, Lucy?" said a voice above me.

I turned and glanced up. Ronald Burkowski, the children's librarian, was peering over the railing of the iron stairs, which spiraled like the inside of a nautilus shell ever higher to the upper levels.

"All clear," I said.

He came down quickly, balancing two large boxes and several bulging shopping bags. A huge bunch of colorful balloons streamed behind him. I went to the door and greeted guests with a finger to my lips while Ronald arranged the balloons, set out paper cups and plates, and hung a silver banner that read HAPPY ANNIVERSARY across the door with the help of Connor McNeil.

I observed the preparations with sheer delight. It was ridiculously funny watching everyone greet everyone else, decorate the room, and lay out snacks and drinks, all while trying not to say a word or make a sound. Butch Greenblatt held the door open for my cousin Josie O'Malley, who was staggering under the weight of a huge white box. She laid the box on a side table and opened it. I peered in with great expectation, and I was not disappointed. "It's marvelous!" I gasped.

"Shush," Ronald whispered.

Josie's cake was decorated to represent five books stacked on top of one another. The icing on the covers and spines resembled old leather, full of intricate scrolls of red or gold; the three edges of each "book" were white for the pages, and the titles were written in ornate black script. A small souvenir figurine of the Bodie Island Lighthouse stood on the topmost book, and the number 10 was written in ornate cursive beside it. "You've outdone yourself," I whispered. "It's much too beautiful to eat."

"That's what they always say," my aunt Ellen said with a soft laugh as she helped Josie carefully peel away the walls of the box. "Until the first cut."

We were gathering to celebrate the tenth anniversary of Bertie James's coming to work at the Lighthouse Library. Bertie was not one to stand on ceremony, and she hadn't even mentioned the occasion. It was only when a longtime friend of hers, Pat Stanton, had called to ask what we were doing to mark the event that we, the library employees— Ronald, Charlene, and I—had heard about it. Two weeks of frantic, and secret, organization had begun.

By six fifteen we were ready. The main room of the library was packed. Everyone shivered in anticipation. We eyed one another, waiting. I switched off the lights, plunging the room into near darkness.

"When's Bertie coming?" Eunice Fitzgerald, the chair of the library board, sat in a wingback chair near the magazine racks, her back straight, cane held in front of her in knarry hands.

"Shush," people chorused.

"Thanks a lot, Bertie," bellowed the normally soft-spoken Charlene.

The assembled partygoers tittered. Charles, another library employee, crouched on the shelf closest to the door to the hallway. He looked as though he was getting ready to pounce the moment Bertie came into the room. I had an image of flying books, falling bodies, a screaming Bertie, and headed to cut him off.

Charlene appeared, saw us all waiting, and, trying to suppress her giggles, called, "Wow! Look at this! Bertie, get out here."

Footsteps came down the hall. Bertie's head popped around the corner. She stopped dead, her mouth hanging open.

"Surprise!" we all yelled.

Charles made his move, but I was ready for him. I leapt into the air and an enormous Himalayan feline hit me full in the chest. I staggered backward as sharp claws dug into my sweater. I crashed into Charlene, who fell into Bertie, who would have hit the floor had the six-foot-five, two-hundred-pound Butch Greenblatt not been approaching our library director at that moment to offer his congratulations.

Butch grabbed Bertie and kept her upright. "This is a surprise, all right," she said, smiling happily in Butch's embrace.

He blushed and mumbled apologies before letting her go.

I put a squirming Charles on the floor. *If looks could kill.* He stalked off, white-and-tan tail held high.

The crowd surged forward, everyone wanting to give the guest of honor a hug and a peck on the cheek and wish her the best.

"Nice one," Ronald said to me. "You almost flattened our boss."

"Blasted cat," I replied.

He chuckled. "You can't fool me, Lucy. You love Charles."

"Best part of working here, I have to admit."

"Present company excepted, I hope. Help me with the refreshments, will you?" he said as the thirsty crowd turned and headed our way.

In the fifteen minutes between library closing and Bertie's entrance, we'd cleared off the circulation desk and set up a makeshift bar. Ronald had poured drinks while Charlene and I passed around canapés. We'd laid bowls of mixed nuts and platters of cheese and crackers on the tables for partygoers to help themselves.

As I served the food, I chatted with our guests. Everyone congratulated me on managing to surprise the unflappable Bertie. The room was full of longtime library patrons, members of the board, and Bertie's close friends, but the one person I'd been hoping to see hadn't arrived yet. I kept checking the door, but no one was arriving late. I put an empty platter of one-bite crab cakes onto a side table and pulled out my phone. No bars, meaning no signal. That was normal: it was difficult to get cell reception inside these thick old stone walls. I made my way slowly across the room, exchanging greetings with partyers. I opened the front door, and someone threw a bucket of cold water into my face. The storm had arrived.

I wiped rainwater away with one hand and checked my phone with the other. I had a text. Sorry. Storm coming. Don't want to leave Mom in case electricity goes out. S.

Phooey. I was disappointed, but I understood. I hadn't known Stephanie Stanton for long, but we'd quickly become friends. She'd come home to Nags Head late in the summer to look after her mother. Pat Stanton had been involved in a serious car accident when a drunk driver hadn't noticed a red light on the Croatan Highway. The drunk got off without a scratch, but Pat had suffered two broken legs and numerous cracked and broken ribs. Her recovery was going to be long and difficult. She was out of the hospital now, but clearly couldn't manage on her own, and Stephanie was Pat's only child. Pat had been a longtime patron of the library and she and Bertie were very close. She'd told Bertie she intended to consider the accident to be a blessing. At last she could spend her days doing what she'd always dreamed of having time to do—just reading.

Despite Pat's determination to look on the bright side, caring for an invalid was always difficult. I knew Stephanie needed the break, and had hoped she could make the party.

Take care, I texted back.

"It was on a night like this one," Louise Jane Mc-Kaughnan was saying to Mrs. Peterson when I'd put my phone away and picked up another round of treats, "that the great ship went down. They say . . ."

Louise Jane was a font of knowledge about the history of the Outer Banks. What she didn't know (or didn't consider dramatic enough), she made up. Usually under the guise of "they say."

"Delightful party, Lucy. Any more of those crab cakes?" Theodore Kowalski, six feet tall and rail thin, peered at me through the plain glass of his spectacles as he chewed on the end of his unlit pipe. He was a passionate lover of literature and a keen and knowledgeable book collector. For reasons known only to himself, he wanted people to think he was English, and dressed like a country squire heading off to the Highlands for a spot of grouse shooting. Theodore was also dead broke, and could be counted on to appear at any library function at which food was served. He was in his midthirties, only a couple of years older than me, but dressed and acted as though he were in his fifties. I guess he thought that made him seem more serious.

"I'll check," I said. "You know not to light that pipe in here, right?"

He beamed at me, clearly pleased. Theodore didn't smoke; the pipe was all for show. Although somehow he managed to ensure that he had tobacco stains on his teeth and the scent of it clung to his Harris Tweed jackets and paisley cravats like barnacles to a barge. "I'm afraid I won't be able to make book club on Wednesday, Lucy. So sorry to have to miss it."

"And we'll miss you," I said dutifully.

"An important business matter. Can't be helped."

Aunt Ellen joined us and nabbed a meatball. "Great party, Lucy. Bertie looks so happy."

"I have exciting news," Theodore said.

"What's that, Teddy?" Ellen asked.

"I've found a buyer for those Agatha Christies I've been trying to unload . . . I mean sell. I've my eye on a set of Dashiell Hammetts in mint condition that I'd like to add to my collection." As I said, Theodore was broke. He earned what money he could from buying and selling books. Unfortunately for his bank account, he was far more interested in buying than in selling. When I'd first begun working here, Bertie had warned me to check his bags and coat when he left the library. He was known to sometimes decide that a rare or valuable volume would be happier in his home library than in this public one.

"How nice," Aunt Ellen said. "Good luck with it. Do you think Bertie was genuinely surprised, Lucy?" She took a second meatball. Ellen and Bertie were long-standing friends. It was through my mother's sister that I landed the job of assistant librarian a few months ago.

"I hope so," I said. "You can imagine how difficult it was to organize all this without her knowing. At five she said she was leaving early today. I just about fainted. Fortunately, quick-witted Ronald told her that Charlene had just called to say she wanted to come in at six to talk something over with Bertie, so Bertie agreed to stay."

"I suppose a chap has to go in search of crab cakes himself," Theodore huffed, and strolled away.

Ellen chuckled. "You just can't get good help in the colonies these days. I see Eunice here, and some of the other members of the library board, but not Diane or Curtis. Did they send their regrets?"

"Gee. It seems that we forgot to invite them. What a shocking oversight."

Ellen laughed. It was no secret that Diane Uppiton and Curtis Gardner were not exactly Bertie's allies on the library board.

Butch approached us, holding a bottle of beer in one hand and a plate piled high with canapés in the other. "You up to a walk on Thursday morning?" he asked me.

"Sure am," I replied.

"Walk?" Aunt Ellen said, her ears practically standing up. She was my mother's sister and I had no doubt Mom had instructed her to report immediately about any potential developments in my life.

"Just a walk," I said.

"I don't go on shift until midmorning that day," Butch explained. "I was telling Lucy how, when I first joined the police, I always tried to take time for a stroll along the beach before work whenever I could. It got me in a good place to face whatever the day had coming."

"And," I added, "that habit, like most good habits, has fallen away. I told him a marsh walk would be just as good, and to make sure he actually does it, he has to take me with him. I'd better get to work. Glasses need to be refreshed. Crab cakes delivered. That's if Theodore leaves any for anyone else." I plunged back into the crowd.

"You three," Bertie said, approaching us with a shake of her head once she'd made her way across the room after greeting her guests. "I can't believe you did all this without my noticing."

"It wasn't easy." Ronald handed her a glass of wine.

"I should have suspected something was up," Bertie said with a laugh, "judging by today's tie." Ronald glanced down. As the children's librarian, he liked to dress up for the kids. His tie was covered with pictures of brightly colored birthday balloons. "Oh," he said, "I didn't even realize."

"Your subconscious at work. Oh, my goodness, will you look at that!" Bertie had spotted the cake. Josie stood beside it, beaming proudly.

In the momentary hush as everyone stopped talking to admire the gorgeous confection, I could hear the wind howling around the curved lighthouse walls, and the steady patter of rain hitting the windows.

"Gonna be a big one," Butch said as he twisted the cap off a bottle of beer.

"I hate to say it," Connor said, "but we should probably suggest people start making their way home once they've had cake."

"Yeah," Butch said. "We don't want anyone caught out in this if it gets any worse."

The library's located about ten miles outside the town of Nags Head. That's ten dark and lonely miles, as the road runs through the Cape Hatteras National Seashore along the edge of the Atlantic Ocean.

"Speech," Ronald shouted.

"Speech, speech," the crowd chorused. A blushing Bertie was pushed to the front of the room. Her eyes sparkled with unshed tears and her voice broke as she began to speak.

"Thank you, friends, so much for coming. You have no

idea how much this means to me. And thank you most of all to the world's best staff, Ronald, Charlene, and Lucy, for this."

Everyone cheered. Ronald took a deep bow.

Charles, who hadn't quite forgiven me for spoiling his fun earlier, leapt up onto the shelf beside Bertie. She laughed. "And thank you, Charles. That storm's building, and fast. I hate to say it, but let's dig into this cake so we can get all of you safely home."

When she'd finished to many cheers, Josie pulled out a knife and began cutting the cake. Bertie got the first piece, and everyone cheered again. I placed slices onto plates and a beaming Bertie handed them around.

While we did that, Butch exchanged a word with Ronald and Charlene, and they nodded. Ronald put the caps back on the wine bottles, and Charlene began collecting crumpled napkins and dirty paper plates. Connor spoke quietly to Bertie.

Soon, all that remained of the gorgeous cake was the bottom layer. Gradually the library began to empty as everyone gave Josie their compliments and said their good-nights. Ronald, Charlene, and I finished tidying up with the help of Aunt Ellen and Josie.

Every time the door opened, rain streamed in and the wind caused the pages of magazines on the rack to shudder. Charles kept himself far away from the door, and I was glad I didn't have to venture out into the wild night. I live here, in the lighthouse, in a delightful, cozy little apartment on the fourth floor. My lighthouse aerie.

Josie packed the last of the cake into small boxes, distributed them among the stragglers, and then she and Aunt Ellen gave me kisses and said good night. Ronald and Charlene, clutching their cake boxes while unfurling umbrellas, escorted Bertie to her car.

At the end of the night, only Butch and Connor remained.

The men eyed each other.

I looked from one to the other. *Oh dear.*

"Good night, Mr. Mayor," Butch said.

"Night, Officer Greenblatt," Connor said.

Neither of them made a move.

"Guess it's time to be going," Connor said.

"Yup," Butch said. "Nice party, Lucy."

Charles sat on the shelf, his head moving from one man to the other as if he were at a tennis match.

"Do you want—?"

"Can I see you—?"

"Good night, gentlemen," I said.

They looked at me. Then they looked at each other. Charles watched them both.

"I'll follow you, Connor," Butch said. "Make sure you get to town safely in that little car of yours. Can't have the mayor going off the road in the dark."

"No need to do that," Connor said. "I've been driving these roads as long as you have."

I crossed the room and opened the door. I peered outside. The night was a wet black void. "Neither of you will get to town if you don't leave now. If anything, that wind is picking up."

"Once I've seen Connor off, I can come back and . . . uh . . . make sure you stay safe here, if you'd like, Lucy," Butch said.

"I don't think that's a particularly good idea," Connor said. "Suppose there's an emergency and you get called to come into work."

"Out. Both of you," I said.

They moved at the same time, squeezing through the doorway, apologizing all over themselves, calling good night to me.

I shut the door behind them and gave the lock a satisfying twist.

Charles jumped off the shelf and headed toward the stairs.

Excellent idea, I thought.

I followed him upstairs with a warm, contented glow.